Instant
Gratification

Instant Gratification

Jill Shalvis

KENSINGTON PUBLISHING CORP.
www.kensingtonbooks.com

KENSINGTON BOOKS are published by

Kensington Publishing Corp.
119 West 40th Street
New York, NY 10018

ISBN-13: 978-1-4967-2084-9
ISBN-10: 1-4967-2084-9

First Brava trade paperback printing: July 2009
First Kensington trade paperback edition (third printing): August 2018

11 10 9 8 7 6 5 4 3

Printed in the United States of America

Also available in an electronic edition:

ISBN-13: 978-0-7582-8416-7
ISBN-10: 0-7582-8416-0

Chapter 1

Hot and bothered, and not in the good way, Dr. Emma Sinclair switched the sign on her father's medical clinic from CLOSED to OPEN. It was eight a.m. sharp, and out of habit, she braced herself to be bombarded.

Not that *that* was going to happen, not here in Mayberry, USA.

Excuse her— Wishful, California. Nothing so simple as Mayberry. Not with the coyotes and bears she knew roamed around the property on a daily basis. She heard the coyotes in the early mornings, their eerie howls making the hair on the back of her neck stand straight up. Even more disconcerting, she'd caught sight of them watching her from the woods lining the property, their hungry eyes making her miss the streets of New York, where the worst predators were grumpy, demanding, homeless people.

She hadn't actually seen a bear yet, but everyone who came through her door had a bear story, so she figured with her karma, it was only a matter of time. Not in a hurry for that, she booted up the computer behind the front desk, remembering with a fond sigh the hustling, bustling rush of her Manhattan

ER, where she literally ran her entire shift; bagging and defib-bing, resuscitating, whatever came her way, with sometimes little more than caffeine in her system.

Yeah, she'd had it all in New York, a promising career with a fantastic sublet near Central Park, a great shift in one of the best ERs in the country . . . it didn't get better than that.

But it certainly got worse.

A world away from her world, Emma was now on the other side of the country, deep in the California Sierras, pining for Starbucks and Thai take-out. Pining for crowds, traffic, and late trains, that's how homesick she was. She missed having a myriad of take-out menus taped to her empty refrigerator, her next meal a simple phone call away.

No one delivered in Wishful. Worse, there was no fast food period, no drive-thrus, nothing unless she wanted to drive the thirty plus miles to South Shore, Lake Tahoe—which meant that she, a professional water burner, was in danger of starving to death.

She missed so much about New York, but what she missed most of all was her mom, who after being invincible and rais-ing Emma on her own while working her fingers to the bone as an RN, had done the unthinkable.

She'd died of one of the few things that Emma hadn't been able to fix—cancer.

Throat tightening, Emma moved through the front room of the old Victorian-turned-clinic, a place that had been deco-rated in the eighties with country chic and hadn't changed much except for the equipment, and some of that was ques-tionable. She opened the country blue, duck-lined curtains, letting in the mid-June sun. She wondered what the day would bring. The usual bee sting? Or maybe for kicks and gig-gles, a stomach flu.

The problem was people in Wishful saw her as Doc's little

girl. They acted as if she was just the key keeper, someone to drop some gossip with, or maybe to talk about her father—her least favorite thing to talk about.

God, what she wouldn't give for a stroke or cardiac infarction, something she could really sink her teeth into

When the front door opened, the silly ceramic cow chime above it jangled, and in came a man, supporting another. Wishful wasn't that big, and after being here for two months, Emma had met quite a few of the locals, including the Wilder brothers. TJ Wilder, tall and big and broad, assisted his equally tall and big and broad brother Stone, who was covered in mud and blood, dripping both all over her floor.

He was limping and grimacing in pain—at least until he saw her, at which point he swiped his face of all expression, going testosterone stoic. "Hey," he murmured. "What's up, Doc?"

Ah, *finally*. Finally something more than a nosy neighbor bringing a casserole and gossip while the real cases went all the way to South Shore. Finally something more than poison oak, something right up her alley, and she moved in to help support Stone, pulling his arm over her shoulder, grabbing his hand to steady him. He had big hands, tough and scarred, much like the man himself even before whatever had happened to him today. "First room," she directed TJ, bypassing the front desk, turning toward the hallway which held two examination rooms. "What happened?"

TJ opened his mouth, but Stone beat him to it. "Just need a few Band-Aids."

"Really." Without her and TJ's support, he'd have slid to the floor. But she was well used to stubborn patients, the majority of which were always of the male persuasion. She figured it had something to do with carrying a penis around all the time. "So you can walk on your own then?"

Stone managed to arch a brow in her direction, though only

one because the other was slashed through, and bleeding down his lean jaw. "Why would I do that, when having you hold me is much more fun?" He gave her more of his weight, which she estimated at approximately one hundred and ninety pounds of solid muscle. "You're softer than old Doc Sinclair," he murmured.

True, though her father was plenty soft. In fact, it was his soft heart that had landed Emma in this situation in the first place, and she wasn't referring to the mild heart attack he'd suffered two months ago—the one that had brought her here to run his business while he recovered.

Nope, she was talking about his inability to concentrate and focus on the things that mattered, such as billing people for services rendered, a problem that had him shockingly near bankruptcy. In the time she'd been in Wishful, she'd discovered he'd not billed more often than he had billed, a mistake she wouldn't be making. Ever. "Well, you're stuck with me at the moment, soft or otherwise."

"That's okay." Stone looked at her. "He always says you're a better doctor than him."

"Whoa. He said that?"

"Yeah, which means you must be really good."

Oddly touched that her father would say such a thing about her, much less anything at all, she didn't respond. She and her father didn't know each other well. Other than the matching MDs, they had nothing in common. Her dad liked the slow, laid-back style of doctoring in a small town, while she preferred the busier, more interesting, fast-paced ER life. Oil and water . . . "What happened to you, Stone? Did someone do this to you?"

"No." His voice was low and hoarse, as if it hurt just to talk. "I'm okay."

Wasn't that just a Wilder for you. Tall, built and sexy, and so completely full of shit. Out of the three brothers, she liked Cam and TJ best, mostly because they spent most of their time out of town.

But Stone . . . well, he was charming and charismatic as hell, but he was also as wild as his name implied—her *least* favorite quality in a man, tough or otherwise. And Stone *was* as tough and impenetrable as they came, the kind of man who could be dropped anywhere on the planet and get on just fine. An admirable characteristic, sure, but she preferred a quiet, more sophisticated guy, preferably another doctor, who understood her world.

Not that it mattered. He was a patient not a prospective lover, and she directed him to an examination table. Not that she could "examine" much with all the mud. "We need to get those dirty things off," she told TJ, and left him to it while she pulled a gown from a drawer.

Stone lay back willingly enough when TJ pushed him down to a prone position. "Just the Band-Aids is all . . . Tell you what, you give me a box, and in return I'll take you on an outdoor adventure. Name it. Anything you want."

The Wilder brothers ran an outdoor adventure/expedition company, which as far as Emma could tell meant that they got paid to be ski and mountain bike bums, playing all day long in the great outdoors.

She skied, but that was about it for the great outdoors for her. "I don't think so," she said, pulling out a tray.

"Ah, come on, the fresh air's good for you." He sounded as if he could barely talk. "How about a rock climb, or getting on a mountain bike?"

She understood the appeal of the area, she really did. It was just that in her world, which she was chomping at the bit to get back to, she didn't have time for such things. "Let's focus on your injuries."

He let loose a slow, bad boy smile, weakened by pain, but still potently sexy. "I'll be fine."

Everything Stone did was slow and sexy. Slow and sexy, slow and easy, and so laid-back she'd often thought he needed to be checked for a pulse.

But not by her. The Wilders were gorgeous, and gorgeously dangerous to female hearts across the land, so yeah, he affected her, but she was a big girl and could resist. There'd be no giving into any smiles, charming or otherwise, thank you very much. Moving to the sink, she began to wash up, no dallying for her.

She had enough going on here trying to keep the clinic up and running and her father on the path of rehabilitation as required by his medical condition—not an easy feat given that the man apparently thought he was still twenty-one instead of sixty-one, hiking and fishing daily at his remote cabin.

After seeing him only a handful of times in all her life, Emma had seen him more in the past two months than she'd ever planned on. But he still hadn't bounced back, and that worried her. She wanted him well and thriving.

And back at work, so she could go home, and back to her work.

Unfortunately, she didn't seem any closer to that than she'd been two months ago. Out of necessity, she'd taken on the additional pressure of handling his books, which were in bad shape, with invoices and reports tossed haphazardly in files in some random system that made absolutely no sense. Apparently her father accepted cash, credit cards, and if she was looking at things correctly, casseroles. *Casseroles.* He had a freezer full of them, and twice this week alone, someone had brought her new ones instead of money when they'd needed services rendered.

Casseroles.

Her father had laughed at her concern, saying a single man enjoyed a home cooked meal once in awhile.

Well, he could eat one every day for a month and still have leftovers.

So could she, for that matter. Yeah, she probably wouldn't starve to death, though she couldn't vouch for the condition of her arteries after all the heavy cuisine.

She dried her hands, grabbed some sterile water and the antiseptic, and headed toward her patient, who was clearly hurting big-time. Stone was lying on the examination table, eyes and mouth strained in spite of his attempt at a relaxed air.

With sympathy, she started with the gash through his left eyebrow, squirting the water over it, gently washing the blood free of the wound, probing, until he hissed out a pained breath.

"Easy, Doc."

She *was* being easy. It was her job to be easy. "This is going to have to be stitched."

TJ nodded.

"No, thanks." Stone spoke lightly enough, but his words came through his teeth now, as if he was barely holding it together. "Seriously, just point me in the direction of those Band-Aids."

"*Seriously?*" she mocked lightly. "Band-Aids aren't going to do it." She stepped in and blocked him from attempting to get up when TJ might have let him. Her hands were on his shoulders, which were tense and strained belying his easy-going nature. "We need to sterilize, scrape, x-ray, and then assess, Stone. No way around it."

"That was a mouthful." He flashed another one of those potent Wilder smiles. "How about we just slow down, relax, maybe take a deep breath. I'm just a little scrapped up, that's all."

"You need stitches," TJ told him. "And you know it." Inside

his pocket, his cell phone began to vibrate. He pulled it out, took one look at the ID and shot Stone an annoyed glance. "You forwarded all the office calls to my cell."

"It was your turn."

"No, it's *your* turn. It's always your turn."

"Exactly," Stone said. "Take the call, it might be important. Maybe it's a client, his pockets flush with cash coming our way. Or maybe it's just another woman dumping your sorry ass." Gritting his teeth, he lay back, looking pale and clammy. "Yeah, that might be fun. Put it on speaker."

"It can wait," TJ insisted. "I need to make sure you behave for the pretty doctor."

"Just get the damn phone. I'll behave."

TJ looked at Emma. He'd been clearly antagonizing his brother in order to distract Stone. Sweet. Level-headed. Yeah, TJ was definitely her favorite Wilder. "I've got him. It's fine."

TJ looked doubtful. "He's a handful."

"I mastered in handfuls."

TJ laughed appreciatively, and Stone sighed. "I'm right here."

Emma hadn't stopped examining Stone during this exchange. She'd found no other head injuries, which was good. He did have a nasty bruise along his jaw, the first of many she suspected, but nothing life threatening. "He's not in any immediate danger," she assured TJ, then slanted a look at Stone when he muttered something beneath his breath about the damned Band-Aids. "Unless I sew his mouth shut."

TJ nodded in amused sympathy, and with worry still in his eyes left the room to answer his phone.

"I thought he'd never leave."

Emma ignored him and went to work on his shirt, which was a short-sleeved performance jersey. Staring at the hem, she lifted it up over a set of defined abs.

Here he was void of mud but not blood. He'd obviously

tumbled along either asphalt or dirt, because he was covered in road rash. It had to hurt like hell.

He wrapped his fingers around her wrist and she raised her gaze to his. California surfer meets angel, she thought. It was the killer combo of that easygoing air and gorgeousness. Maybe also that light brown hair, streaked gold by the sun, wind-tousled and wild and inviting enough that a woman would want to run her fingers through it. Maybe it was his strong, lean, unshaved jaw. Or maybe it was his fathomless green eyes that made a person—or in this case, one grumpy doctor—feel as if he could see her soul.

And the way he looked at her.

Yeah. It was most definitely that, and she knew right then and there—as if she hadn't already known—that he was trouble.

Crazy, big, bad trouble.

"No need to fuss," he told her. "I heal fast."

She could believe that. His body was in prime shape, sinewy and hard. Given what he did for a living—play basically—she knew that body wasn't gym-made but the real deal, born of actual outdoor activity. She got to his ribs and he winced. "Did you fall?"

"Falling is a way of life for a guy like me."

"A guy like you?"

He sucked in a hard breath as she probed her way over his torso. "Yeah. A mountain bum."

He was long and lean, not an extra ounce of fat on him, so she had no trouble accessing the ribs. Unfortunately, she had to use her fingers, and as she did, his flat, ridged belly rose and fell with his agitated breathing. "Stone?"

He opened his eyes.

"Tell me what happened," she said, looking at his pupils, which were the same size and reactive.

"It's complicated."

She'd been born here, but raised in New York by a tough-as-nails woman who'd taken no bullshit. As a result, Emma had either heard or seen it all, and nothing surprised her. Nothing. "I think I can handle it."

He let out another hard breath when she pressed on his ribs. "It's all a little fuzzy."

She frowned and eyed the bump on his head again. "Fuzzy? Are you dizzy? Spots?"

"No."

She checked his pupils again. "You can't remember what happened?"

"Well . . ." He smiled faintly. "There were these three crazy women."

Her eyes flew to his in time to see his mouth quirk slightly. "Three women," she repeated.

"Uh huh."

She narrowed her eyes. "And?"

"They jumped me at Moody's."

The single bar and grill in town, where the only nightlife for thirty miles happened. Emma once again took in the road rash all over him. "Bar fight, my ass."

He laughed, then sucked in a harsh breath. "Oh, Jesus. Laughing isn't good. Laughing is bad."

"So save your breath." His jersey was snug, fitted for outdoor activity such as mountain biking or hiking. She wasn't going to be able to pull it off him without causing him considerable pain, and besides it was already torn and destroyed, so she grabbed her scissors.

"Hey—"

And cut it up the center of his chest, spreading it wide, revealing more road rash, bleeding sullenly and clogged with dirt wherever his shirt had torn.

A huge infection waiting to happen.

She set about checking his upper ribs. "Not broken, I don't think," she murmured, feeling the one giving him trouble as he held his breath. "Wait—"

"*Christ.*"

"Yeah, that one's probably cracked," she said as he went green and closed his eyes again. "We'll x-ray it along with the rest of you. Head injury first. I'm going to give you a shot to numb the area. Then stitches."

His eyes popped open, sharp and deep, *deep* jade. "With a needle?"

"That's usually how stitches become stitches."

"I vote for super glue. I used it last year on a gash right here . . ." He gestured to his chin with a bloody hand. "Worked like a charm."

"And you have the scar to prove it," she noted, leaning over him to check it out. "Don't worry, I'm good. Damn good. You won't scar from my work."

"I don't mind the scar."

"Ah, but there's no need to mess up that pretty face of yours." She waved the gown at him. "So, back to that stripping."

"You going to have to buy me dinner first."

She gave him a long look that was wasted on him because his eyes were closed again, his mouth white and tight, his face green, and she sighed. "You want me to get TJ to help you?"

"I've got it." Grimacing, he sat up. With a shrug, he let the cut shirt fall off shoulders that were approximately as broad as a mountain. He grabbed the gown from her, which was what she'd expected. In her experience, men rarely wanted help, even when dripping DNA all over her floor.

She moved to her station to gather what she'd need, hearing some rustling behind her, and then a low, heartfelt, rough oath. When she turned back, he was struggling to remove his biker cleats, and she did mean struggling. Bent over, his shoulders hunched as the ties on the cleats eluded his bloody fingers. She moved in to assist, eyeing that horrific road rash, some of which vanished up beneath the only thing left on him—his biker shorts.

She'd seen countless nude bodies, young, old, and halfway in between, and never, not once, had she felt even a fraction of a sexual awareness while in her doctor's coat.

Her best friend and fellow ER-mate, and sometimes friends-with-benefits buddy Dr. Spencer Jenks didn't believe her, but it was true. She simply wasn't attracted to a person in need of medical help.

Fascinated, yes.

Excited to dig in, always.

Attracted?

Never.

Until now.

It wasn't the sun-kissed hair, or those green eyes, or even that tough and rugged physique.

In truth, she didn't know what attracted her exactly. But she knew what bothered her—he wasn't her type. Not even close. He was laid-back and easygoing, and had one of those lackadaisical attitudes about life. One that said he was all play and no substance.

Hell, he skied and biked for a living.

Bottom line, she wasn't into guys like him. So why she felt that frisson of awareness—lust—skitter up her spine, was one of the biological, maybe also chemical, mysteries of attraction, and she shoved it aside as completely inappropriate as Stone fumbled with the gown, wincing at every movement.

She shook her head and moved closer. "Forget it for now, it'll just stick to your wounds." She pulled out the needle encasement, and he went still, eyes locked on her fingers.

"I don't need that," he said.

That's what they all claimed. She drew Lidocaine into the syringe. "When did you last have a tetanus shot?"

Still staring at the needle, he shook his head. "I don't remember, but I'm good. On both counts."

She put a hand on her hip and studied him, all long, lean, sinewy, bleeding grace. The man was six-two, maybe six-three, and as already noted, every one of those inches was hard, toned muscle. She knew that when he wasn't hurt, he moved with an easiness that spoke of great confidence. Hell, she'd personally seen him ski right off a cliff without a twinge of nerves.

Yet he was afraid of a needle.

It might have amused her, if she wasn't genuinely worried about getting him taken care of properly, and that involved a shot. "Close your eyes."

"No."

She wondered just how hard he would be to hold down. She was pretty damn good at immobilizing people, having cut her teeth on drug addicts in the ER, but he was just big enough to worry her. "I promise to be quick."

"Yeah, I don't think so." Accompanying this, he scooted backwards, a mean feat given what his ribs must feel like.

"Stone—"

"Really," he said, sweating, pupils dilated now. "I don't need it."

She put a hand in the middle of his chest to keep track of him. And to hold him still. "Don't make me call your brother back in here to help me hold you down."

"Ah, now you're just being mean."

She smiled. "Stop dragging this out."

"Wow."

"Wow what?"

"You *do* own a smile," he said, giving her one of his own, pain-tinged as it was.

It took her aback for the briefest moment, but it was hard to be insulted by the truth. Irritation and Grumpy *had* been her two closest friends lately, she could admit that much.

"It's a pretty one, too," he murmured. "You ought to use it more often.

"Flattery will get you nowhere." She flicked her finger at the syringe, shaking out the excess air. "You're still getting the shot."

Chapter 2

Stone sat straight up on the examination table, a table he shouldn't even be at, but his stupid brother had insisted.

"You're hurt and you know it," TJ had said, up on the mountain. "I can't bring you home without x-rays, Annie'll kill me."

Their aunt was the least of Stone's worries at the moment, with the pretty, mean doc waving that needle around. He gave a brief thought to making a run for it, but he didn't like to move fast unless he was on skis or a mountain bike.

The deciding factor was simple—just thinking about running made him queasy. Especially since sitting up had nearly killed him dead right there on the spot. "Oh, fuck," he gasped, clutching his ribs as fire torched its way through his insides. "*Fuck.*"

"I've got you."

Hard to believe that sweet-as-honey voice belonged to the razor tongued, cool-as-a-cucumber snooty doctor still waving that damn needle in one hand, supporting him with her other.

Old man Doc had warned him that his daughter was tough, edgy, and abrupt, and he hadn't been kidding. During the time she'd been in Wishful, she'd both turned him down for a get-to-know-you drink, and then again when she'd kicked his ass on Wilder's Run back when they'd still had snow. Since he'd been skiing since he could walk, that one had hurt, but his binding had been loose, a fact she refused to believe, and . . .

And, hell.

He liked her and he didn't even know why, especially since it wasn't reciprocated.

Not even close. Not only that, she was cold, and . . . and smart and funny and hot. So damn hot in those fancy trousers and those fitted silk button downs and fancy doctor coat, like she was still in New York instead of the wild, remote Sierra Mountains. It didn't hurt that she was five-foot-seven-ish, curvy, an auburn-haired beauty who looked like Barbie's mean sister.

Dr. Barbie.

"Keep breathing," she said, cool, calm and collected.

Stone was cool, too. Cool and calm, and possibly maybe getting a little turned on despite the fact that he hurt like hell.

It wasn't her slight New York accent, he decided. It wasn't the elegant, sophisticated clothes she wore that had probably cost more than his Jeep. It wasn't that she was stacked and *far* too pretty for one so tough, or that she moved with quick efficiency, wasting not a single movement.

He actually didn't know what drew him, and that bugged the hell out of him, too.

So did the fact that he couldn't take a breath without wanting to whimper like a baby. If he'd ever been in more freaking pain, he couldn't remember it.

Pathetic.

"Keep breathing," she reminded him.

Yeah, easy for her to say. Breathing burned like fire.

"Need a smelling salt?" Her eyes were baby blue, and as cool as the rest of her.

"Your dad's better at the bedside manners."

"Unfortunately for you, he's not here."

"That's okay. You're nicer to look at." Everyone in Wishful loved and adored old man Doc, who for the past forty years had patched and stitched the entire population of Wishful, day or night, without complaint. Stone missed him. "But he'd have just given me the damn Band-Aids."

"Well, then maybe you should have waited until he was back at work to . . . what did you say happened?" She slanted him a long, droll look. "Got beat up by three women?"

"Uh huh." But his attention was now on her hands as she set down the needle—thank you, Jesus—and picked up a gauze.

A gauze he could deal with. A gauze he could be friends with. A gauze wouldn't make him want to pass out. "Last I heard, you were working in New York," he said, desperately trying to distract himself. "Running an ER."

She hesitated briefly, then poured antiseptic onto the gauze, brushing the wound at his temple. Her blouse was smooth and silky. She had a crease down the center of her pants leg, and she wore heels that clicked on the linoleum floor. She was careful, organized, and obsessively focused. Maybe a bit anal to boot. It should have turned him off.

It didn't.

The opposite actually, and he had no idea what that said about him. Her lab coat added a serious sexy factor to the ensemble. Her fiery hair was shiny and straight, and pulled back at the nape of her neck, held there by a pretty silver clip. The silky strands smelled good, too. God, he loved it when women smelled good. "Never noticed you coming back this way to visit."

"My dad's busy."

"Not that busy."

"Okay, *I've* been busy." She paused. "We've seen each other. He occasionally came to New York to visit me."

Ah, there it was. The war between pride and censure. She didn't like the idea of Stone thinking she didn't care.

Stone had one parent who'd walked. The other was dead so he wasn't one to judge a parent/child relationship. He loved Doc, but there was no doubt the guy had made mistakes with his daughter, and he knew Doc would be the first to admit it to anyone who asked. "It's nice to see you here," he said. "Taking care of this place for him."

"Just until he's back on his feet. Then I'm going home."

He studied her face. She was a good doctor. He knew because Doc had followed her career and bragged about her often, but something about the way she was taking care of him so efficiently and professionally made him want to ruffle her up and show her how much more fun being even a little relaxed could be. "Once upon a time this place was your home."

"A very long time ago."

True enough. Twenty-four years ago, her mother had left Doc Sinclair and the California Sierras, taking their six-year-old daughter with her, never to return. They'd gone big city, complete with the attitude that went with, apparently—

Whoa. There she went, picking up that big ass needle again. As she came close with it, sweat beaded on his forehead, "Yeah, I don't—"

Her hand, gentle but firm, pressed on an uninjured portion of his chest and pushed him flat to the table, and in the next second, she stuck him.

"Ouch!"

"Hold still."

He didn't have a choice. She wasn't a big woman by any means, but she had strength. Sturdy as a rock, she managed to both hold him down and shoot him full of the stuff that was supposed to make him numb. Picturing the needle going into his head, nausea rolled through him.

"You're doing fine." She promptly pulled the needle out and poked him again.

He saw spots.

"Stay with me," she said.

"He's a wuss with needles." This from TJ, who'd apparently finally finished on the phone and was getting his ass back in the room. "They make him faint."

"They do not," Stone grated out, sweat pouring down his back.

Emma's baby blues met his. "If you're good, I'll"—she paused to move the goddamn needle around—in his head!—"give you a sticker when we're done here."

TJ snickered.

Yeah. His brother was going to have to die.

Then TJ leaned over him, peering closely at the cut on Stone's forehead. "That's nasty."

"Thanks, man."

"You probably shouldn't have tried to stop yourself with your face." He shook his head. "Rookie mistake."

"Again," Stone said tightly. "Thanks, man."

TJ looked up at Emma. "So what do you think, Doc? Four stitches? Five? Twenty?"

"Oh, God," Stone muttered, sweating profusely.

"Maybe we should just amputate at the neck, what do you think?" his soon-to-be dead brother asked with a crooked grin. "I could sit on him for you."

"Seven." Emma looked at Stone. "Just seven stitches. It'll only take a few minutes."

Stone closed his eyes as she began. TJ wasn't sitting on him, but he *was* holding him down just in case, though just in case of what, Stone had no idea. The bones in his legs were imitating overcooked noodles and he wasn't going anywhere.

He was fine with that, except . . . except, Jesus. He could

feel the tug of the stitches, but no real pain, not that *that* helped when he could feel the slide of the needle going into his head.

In and out.

In and out.

Oh yeah, he might be sick . . .

He was doing his damnedest to pretend he was somewhere else, *anywhere* else, when Emma patted him gently on the shoulder. "Done."

Thank God. He opened his eyes and met hers, expecting to find a wry amusement at his expense, but he didn't see anything but a sharp intelligence and steadfast determination to simply do her job.

He looked at her for a long beat, admitting to himself that he was waiting for something more from her; a heat, a flicker of awareness of him as a man, a hint of an attraction, but she turned away without giving up anything of herself, heading to the sink to drop in her used equipment while Stone once again struggled to sit.

TJ helped him, but when Stone would have gotten down off the table, Emma glanced back over her shoulder. "Where do you think you're going?"

He didn't know, but it was going to be as far and fast from here and any more needles as he could get. "A drink. I need one. You?"

"We're not done here, Stone."

Oh, yes they were. So done. "We could go swimming at Fallen Rocks, it's going to be a hot one."

Dr. Uptight Barbie merely jerked her chin in TJ's direction.

Stone knew that look, the intent behind the chin movement, but before he could process and move his aching-like-a-sonuvabitch body, his brother was suddenly blocking him from getting off the table.

The doc was right there, too, standing at his hip again, holding a tray filled with a stack of fresh gauzes and some antiseptic that looked as if it was going to hurt like hell. "Yeah, I don't think so," he said.

"You have gravel in your wounds, Stone." She picked up a piece of gauze and doused it, then picked up a tool that looked like a fancy set of tweezers.

TJ had the decency to look queasy, which didn't help Stone any.

"Really," Stone told them both. "I'm good. Some Band-Aids, that's all I need." *Why wasn't anyone listening?*

Emma eyed his shorts, specifically the areas where blood was leaking through. With a very bad feeling, he shook his head. "No. No way. They're staying on."

"I have to clean the wounds," she repeated. "All of them."

Oh, Christ. Dr. Barbie? Try Dr. *Evil.* She wasn't backing down, and rather than suffer the indignity of letting her—or even worse, TJ—take down his shorts, he did it himself, and then lay there buck ass naked with his eyes closed. "I feel so cheap," he muttered. "You didn't even buy me dinner first."

TJ snorted, but the doc ignored him. "I also want to x-ray your ribs and your head," she murmured as she began the torture. "And anything else you haven't yet revealed to me that might be cracked, fractured or broken besides your good sense."

Wow. She was even meaner than he'd thought.

It got worse, way worse.

An hour later, she'd seen every single inch of him up close and personal, and he did mean up close and personal. She'd left no wound unprobed. He'd been stitched, x-rayed and bandaged, and feeling more than moderately violated, was finally shown the door with stern directions to ice, elevate and rest.

Dr. Evil had wanted to give him a tetanus shot, but since he hadn't been injured on anything rusty, she'd made some crack about torturing him enough for the day, requesting he come back next week for the shot.

Yeah. He'd be back. When hell froze over.

Crawling into TJ's truck, he leaned back in the passenger seat and sighed. "I miss Doc."

"She fixed you up just fine."

"Evil. She's Dr. Evil."

TJ smiled. "Maybe. But she's the hottest Dr. Evil I've ever seen." He pulled them out of the lot, driving through Wishful, a town holding three thousand year-round residents inside its heavily Victorian-influenced architecture.

The town had been around since the 1800s, where it'd once thrived as a vital part of the wild, wild west. The gold rush had come and gone, and then the lumber boom, but Wishful, located at over six thousand feet, had put itself on the map thanks to the ice it'd shipped out by the truckload to the rest of the country at the turn of the century.

Now it was an outdoor enthusiast's tourist stop on the way to Lake Tahoe, and the Wilder brothers had taken full advantage of that, running their adventure expedition company on the outskirts of town, taking people on any kind of mountain outdoor adventure there was; skiing, snowmobiling, dirt biking, hiking . . . anything. Baby brother Cam had put up the money, having amassed a considerable fortune being a world renowned snow boarder for fourteen years. Stone had located the thirty acres for sale, then designed and built the lodge, along with a series of smaller cabins for staff and family. TJ had come up with the business plan and initial contacts, getting them paying clients and taking those clients on the longer treks. It worked. Now they spent their days giving people the adventures they'd only dreamed about.

Not a bad way to earn a living.

Unless, of course, one of the idiots—er, clients—deciding to take his own adventure without knowing what he was doing, ended up needing the volunteer Search and Rescue team's help, of which Stone was a member. Stone had found the guy on a rope hanging off the cliff he'd slid down. He'd waited until Stone reached him to panic, sending Stone rocketing down a sheer rock fifty feet, landing him in the Urgent Care being taken care of by Dr. Evil.

"She said she was going to come check on you in a few days." As he drove, TJ tossed a grin Stone's way. "Maybe give you a shot of antibiotics. With a needle."

"You are such an asshole."

"Aw. She promised to bring you a lollipop if you didn't cry this time."

"A *fucking* asshole."

TJ laughed and kept driving, passing town, heading toward the Wilder Lodge. The sharp, craggy mountains all around them were still brilliant green from snow melt. They'd had a hell of a wet winter and spring, and were enjoying the effects of late June. The creeks were full to overflowing, feeding the meadows. Wildflowers, swayed in the hot breeze. Stone loved each season, but at the moment, with his poor abused body on fire, he missed the cool snow of winter.

"You should have seen your face when she brandished that needle." TJ turned at the Wilder Adventures turn-off. "I thought you were going to crawl off that table with your ass cheeks."

That was the Wilders for you. Lots of love all the way around.

"Your bare ass cheeks." TJ grinned. "Ah, man. Good times."

"TJ?"

"Yeah?"

"Shut up."

TJ nodded, trying to go solemn and not quite making it. "You're right. That was rude."

"Thank you." Stone let out a long breath, trying to relax.

"So." TJ tossed him a look.

"So?"

"What's it like knowing she's seen your junk, and not from your best angle?"

Stone craned his neck and gave him a death stare.

"Sorry. Not funny yet?"

Stone just sighed and closed his eyes.

Chapter 3

Two days later, the pain from Stone's cracked rib, aching joints and open wounds had subsided just enough that he could move around.

Sort of.

He got out of bed and left his cabin, heading up the trail toward the big lodge that housed Wilder Adventures. Pine needles crunched beneath his boots. The early morning air was chilly, only about fifty degrees, but by noon it would probably hit closer to ninety-five.

Around him, birds screeched. Insects hummed. He was dive-bombed by an errant wasp. He swatted at it and kept going through the woods. The trail was well kept but beyond it, nothing but remote wilderness. Approximately 75,000 acres of subalpine and alpine forest, granite peaks, and glacially formed valleys and lakes, all government owned and available for exploring.

He knew every inch of it.

By the time he climbed the steps to the lodge and got to his second story office, he was already tired. Still, he began the uphill battle against the mess on his desk. Over the next few months, he would plan and lead many varied treks—but for now he was diving into the mountain of paperwork required for those treks. There were permits to secure, equipment to order, treks to map, billing . . . and he did it all while fantasizing about playing doctor with a certain Dr. Evil in fancy clothes, with a set of baby blue eyes and a mouth that was made for—

His door opened and Annie walked in. Though she was only ten years his senior, his aunt—and Wilder Adventure's chef—could kick his ass on a bad day, and given her scowl, it would appear it was exactly that. "Don't go away mad," he murmured wearily. "Just go away."

"No can do." She was wearing an apron that read: I'D TELL YOU THE RECIPE, BUT THEN I'D HAVE TO KILL YOU, which pretty much summed up her usual attitude.

An attitude that today, happened to match his. "You didn't knock," he said.

"Because you wouldn't have said come in."

Good point.

Definitely not leaving, she picked up the scrawny cat sitting in his spare chair—Chuck, a stray who'd adopted them nearly a year ago—and sat herself, where she studied Stone like a hawk.

A mother hawk.

Chuck yawned wildly and settled on Annie's legs. Only a few months ago, the cat had been so skittish no one could even feed him, but Katie, their bookkeeper and now keeper of his brother Cam's heart, had tamed both the man and the cat in one fell swoop.

Annie absently stroked Chuck's chin as she eyed Stone.

Uncomfortable with the scrutiny, he shifted, jarred his poor body, and paid for it with a stab of pain. "Don't ask me if I feel as bad as I look."

"Okay." She petted the cat some more. "But do you?"

He let out a careful breath. *Yes.* "No."

"Liar."

Ignoring her, he went on with his paperwork. Or tried. It wasn't easy with every movement pulling on a wound or bruise. Ignoring that too, he pulled his keyboard closer. Once upon a time, he'd loved handling the paperwork for Wilder Adventures. But then they'd gotten busy and it'd become a real pain in his ass. He'd hired a bookkeeper, Riley, who'd then decided to become Mr. Mom, so he'd hired Katie, who'd fallen in love with his brother and was currently traipsing across the Andes on an extended pre-wedding honeymoon.

Leaving just him, TJ and Annie. Since neither TJ nor Annie ever touched the paperwork, he was on his own—and it was killing him.

He just needed a break, he thought. And an entire bottle of Advil.

Annie put her feet up on his desk, getting comfy, which meant he was going to be stuck with her for a while. Her long dark hair was back in a single braid. With her Wilder hoodie and dark jeans, she might have been sixteen rather than forty.

"Seriously," she said. "You look like something Chuck dragged in."

She acted as if she was either his boss or his mother, and though officially she was neither, unofficially she'd taken on both roles years ago, running the lodge and their hearts with equal ease.

She had help. Her husband Nick was one of TJ's oldest friends. Nick worked as their mechanic and helicopter pilot, and was as indispensable to Wilder Adventures as the rest of them. "Okay," he admitted. "I feel like shit. Happy?"

"Aw, baby. Here." She pulled Advil out of her pocket and handed them over.

"Bless your black heart."

She watched him swallow three tablets dry, then turn to organize some invoicing, swearing as he did. "I did warn you," she murmured, "About letting Cam fall in love with the book-keeper."

"They're meant to be," Stone said, and meant it. Cam had never been so happy, not even when he'd been a world champion snowboarder. "They deserve each other."

"You sound like a chick. You sure you didn't have a concussion after that fall?"

Stone shook his head. "You know, I actually tell people you love me."

"I do love you. Cam will be back from taking Katie through the Andes in a few weeks, so stop moping. We're doing just fine."

Fine was relative.

Their business had grown in huge proportions this past year, especially with all three of the brothers now leading various treks. But with Cam gone for the past month, wooing the woman he intended to bring into the Wilder fold permanently, it'd left a void.

And not just in the office.

He missed the sonofabitch. TJ was around, and indispensable, but he handled all the long treks, meaning he'd be gone soon enough as well.

Leaving Stone by himself.

"It's not brain surgery," Annie said.

He laughed softly—ouch—and looked at her. "You know, with you and Nick tossing out your divorce papers instead of filing them, I figured you'd be all warm and fuzzy."

"I dressed up as warm and fuzzy once for Halloween." Annie dropped Chuck to the floor and stood to pace.

Stone watched her a moment, realizing she wasn't here just to drive him crazy. Something was wrong, and his gut tightened. "What?"

"He wants a baby."

He blinked. "Nick?"

"No, the damn Easter Bunny. Yes, Nick. Jesus, Stone, keep up."

"So what's wrong with wanting a baby? You're only forty."

She shoved her hands in her pockets and looked . . . scared. "I already raised the three of you. I don't want to start over."

She'd been little more than a kid herself when she'd taken them on, but she'd kept them fed and out of jail—above and beyond the call of duty as far as he was concerned—and she'd been good at it. No, raising another kid wasn't what was bothering her. "That's not why."

"Okay." She walked the length of the office, pivoted, and did it again. "I'm not ready to take our relationship to that level."

"Come on." He had to laugh at that. "You've been together twenty years. A baby would be fun."

"*Fun?*" She whipped around to face him. "Fun? Let's see you breastfeed it. That we could call fun."

He shuddered. "I'm just saying."

"Well *I'm* just saying! I can't have a baby, I'm already getting fat just *thinking* about it." She plopped herself back down and glared at him. "I started running."

She hated exercise with the same passion she reserved for hating spiders. "Why would you do that?" he asked, alarmed not just for the guests they needed her to be nice to, but for him and his brothers. Running would only make her all that much more distant from warm and fuzzy. "Don't do that. Don't take up running."

"I have to. This body isn't what it used to be. Things aren't holding the way they used to." To show him, she cupped her breasts and jiggled them.

"Jesus!" He slapped a hand over his eyes. "Stop that."

"And my ass." She cupped that next. "It's falling, Stone. Losing the fight against gravity."

"Shoot me, *please.*"

"So I'm running." She sagged back. "Dammit."

"There's got to be a better way. Surgery."

"Hell no." She pointed at him. "You, the wussiest of the Wilders, are not alone in your needle phobia."

"TJ told you."

"Oh, yeah. He told me. Dr. Evil? Really?"

Stone shook his head in disgust. "He has a big mouth."

Annie laughed. "Yeah, he does. But we spent all last year worrying ourselves to death over Cam before the kid got his shit together, and apparently now we need a new obsession. We picked you."

"When? When did you pick me?"

"When TJ and I talked to Cam on the phone last night."

Stone shook his head. Last year he and TJ and Annie had nearly killed themselves trying to save a devastated Cam, who'd lost his life's passion—racing—to an injury. They hadn't been able to reach him, to help. But then Katie had come along and done it for them.

But Stone didn't need anyone worrying about him. He was fine.

"You're not yourself lately."

"Am too."

She slanted him a glance.

"Okay, I'm not." He shoved his hands in his hair. "But I'm fine."

"Fine as in you're going to vanish for a year?"

"That was Cam." He blew out a breath. "Not me. I wouldn't vanish. I love it here, you know that."

"But . . . ?" she pressed. "'Cause I definitely hear a but at the end of that sentence."

"But . . ." The truth was, the business had been TJ's love child, funded by Cam's professional athlete winnings, and run by Stone.

Which was fine. Great. Because how many people could say that they, literally, played for a living? Plus, it'd kept him and his brothers together, when once upon a time he'd wondered if they'd ever be okay.

But the guiding, the business end of things, none of it had been what Stone had seen himself doing with his life. Truth was, he was so damn far from his own dreams of renovating and restoring the glorious old historicals in the area that he couldn't even picture it anymore. He shrugged. "But we're busy. Really busy. And yeah, I know it's fun stuff we're busy with, but it's a lot of work."

"Oh, baby. You're tired is all."

"Yeah." It'd been ten years since he'd bought his first falling-down-on-its-axis Victorian in town and flipped it. He'd managed only two houses since then, and he wanted to do more, but he didn't have the time. He could buy something and hire out and get things moving, but he didn't want that either.

He refused to be a Cadillac contractor. He wanted to strap on the tool belt himself.

For that, he needed time.

Lots of it. "I want to do another building renovation."

"Oh." Annie lifted a brow. "I didn't know you were still thinking about that."

"Yeah, I—" On his desk, his Nextel beeped. Then came TJ's voice. "Stone you there? Over."

"See?" he said to Annie. "Busy. Too busy. I'm here," he said to TJ. "Over."

"Get the Doc and meet me at the base of Granite Meadows. ASAP. Or yesterday. Yesterday would be better. Over."

TJ was at Granite Meadows with clients, two women who'd

wanted to be taken to the top of the peak for a photo session. TJ had taken them up there in his Jeep. It was a four-wheel trek but an easy one, no hiking required. "What happened?"

"You're not going to believe this, but one of them is having a fucking baby."

Indeed, in the background a woman screamed, long and loud, bringing goose bumps to Stone's flesh. He leapt up, the movement agony. "Call Doc," he said to Annie, grimacing at his own quick movements. Shit, he hurt. "Tell him I'm coming for him—"

Ah, hell.

It wasn't old man Doc anymore at the clinic.

It was sexy Dr. Evil, who'd last seen Stone sprawled out on her examination table, naked and bloody. He'd had x-rated dreams about her for two nights running, dreams involving her white coat and nothing beneath it. Well, and maybe those prim heels . . .

Jesus, he needed his head examined. "Tell Emma I'll be there in five minutes and to be ready for a birth." He pushed the button on his Nextel as he moved fast enough that his still healing ribs protested. "On my way, TJ. Over."

"Hurry."

TJ sounded panicked, and hell, Stone couldn't blame him. He'd have said over the years that they'd seen and done it all, but this was new.

A baby on the trail.

Yeah, it was new, and not a good idea. He had basic medical training from working volunteer Search and Rescue, but none of them had delivered a baby. Just the thought left him a little wobbly.

Or maybe that was leftover from his own body recovering, but he was at the Urgent Care's driveway in seven minutes flat. It was a duplex, with the living quarters above the medical facility. He was relieved to see Emma running down the stairs toward him without him having to take the time to go get her.

So far so good.

She was wearing another pair of her fancy trousers, black this time, and a pale peach silky number on top that defined her very definable breasts.

Yeah, he was noticing. He'd have to be a hell of a lot more tired not to. She had real breasts and real hips and they drew him in like a magnet. Just last night, in his most excellent fantasy, she'd been straddling him with those hips, and—

She hopped up into his truck, dropped her medical bag into her lap and looked at him. "A baby on the trail? Are you kidding me?"

He liked that she didn't waste time with pleasantries. "It's a new one to me, too."

"People just can't go having babies out in the middle of nowhere. The nearest hospital is thirty miles away."

As he knew all too well.

"Did you call and put them on alert?" she asked.

"Yes, they're standing by if we need a heli."

"So no one is coming but you?"

"And you."

She just gave him a banal look. "Speaking of that, why me?"

"Well I thought maybe it was the only way to get you to go out with me."

When she narrowed her eyes, he offered a smile.

She didn't return it. "Is there really a baby or not?"

"There's really a baby. Well, not yet, but soon."

"On the trail," she clarified. "Where there are bears and dirt and bugs and oh, I don't know, a thousand different germs and bugs, not to mention things that could go wrong?"

"Yeah."

"*Shit*."

Stone out and out grinned. She might be edgy and bossy and seriously tense, not to mention bad-tempered, but she wasn't boring. "I hope you weren't too busy."

"Are you kidding?" She was going through her bag. "The people here look at me like I'm an alien. I was considering cutting off my own finger for something to treat."

Ah, there it was. His opening, which he unabashedly took. "So you should be thanking me for bringing you something exciting."

"A baby," she murmured, definitely not thanking him. "On the trail. Good Lord." She sighed. "Definitely not in New York anymore, Dorothy."

He laughed, something he'd done far too little of lately—which meant Dr. Emma wasn't just good for erotic dreams, but maybe . . . just maybe something more as well.

Chapter 4

Stone drove with a controlled speed and intensity that rivaled any cabbie Emma had ever met. In the city, crazy driving had never bothered her for some reason, but here in the remote wild, wild west, with nothing but trees, trees and more trees surrounding them, it seemed more than a little terrifying.

Stone took a hard turn and she slid in her seat against the constraints of the seatbelt. Not her driver. Nope, Stone leaned with the car—though he did wince, probably his ribs—and continued driving without missing a beat.

She watched him. Actually, she couldn't seem to take her eyes off him. His jeans were clearly beloved old friends, soft-looking and faded. There was a rip over one knee and the opposite thigh, which brought her attention to his long legs folded even in the large cab of his truck. His long-sleeved performance jersey was shoved up to his elbows and read Wilder Adventures over one hard pec. His arms, tanned and sinewy, flexing as he worked the wheel over the roads, still had medical wrap covering the worst of his cuts and scrapes.

Luckily the dirt roads, narrow and curvy as they were, were at least in fairly decent condition. They'd had a lot of precipitation lately. She'd caught the tail end of an unreal spring first-hand, which had caused all the thick, impenetrable growth on either side of the road.

A little too *Twilight Zone* for her taste, even in the middle of the day. The air smelled like fresh pine and dirt, and at this altitude, felt hotter than hell as it blew in the opened windows. Stone glanced at her and caught her looking at him.

"You're tough to read," he said.

"What are you trying to figure out?"

"The last time I saw you, you saw a whole hell of a lot of me."

"True."

"I was just thinking that you must have some reaction to seeing me naked before we've even shared a coffee . . ."

Yes. Yes, she'd had a reaction. A very private one. "That was my job."

He nodded. "And sharing a coffee—"

"Would be a major mistake."

"Why?"

Because I keep picturing you naked. "Because I don't mix business and pleasure."

"Ever?"

"Ever."

He took a hard right and headed up a narrow fire road.

"Where are we going?"

"Up past the summit, which is where TJ took Neely and Lilah, our clients."

As they climbed, and as the road narrowed even more, with the wild growth on either side closing in on them, Emma gripped the console as he sped them around a tight corner on the dirt road, nearly getting some air beneath the tires.

He shot her another glance, his eyes touching on her white-knuckled grip on the dash. "You okay?"

"I'll let you know if you get me there alive." She pried her gaze off the road and studied his face. He was totally at ease, his big, scraped-up hands on the wheel. The wound over his eye was covered with several large Band-Aids, his apparent fix-all for everything. The stitching didn't appear inflamed or swollen but he had shadows under his eyes. "And you?" she asked. "How are you feeling?"

"Peachy."

"Liar. You look like hell."

"Aw, thanks."

"Ibuprophen? Icing? Rest?"

Instead of answering, he pulled his vibrating cell phone from his pocket and pushed TALK.

TJ's voice filled the cab. "Where the fuck are you, over?"

"On my way." Stone glanced at Emma. "With the doc, over." He sped up a little, wincing as they took a tight corner and he had to shift.

Yeah, definitely his ribs. "So?" she pressed. "Advil at least?"

"Yeah, I've taken plenty of good old Vitamin A, not that it's helped. As for resting? Hasn't happened."

"Why not?"

"Don't have the time, not with Cam in the Andes and TJ accepting every trip that comes our way." He flashed a grim smile. "Being a mountain bum is hard work."

"You need rest to heal, Stone"

"Yeah, I'll get around to that." He pulled the truck into the small clearing at the top of the hill next to a Jeep with the Wilder logo on the side. "But for now, let's have a baby."

As Stone and Emma got out of the truck, a woman screamed, and every single hair on Stone's body stood straight up. "It's killing her."

Emma didn't respond. Whatever she was thinking, she kept it to herself as she moved quickly but calmly, her face cool and quiet.

Her game face.

Man, she'd gotten grace and poise in spades, he thought, following her to the front of the Jeep, where on the ground, on a large blanket overlooking the entire valley below, lay a woman writhing in pain, another woman kneeling at her side.

TJ was there too, but he came toward Stone, heading him off, looking pale and shaky.

"How the hell did you not know one of them was pregnant?" Stone asked him.

"She hid it under a big sweatshirt." TJ shoved his fingers through his hair. "I had no clue. What about you? *You're* the one who took their applications."

"Sorry, but we don't have the 'are you pregnant' question on the forms."

"It doesn't matter how it happened now." TJ let down the tailgate of Stone's truck and sat heavily. "It happened."

From the ground, Lilah screamed again. Both brothers jumped.

"She *planned* this," TJ whispered in horror. "She *wanted* this. They're a couple, a lesbian couple, and hardcore hikers. They wanted their baby born on the trail. A natural birth, Lilah said. Before she started screaming." TJ swiped a shaky hand over his face. "And then Neely panicked and said she thought something was wrong, and I—"

"Panicked too?"

"Hell, yeah."

"Guys." This was from Emma. "Come here."

TJ swiveled his head toward Stone in sharp panic. "She can't make me."

Emma pulled on a pair of medical gloves. "I'm going to need one of you to strap on your big boy pants and man up. I need another set of hands."

One minute Stone was standing there thinking "fuck no",

and in the next, TJ ever so helpfully gave him a shove toward her.

Emma looked up and locked gazes with him, nodding her thanks.

Ah, hell. He wouldn't have walked away from a stranger in need, and he wouldn't walk away from this. Funny how he'd always thought he'd done it all in his thirty-two years, but as it turned out he hadn't, and though he knew next to nothing about birthing a baby, he knew two things. One, it was going to be damned messy, and two, *intimate.*

Which meant he was about to get messy and intimate with a woman he didn't know how he felt about.

Then Lilah's next scream tore his soul, and incapable of just standing there, he moved closer.

"Support her from behind," Emma demanded when he dropped to his knees beside her, trying desperately not to look. "Don't let her lie flat. She needs to be propped up. Neely, help me get this Chux pad beneath her for a clean area."

Oh, Jesus. He was going to have to look.

"There are no needles," Emma told him. "I'm fresh out."

He met her eyes, and there in those sharp baby blues, behind the fierce determination he was coming to think of as her game face, he caught a flash of amusement.

Then it was gone. "The baby's head is crowning," she said quietly. "We don't have time to get her out of here. I need to know. Are you in this or not?"

Hell. If she could do this so calmly, he sure as hell could, too. "In."

Lilah cried out and fisted a hand in Stone's shirt, pulling hard against his hurting ribs. "I need to push!" she yelled, panting.

"Okay," Emma soothed. "But let's get you into a better position first." She looked at Stone, and he nodded.

Smiling as reassuringly at Lilah as he could muster, he moved in behind her, taking her weight against him, which prompted a sigh from her. "Better?"

"Yes." Cradled, her back to his front, she gripped both his arms and immediately started writhing. "Oh God, oh God, another one. Another contraction already!"

"It's okay," Neely told her, but her eyes were wild. "It's all going to be okay. We planned this, we knew it was going to be rough."

"*Rough on who?*" Lilah, lost in her pain, squeezed Stone's arms like a vice. "Listen, I changed my mind. I don't want to do this anymore."

"Lilah." Emma looked up from between Lilah's propped knees. "I can see the head. I need you to push now."

"This was a bad idea," Lilah gasped. "I don't want to push anymore." She lifted her head up to Neely. "Let's just go home, okay? You don't mind, right? I'll push tomorrow, I promise."

"Oh, baby," Neely whispered with tears in her eyes as she stroked Lilah's hair. "You can do this. I know you can."

"But I can't." Lilah started sobbing. "I just can't. You do it for me, okay? Please, Neely? Please do it for me."

She sounded so terrified that even Stone was wishing he could do it for her, but once again Emma took charge. "Lilah, this is all you. Just some pushing, and then you're done. You can do this."

"No, I can't—ohmigod, another one!" She screamed, thrashing around in agony while Stone tried to keep her on the clean pad.

Neely whirled on Emma, tears streaming down her face as she grabbed Emma by the front of the shirt. "Goddammit, do something for her!"

"Whoa." Stone leaned over Lilah, intending to pry Neely's hands off of Emma. She was in this position because of him, which made him responsible for her, but he forgot one thing.

Emma could hold her own.

She simply shrugged off Neely and put her hands on the woman's shoulders. "Get it together," she told Neely quietly and firmly. "Lilah needs to see that you have it together." Then without waiting for Neely to decide whether she could or couldn't handle it, Emma came up on her knees and leaned into Lilah, getting right in her face, which by default was also right in Stone's. "Lilah, listen to me. I need you to—"

"I can't!"

"Yes, you can, and you will. *Push*."

When she spoke like that, with all that authority and certainness, even Stone wanted to push.

"I can't"!" Lilah cried again.

If he'd been Emma, he might have been tempted to remind Lilah that she'd wanted this, that if she'd gotten herself to a hospital like common sense dictated, she might have been given pain medications, maybe an epidural, but she'd come here.

By her own choice.

"Look," Emma said, in all her glorious New York tough-ass edginess. "Yes, this sucks golf balls, the pain is like being ripped in two. But the baby is here, Lilah. *Right* here. All you have to do is push and it'll be over and you'll be able to hold your baby."

"My baby," Lilah repeated weakly, sweat running down her temples.

"That's right," Emma said firmly, hair falling loose, her clothes smeared with blood and her own sweat, kneeling on the blanket out in the wilderness that Stone knew she wasn't too fond of.

It was fascinating to him. *She* was fascinating to him, and elegant and sophisticated, and so *not* the priss he'd thought. Not anywhere close.

"*Your* baby," Emma reminded Lilah. "There's a big prize at

the end of this hell, and it's your beautiful baby. Now let's do this."

Stone watched amazed as Lilah let out a breath, stopped crying and nodded. "Okay," she said. "Let's do this."

It boggled Stone's mind. Emma hadn't coddled. It certainly wasn't in her nature to be particularly sweet or gentle in her firm determination either, but she was undoubtedly extremely, undeniably, kind as she bulldogged through and got her way.

Right then and there, Stone felt a little catch in his gut. Not a crush, not exactly, but something that might be worse.

Far worse. Which was going to be damned inconvenient.

"A baby," Lilah murmured roughly to Neely as they kissed. "I actually almost forgot."

Neely laughed through her tears, and back on track now, swiped Lilah's face, stroked her legs, doing the deep breathing with her.

"On the count of three," Emma said, in charge of her world, and at the moment, also Stone's. "One, two, *three*!"

Lilah pushed, and screamed, and pushed some more, and Stone thought she was going to break both his wrists, but then she sagged back against his very sore chest, panting for breath. Realizing his pain was nothing compared to hers, he didn't mention it. "Doing great," he said, hoping it was true, and also hoping he had some unbroken bones left when she was done.

"The head's out," Emma said, doing something with a suction bulb between Lilah's legs that Stone didn't want to know about.

"Push again," Emma directed.

"Oh, God."

"You can do this, Lilah. I can see your baby's beautiful head. Now sit up and push!"

Stone braced himself, said goodbye to the rest of his bones, and kept his eyes on the sky while Lilah straightened and pushed.

And pushed.

This was accompanied by plenty of screaming, more squeezing, and out of the corner of Stone's eye he saw TJ standing out of the way, his back turned, on the phone to the hospital, the bastard, not getting bled on and not getting his bones broken.

"Look," Neely suddenly cried. "Ohmigod, look!"

Stone instinctively looked. He saw . . .

Oh, Jesus. He saw blood and gore, and female parts stretched to limits that boggled his mind and made him want to beg for forgiveness for his entire race.

The screaming echoed in his head, which suddenly felt detached from his body, and if he'd been standing, he'd be flat on his ass by now, but he had Lilah squeezing the holy hell out of him, keeping him conscious.

"I've got her!" Emma said in triumph. She came up on her knees, cradling her bundle in a towel, vigorously drying the baby and suctioning the nose and mouth at the same time. She expertly swapped out the wet towel for a dry one as the baby began to wail. "A gorgeous baby girl," she declared, and set her on Lilah's belly.

The baby squawked and let out a gusty cry.

Stone stared down at the sticky, gooped up baby in shocked awe.

A living, breathing person.

Emma was evaluating the baby for color, respirations, muscle movement, anything unusual as she clamped the umbilical cord, and then turned her attention to the placenta, while Stone's head just spun.

It was truly the most amazing thing he'd ever seen, and he lifted his gaze to Emma and found her already looking at him, her eyes suspiciously bright and misty.

And then she did something totally unexpected. She smiled at him.

Yeah, she was tough as nails and cynical and blunt. And sometimes just a little mean.

And she cried over a newborn.

Neely and Lilah were both laughing and sobbing. Once Emma said that everything was okay, Stone and TJ carried Lilah to TJ's Jeep. They got her and the baby settled in and TJ drove them down the hill to Neely's sister, who was a midwife and registered nurse in South Shore.

Which left Stone and Emma alone.

He walked to where she stood at the cliff overlooking the open meadow below. "You okay?"

"Always." She turned her head toward him and did the damnedest thing. She smiled again, a God-given, sweet, warm, real smile that met her eyes and curved her mouth, and rocked his world. "And how are you?" she asked.

He let out a low laugh. "I'll come right out and admit it. My knees are still shaking."

She smiled again and blew at least a thousand more of his brain cells, which didn't leave him with much. But wow, the smile softened her. Made her seem gentle.

Sweet.

All the things he'd thought her void of, all the things he tended to love in a woman, and he had one thought as he felt another catch from deep inside him, as his body went still on high alert and his pulse picked up speed—

Oh, shit.

He needed to back up. Or better yet, turn and walk away. That was the easy thing to do at this point. But did he ever take the easy route? Hell, no. The hard way was his only way, always, and he stepped close.

Her smile deepened, and his next thought was hell yeah, here it came, the thank you for his help. He'd shrug and say it'd been his pleasure, and she'd maybe move in for a hug, or better yet . . .

A kiss.

Yeah, a slow, hot, melting thank you kiss would suit him just fine, with lots of tongue and busy hands—

"So you're afraid of needles *and* pass out at the sight of blood, huh?" she asked, amused.

She wasn't thanking him.

She was laughing at him. *Openly.* He tried to be insulted, but Jesus, when she smiled? It was amazing.

She was amazing. "Really?" he asked, letting loose of a stupid smile himself. "You're going to go there?"

Still laughing, she nodded. "Yeah."

"That's cruel, Emma. Very cruel."

"Sorry."

Sorry, his ass.

She wasn't sorry, she wasn't anywhere close to sorry. She was cracking up, and he should be annoyed. But she looked so damned sexy as she laughed at him.

"I thought you were going to pass out a few times," she said.

"Well you'll have to excuse me, I've never seen a vagina from that angle before."

She only laughed harder and patted his arm like he was a four-year-old, before heading toward his truck in her fancy clothes now streaked with dirt, blood and other stuff he didn't want to think about.

God, she was hot as hell.

They weren't finished, not by a long shot, so he followed her. "For the record, I *didn't* pass out. I was in it, all the way."

She stopped at the hood of his truck on the passenger side. "You were, for which I'm most thankful. But seeing as you're so weak-kneed and all, maybe I should drive."

Yeah, she was sweet and gentle and soft, all right. Like a sleeping lion.

"We need to hurry." She glanced at her watch. "I'm on a schedule here."

He leaned toward her, his hands on the hood as he faced her. "What are you in such a hurry to go back to?"

"I have things to do."

He had to laugh. "You ever slow down and smell the roses, Doc?"

"I'm not a roses kind of woman."

"How about relaxing?" he asked, thinking he figured he knew the answer. She wasn't much into that either.

"Relaxing bores me."

"How about fun. Do you ever have fun?"

"Yes," she said. "But not when I'm three thousand miles from home, in a town that pays in cholesterol-laden casseroles and looks at me like I'm an alien."

An uptight, anal, sleeping lion, with *teeth*. "I don't look at you like you're an alien," he said.

"Yes, but you don't count."

"Why don't I count?"

She hesitated. "Because you look at me in a different way."

"Like?"

"Like . . ." Interestingly enough, she blushed.

"Like I'm attracted to you?" he pressed, amused.

Her eyes met his. "Yes. Like that."

"Because I am. Very much."

She eyed him a long beat before hopping up into his truck without a word. Not exactly a glowing recommendation but she hadn't slammed the door on that admitted attraction either, a fact he decided meant good things.

Or so he hoped.

Chapter 5

Emma's dad had called her twice, and she'd missed both calls, so that night she hopped into his spare truck to go visit him.

His small, remote cabin was outside of town, about ten miles up a dirt road on the shores of Jackson Lake, where he spent his days rehabbing by fly-fishing to his heart's content.

The problem wasn't the dirt road, or the ten miles.

Okay, that was the problem. As was the fact that she drove like shit.

She didn't drive in New York, though she did have her license. She actually liked to drive, but she didn't have much opportunity to do so.

Until she'd come here. First of all, the truck was huge. And crotchety. And not exactly easy to handle. She held her breath each of the ten miles, but luckily it was a dry day and she managed only one or two near misses with wayward branches, and that one kamikaze squirrel, but they'd both survived.

By the time she arrived, she was sweating buckets and her father was just coming in from fishing. He was medium built, with only a slight pudge to belie his years. He had a full head of curly gray hair that stuck straight up, whether from its own mind or lack of a brush, she had no idea. "You called. Twice."

"Sorry," he said. "I just wanted to . . . connect. See if you were doing okay."

"That was my question for you."

"I'm doing good. The clinic driving you crazy?"

"No." A lie.

He just looked at her, patient. Understanding. And she caved. "Yes."

He smiled sympathetically. "Sorry. I know it's a different pace than you're used to. I guess I was hoping you'd enjoy it."

"Jury is still out," she said kindly. No use in telling him how restless she felt. "I brought more casseroles. The healthy ones."

"I like the unhealthy ones better." He had laughing eyes and an easy smile, but she didn't find this funny.

"No fat," she said, and he sighed.

"Your medical records?" she asked, as she did every visit.

"I forgot. Next time," he said as he did every visit.

After the initial pleasantries, they stood inside his cabin, him in his fishing vest, she in the doctor coat she'd forgotten to remove, staring awkwardly at each other.

She wondered, as she did every single day—why had she come?

Because for better or worse, they were all each other had. In spite of being all work and no play, that meant something to her.

He meant something to her.

They had nothing in common, nothing to talk about, and he didn't have cable, but they were family.

That didn't mean that they actually liked each other. Truthfully, he looked just as grateful as she felt when she left.

She sweated off another two pounds on the way back, and then stayed up late reading some medical journals and eating a mystery casserole from the freezer. It was one that had looked like maybe it was too high in fat content for her father, and as she chewed she could feel her arteries clog up as she gained back her two pounds.

Damn, she needed something to do other than eat, but Wishful tended to roll up its collective sidewalks at sunset. The baby delivery today had been great, but that had been the only exciting thing to happen to her in days. Weeks.

Two months.

Already she was drowning in boredom again, as in head under, going down for the count, drowning.

She didn't want to resent her father for this, she really didn't. It wasn't his fault he'd had a heart attack, that he needed help to keep this place going until he made a full recovery.

Or that they were all each other had left, which essentially meant he was as stuck with her as she was with him.

Nope, she didn't blame him. She just wished things were different. Wished she could look at his records and make sure he was recouping okay, or if there was something—*anything*—she could do to expedite it.

She had far too much time to obsess over that. Too much time for everything, especially at night when she had nothing left to do except watch the one channel she got—which ran nothing but screwball romantic comedies.

Her mom would be pestering her to get the hell out. God, she missed that noisy, pushy, bossy woman with her whole heart. Sandy wouldn't be happy to know Emma was here, not one little bit.

Emma wasn't happy either.

But . . . but now that she knew how bad her dad was at the bookkeeping and billing, she was worried that he'd run out of money by year's end if he didn't make some changes.

She had ideas for those changes. He could be treating bigger cases, could be far more successful if he tried to compete with the South Shore clinics.

But Eddie Sinclair didn't think like that. He was much more laid-back than she, preferring to just let things happen. Every time she'd tried to bring up business talk, he got an amused look on his face and told her everything would be fine if she remembered to keep breathing.

She *was* breathing, dammit, but his lackadaisical ways didn't help. How he'd ever lived alone all these years was beyond her. He'd *chosen* to do so. *Chosen* to let her mom leave, *chosen* not to have joint custody, or any sort of visitation.

Old wounds, she reminded herself. She was over it. So over it. She got over things quickly, always had. Except usually she had something to occupy her mind, something like work.

At least Spencer was flying in for a few days. She was counting on her co-worker and closest friend to liven things up around there.

She set down her casserole and walked through her father's place. It was familiar to her. It should be, she'd lived here for her first six years, and being here gave her an undeniable sense of nostalgia. Oddly enough, she remembered every nook and cranny of the three tiny bedrooms, two tinier bathrooms and postage stamp size living area and kitchen. She remembered her mom cooking in that kitchen . . .

She swallowed the sorrow that never seemed to go all the way down, and right there in the middle of the living room, she let it all wash over her.

Her mom had been born in New York. A city girl at heart, she'd fallen in love on a college science field trip in the Sierras with the brand new young doctor teaching the course.

Her father.

Blinded by nineteen-year-old love, Sandy had given up everything and moved across the country to be with him. They'd lived in wedded bliss until her first Sierra winter.

It'd hit hard.

The twenty feet of snow had been a rough shock, but going

weeks at a time with no contact with the outside world had slowly done her mom in. When a bear had broken into their kitchen and eaten the Junior's Cheesecake she'd had shipped from Manhattan, she'd tossed up her hands, said, "Stick a fork in me, I'm done, Eddie", and had packed herself and Emma up.

Eddie hadn't tried to stop her.

Back in New York, Sandy had rented a one room flat, and though Emma knew now that money had been tight as Sandy worked sixty hour weeks nursing, Sandy had never once let on.

Emma wandered to the log mantle over the fireplace, and looked at the frames. There was one of herself as a newborn, another of her around five and missing her two front teeth. Then there was a glaring gap in the pictures because the next frame was of Emma at her college graduation, when her father had made an unscheduled appearance.

But the one that caught her by surprise, the one that grabbed her by the throat, was of her mom. She looked to be in her early twenties, and was smiling with easy whimsy into the camera. Emma reached for the frame, picking it up, running her finger over the glass as if she could touch her mom one more time. "I'm back," she whispered. "Back in Wishful. Who'd have thought it, huh?"

Yes, well, make sure you check for spiders before you get into bed, darling. Those wolf spiders are everywhere.

Her mom's soft, laughing voice echoed in Emma's head, clear as a bell, making her laugh in shock. Clearly, she was far more tired than she thought. That, or she needed a mocha latte pretty damn bad.

She settled on sleep.

The next day, Stone took a group on a moonlight hike up Sierra Point. It'd been five days since his accident, and he felt much better. Finally. After the hike, his guests, who were up from the Bay Area, requested he drop them off at a local bar, where they could drink the rest of the night away.

Though there wasn't much left to it—it was nearly one in the morning—he dropped them off at Moody's, then walked back out to his truck and faced an annoying dilemma.

A flat tire.

He pulled out the tools and changed it himself, somehow managing to kneel on a rusty nail, cutting open his knee in the process. Probably the same rusty nail that had wrecked his tire to begin with, and besides bleeding down his leg, it hurt like a son-of-a-bitch.

As if he didn't have enough injuries to deal with.

With a sigh, he went to the glove box for his first-aid kit, and found . . . nothing. "Goddammit, TJ."

TJ was always too lazy to restock his own kit, far preferring to grab Stone's. He looked down. He was bleeding like a stuck pig through the new hole in his favorite Levi's. Shit. Maybe if he just cleaned it out really good, he'd be fine—which seemed to be the theme of his life lately.

Problem was, he didn't want to die of tetanus. He could go the twenty minutes home to clean out the cut, or be at Doc's in two.

In the old days, he'd have had no problem showing up on Doc's doorstep in the middle of the night. Hell, Doc had given each of the Wilders a key, and there'd been many, many times when Stone had just let himself into the clinic, grabbed what he needed, gone on his merry way without waking Doc, who'd appreciated not having to get up.

Hoping the apple didn't fall too far from the tree, even while knowing it had, Stone put the truck into gear and drove to the clinic. It was locked up tighter than a drum, all lights off. Limping now, dammit, he knocked lightly on the door to be polite, then fished out his key and let himself in. He flipped on the reception room light because if Emma woke up, he didn't want to scare her. Doc had always kept the staff kitchen stocked up for the few times he had to use it as a third exam room. Stone limped across the room and flipped on that light as well, heading for the supply closet. He pulled out the hydrogen peroxide, some gauzes and—

"Hands where I can see them, asshole, or I'll kick your balls into next week."

He raised his hands in the air—slowly because he was still aching like crazy—and turned. Emma stood in the doorway in a pair of men's boxers and a thin camisole, wielding a baseball bat like she knew how to use it. Her hair was loose and a bit wild, but her eyes were ice. She wore no make up, which he loved, and he really loved the bed head, but mostly his brain stuttered and came to a screeching halt on the fact that she wasn't wearing a bra.

He really, really loved that part. "Just me," he said lightly. "And FYI, you can't threaten a guy's balls when he's facing the other way."

She didn't lower her bat, not a single inch. "I can threaten them now."

He resisted the urge to cover them. "Okay, let's all just relax."

"Relax? You broke in!"

She was looking and sounding very New York, and maybe he was sick, but he liked it.

A lot.

And maybe, just maybe, he'd meant for this to happen tonight. "I didn't break in, I have a key. Your father gave it to me. I tend to have a lot of emergencies . . ." He flashed a smile. "And he liked his sleep."

"You want me to believe that my father let you come and go through his medical supplies whenever you wanted?"

"As the situation required," he corrected, trying another smile.

She still didn't match it. She was scowling, actually, and that sharp gaze ran down his body, stopping on a dime at the hole in his jeans revealing the bloody knee. "You're hurt."

"Just a little. I want to clean it out and—"

"Let me guess. Get a Band-Aid." With a sigh, she finally lowered the baseball bat and jabbed it toward a chair. "Sit."

Instead he pulled himself up on the counter and eyed the bat as she set it down. "You actually ever use that thing?"

"Didn't I just threaten to kick your ass?" She smiled grimly. "Trust me, I could have done it."

Maybe. Only because he'd been too busy dropping his jaw to the floor to protect himself. Holy shit, the woman had been hiding a smoking hot bod; full breasts with nipples that were pressing up against the material of her cami, a sweet set of hips and a strip of bared belly, revealed by the boxer shorts she'd rolled over several times to adjust to her frame.

She moved past him, picked up one of the doctor's coats hanging on a rack and slipped into it. Damn.

"Sorry," she said at his expression. "Only invited midnight callers get to see me in my pj's."

"Can I get an invite?"

Her laugh told him no way in hell was he getting an invite, but he smiled anyway. "You look pretty when you laugh."

She was still smiling when she came close and bent, peering at his knee. "No stitches this time."

"Good."

She straightened and eyed the cut over his eye. "And that looks to be healing. I thought maybe you'd need some antibiotics, but you don't. *But.*"

Ah, hell.

"You need a tetanus shot. You know that, right?"

"Yeah." He felt his vision go a little fuzzy. Jesus, he was fucking pathetic.

"You going to pass out on me?"

"Not if you take your coat off again."

"Nice try." She was preparing the tetanus shot, and he was sweating and feeling sick when she glanced over at him. She shook her head and sighed. "Unbelievable."

"I know." He swiped his brow. "I—"

"Not you. Me. I can't believe I'm going to do this for you, but . . ." She let the coat hit the floor. "Consider it a present, from me to you."

It was a great present. She had great legs, long and toned. Great arms, too. But his gaze dropped to her breasts as she came to a stop at his hip, shoved up the sleeve of his shirt and swiped his skin with an antiseptic gauze. Her skin was smooth and creamy, and his mouth watered. She smelled amazing, too, like— "Ouch!"

She slapped a Band-Aid on him. "You might have a sore arm for the next few days."

"I have to rock climb tomorrow."

"Maybe I should have given it to you in the ass then?"

He laughed, but when he looked at her face, he realized she wasn't kidding. "You really are mean."

She smiled as she bent for the doctor's coat, giving him a heart-stopping view. "I know. And honestly? You shouldn't be rock climbing. Not with your ribs and stitches and other various injuries. You shouldn't be doing anything tomorrow."

That said, she covered up again and was ushering him to the door, pushing him out into the night, the sound of the bolt sliding home his only company.

Well, that and the memory of her in those little boxers and cami, took him all the way home, followed him into his shower and through a whole night of new and even more erotic dreams.

The next morning, Emma opened the clinic's doors for all the patients who hadn't broken into the place in the middle of the night. It was eight sharp, and she had one patient. Cece Potter, Moody's waitress. The young twenty-ish woman needed an antibiotics prescription for a throat infection, and alternately called her "Dr. Sinclair"—in a snooty tone, and "that woman that Stone's seeing"—also in a snooty tone—which was more disconcerting.

"I'm not—" Emma started.

But Cece Potter, not interested in explanations, was gone, and Emma had no other patients to distract her.

That woman Stone was seeing?

Seriously?

By noon she was ready to tear out her hair when Missy Thorton showed up with a sprained thumb. Missy was the cashier at Thorton's Hardware store in town. She'd been in Wishful since the dawn of time, or close to it. She had a sweet face and a grandmotherly shape that lowered Emma's resistance because she had a soft spot for women who looked like they'd lived and lived well.

"Is your daddy back at work yet?" Missy asked as Emma x-rayed her thumb.

"Not yet. Nothing's broken. I'll just wrap it and—"

"Maybe I should go to South Shore for a second opinion."

"You could, but this isn't complicated."

"Hmmm . . ."

It took some convincing, but finally Emma was wrapping the woman's sprained thumb. Outside the window, the street was busy with the lunchtime crunch. The shops were doing a good business. Everyone was doing a good business but Emma.

"Hmmm," the woman said again.

Emma looked up into Missy's face. "Is something wrong?"

"What if it's broken?"

"I showed you the x-ray. There's no break."

"Hmmm."

Across the street, a pickup pulled up and parked. Stone's. He wore loose jeans and a polo shirt. Tall and sure of himself, he pulled out a clipboard and headed toward the corner building, moving with the carefulness of someone who'd been beaten up by three women in a bar only a week ago.

Or whatever had really happened to him.

Oblivious to her eyes on him, he headed—limping slightly—down the sidewalk, stopping in front of the old, rundown building on the corner. It had a FOR SALE sign on it.

Bending his head, he wrote something on the clipboard.

"I hear you treated him," Missy said.

"Who?"

"The man you're staring at instead of concentrating on your patient who."

Yeah. Point taken. But just looking at Stone invoked memories, his bad boy eyes, filled with wicked intent, his smile, the one that backed up that intent.

His naked body sprawled on her examination table.

She gave herself a second to digest that image.

"He is a fine boy." Missy was smiling shrewdly. "Very fine."

Except Stone Wilder was no boy. In fact, just remembering how little he resembled a boy brought a little secret tingle to certain places she hadn't thought about in a while.

"And he's very good at what he does," Missy went on.

Yes, well, how hard could it be to play all day long?

"My niece's boy was heading straight for juvie last year," the older woman said. "And landed himself on one of those treks the Wilders take troubled kids out on. He did really well, but when he wanted to go again, Stone told him that he couldn't go out if he kept up the stealing. So Trevor gave it up. The trek changed him, calmed him down. That was Stone's doing, pure and simple."

Okay, that didn't sound like he was all mountain bum.

"Women love him." Missy eyed her wrapped thumb this way and that. "So don't blame yourself for having a crush on him."

"I don't—"

"Of course you do, dear. You were practically drooling. Don't worry, there's far worse things to be than Stone's woman."

Okay, that was two times now she'd been called that. "I'm not his woman."

"Maybe we should consult with Doc about the possible break?" Missy asked, still eyeing her thumb.

Emma tried a deep breath. Didn't help. "I can assure you, Missy, I know what I'm doing."

"*Hmmm.*"

How she managed such a wealth of doubt in that single syllable, Emma had no idea but she'd become used to it. Four years of undergrad and four years of medical school at Columbia, residency at NY Presbyterian, two years in the NY Bellevue ER—one of the busiest in the country—and yet the people here *still* saw her as Doc's kid, not a "real" doctor. She pulled Missy's chart close to document today's visit.

"Did you know I knew your momma?"

"I didn't, no." Under diagnosis, Emma wrote: sprained thumb. She refrained from adding: pain in the ass.

"She was a good woman. A hard worker, too."

Her mom *had* been a good person, and a very hard worker, up until the day she'd died six months ago, and the kind words softened Emma's heart with memories. "Thank you."

"I don't know what happened to change her, none of us ever knew."

Emma managed to keep the smile in place by sheer will as she stood. "Keep the thumb elevated, Mrs. Thorton. Aspirin as needed for the pain."

"I mean she just up and left your father, one of the best men in Wishful. Crazy, right?"

Emma didn't mean to respond but she found she couldn't help but defend her mom. "She had her reasons."

"Yes." Missy nodded slowly. "I remember quite clearly how she—"

"I'm sorry." Emma forced a smile. "But I don't want to get into this now." Or ever. "I'm busy and—"

The bell jangled out front, for once not annoying her. Saved by the ceramic cow bell. "I'll print you a bill."

"Oh." Missy looked startled. "But your father just sends them to me at home."

Where they were ignored. "Things have changed." She moved out of the treatment room toward the front desk, where she'd hoped to have a receptionist by now, except for the lack of money with which to pay one.

"Got stung by a bee on the jobsite," a twentysomething guy said to her from the front door, waving a hand supported by a wrist in a cast. "I can't get the stinger out. The boss wanted me to go to South Shore, but I didn't have enough gas."

"Oh, the doctor's not in," Missy told him. "He's still recouping."

"Bummer."

"The doctor *is* in," Emma corrected, resisting the urge to thunk her head down on the counter. "Come on in. Please. I can help you."

The would-be patient swiveled his head to Missy for reassurance.

Missy shrugged as if to say *It's your risk.*

Emma ground her back teeth to powder and pointed to the guy's cast. "What happened there?"

"Oh, I fell hiking up the summit this past weekend. Tripped over my own laces and broke my wrist."

The summit was only three miles from here. A quick five minute ride, tops. "Where did you get it cast?"

"South Shore."

Lake Tahoe, which was at least forty-five minutes away at the best of times. She nearly did thunk her head down at that.

"I needed a doctor," he said.

"I *am* a doctor."

"Okay, cool. You remove stingers?"

Chapter 6

That night, Emma risked driving the roads out to her father's cabin again under the guise of bringing him another casserole, hoping for a sign that her torture would be coming to an end.

He accepted the casserole, but still couldn't produce his medical records—shocker.

On the way home, there was a wind that knocked the truck around some, and she found herself holding her breath all the way back. By the time she got into town, she needed chocolate.

Lots of chocolate.

She parked at Wishful's one and only grocery store in desperate search of a sugar rush. She ran into Missy in the dairy aisle and Annie in the cereal aisle.

Small town living.

She was deciding between *Time* and *Scientific Weekly* when she felt the odd tingle of awareness race down her back and settle into her good spots.

Oh, boy.

Even without looking, she knew what that meant. Turning,

she locked gazes with Stone, trying to reconcile the laid-back guy she thought she'd figured out with the guy Missy had talked about.

He was propping up a vitamin display with his shoulder—which he did quite nicely, she noted, in his loose cargoes and plain T-shirt, iPod ear-pieces hanging around his neck. He didn't move, doing his best to perpetuate that lazy guy image he seemed to enjoy so much.

"Doc."

"Stone."

He smiled, slow as a Cheshire cat, and lifted his hand, revealing the bottle of Advil he held. "Getting some more of that good vitamin A."

"You're still hurting?" she asked while trying to decide who he was—mountain bum, or saint. Neither, she decided, but the jury was still out on who he might really be.

Strangely enough, her heart was suddenly racing as if she'd run down the aisles. An odd physical reaction to a patient.

Except not just a patient.

Funny how her mother's voice turned up in her head at the least expected times. Like now.

He's a mountain hottie, darling. Ignore mountain hotties. They'll snag your heart, and then stomp on it.

Oh, for God's sake. She focused on Stone. Not exactly a hardship. "How are you feeling?" she asked since he hadn't answered her question.

"Better. I've been wanting to thank you."

"For?"

"First for the medical care."

"No problem."

"And second for helping out with Lilah."

"Again, no problem."

"And third—and possibly most importantly, for not beating me with your bat."

She felt a smile tug at her mouth. "You got lucky." She moved toward the next aisle—fruits and veggies, dammit, but she couldn't just grab a fistful of candy bars right in front of him. So she grabbed some grapes even though she didn't like grapes, and dropped them in her cart.

Shifting a little closer, he reached for the bag dispenser, just over her head, making her hyperaware of his big body and the fact that he smelled amazing.

A woman came down the aisle with four young kids, each of them screaming and yelling and beating each other with light sabers from the toy aisle. The woman started to pass by them with an apologetic smile, but stopped at the sight of Stone. "Hey, you," she said with familiarity. "I've been wanting to thank you for the bag of t-shirts, the kids loved them."

Stone smiled easily, picking up one of the boys before he could climb the banana display, setting him down by his mother. "No problem, glad you could use them. Alice, this is—"

"Doctor Sinclair," Alice said with a much more formal tone than she'd used with Stone. "I've heard about you. How's your wonderful father doing?"

"Better, thank you," Emma said, hoping to God that was actually true.

"Good." With one last sweet smile for Stone, Alice moved on, surrounded by chaos.

"We went to school together," Stone told Emma, once again following her as she turned into the next aisle. The woman shelving soups sent Stone a hopeful smile combining a sultry invitation and a knowing satisfaction. "Hi there, Stone."

"Hey, Tina," Stone said with more easy familiarity. "How's Danny?"

"Oh, I'm not seeing him anymore." Cocking her head, she eyeballed Stone up and down, as if maybe he was a twelve course meal and she was starving. "I signed up for another rock climbing class. Requested you."

He laughed softly and shook his head. "Cam takes those now."

"Yeah? Well, maybe you could make an exception?"

"The schedule's pretty set."

"Well damn then."

"An ex?" Emma asked dryly in the next aisle.

He slipped his hands into his pockets. "Sort of. We went out once."

Uh huh. Telling herself she didn't care, she headed up the frozen aisle toward the checkout. A beautiful dark brunette in a white tank top and a black skirt was in the middle of the aisle inspecting two different bags of frozen peas. Surprise, surprise, she nodded at Stone, though without a smile. "Hey, Wilder."

"Serena."

"Tell Annie her pies are ready."

"Will do."

"And tell your brother I hope Katie-the-new-girlfriend has dumped his sorry ass."

"She's the fiancé now," Stone told her.

"Yeah, I know. With any luck, she'll wise up in time." The woman gave Emma a long, speculative look, then strode off.

Stone turned to Emma who shook her head. "Are you three the only guys in town or something?" she asked.

"Nah." He smiled a little wryly. "But somehow we have this reputation."

"*Somehow*, huh?"

"It goes back several generations."

"Really?"

"Yeah. My great, great, great, great grandfather hung out with Jesse James. He ended up six feet under after a bar fight. That was the beginning of the legend. Or so they say."

"The legend?"

"That the Wilder men will never amount to much."

She watched him lift a broad shoulder as if that didn't hurt in the least, but something in his eyes gave him away, and her amusement faded. "That's quite a legacy to have to live with."

"We've managed to do just that for generations."

"How about *this* generation?"

He slanted her a glance, as if surprised she'd even bothered to ask, but she knew a little bit about living up to expectations. Her mother, as wonderful as she'd been, had pinned her hopes and dreams for the elusive "great life" on her only child and that hadn't been easy to face.

"Still waiting on the final vote," Stone said.

Interesting. They headed to the checkout, with Stone nodding to two more people along the way.

"Everyone knows everyone here," she murmured, unloading her cart, staring at the candy bars above the row of batteries on the last-minute stand above the conveyor belt. "I feel like I'm in Mayberry."

"Yeah. I call it Mayberry with Attitude. But as for feeling like you don't fit in, that could be fixed."

"How?"

He met her gaze. "We could go out."

"Out," she repeated, her pulse kicking into gear.

"Get to know each other. Have fun."

"How would that help?"

"Well . . ." He eyed her as he rubbed his jaw, the sound of his stubble doing something funny deep inside her belly. "Maybe it'd help you relax a little. If you were less uptight, maybe people would find you more approachable."

Hard to dispute the truth, but didn't make it easier to swallow. To take the moment she needed, she grabbed some batteries instead of the chocolate she really wanted. AAA's, not on sale. "Yeah, I don't think that's a good idea. The having fun thing."

"No?"

"No." She grabbed more batteries. "It's nothing personal."
His eyes revealed the skepticism of that statement.

"It's just that I'm not going to be here long, and—" More
batteries, because they were helping so much.

He eyed her cart with wry amusement. "You either have a
lot of very little flashlights, or a busy vibrator."

She looked down at the six packs of batteries and grimaced.

"You know, I have a better way to relax," Stone murmured
in her ear, his voice low and husky, and dammit, hypnotizing.

"The batteries are for my . . ." What? They were for what?
She was drawing a big, fat blank.

He just raised a curious brow.

And she deflated. "Oh, be quiet." In turn to his soft chuckle,
she put the batteries back. It was time—past time—for her to
blow that popsicle stand, cute mountain bums and all.

After a night of heavy rain, Stone and TJ took a group kayaking down the Cascade River. It was Mr. Toad's Wild Ride,
mostly because their guests had lied about their kayaking skills,
and also because the rains had the river rushing and swollen.

Taking a break from keeping their clients alive, Stone and
TJ pulled everyone off the river for a late afternoon lunch.
Their guests stretched out, enjoying some sun and Annie's
sandwiches.

TJ and Stone sat a short distance away, trying to recover
when Cam called Stone's cell. He listened to their complaints
and laughed from 7500 miles away. "What do you mean you're
exhausted? You going to let a couple of clients kick your collective asses?"

"You have no idea," Stone muttered.

"Actually, you would have an idea," TJ said. "If you'd get
your ass back here."

"Couple more weeks," Cam said. "We're going to Costa
Rica first—unless you need us sooner?"

Stone looked at TJ, who sighed. Neither of them wanted to rush Cam, not when he was happy for the first time in recent memory. "We're fine," Stone told him. "You just lounge around with your fiancé and we'll earn your keep."

Cam laughed. "Sounds good to me. So what's going on?"

"You mean besides the fact that the river's crazy today and that our clients lied on their applications?"

"Sort of like the pregnant woman?" Cam asked. "You guys are losing your touch."

"Okay, you know what?" Stone said. "People getting lots of sex don't get an opinion." He shut the cell phone.

"Now see," TJ said. "This is why I like the long treks. No baby deliveries. No beginner kayakers. Only the hardcore people who know what they're doing. I have three separate requests for that six week Alaska trip alone." Lying back, he shoved his hands behind his head and smiled up at the sky. "I could get into taking three long trips in a row."

Stone tried not to panic. "Which would leave me alone here." Again.

"You love being in charge."

Stone cranked his neck to look at his brother. "No, I don't."

"Yes, you do."

"No. I really don't."

"Then why do you always handle all of the behind the scenes stuff?"

"Uh, because you don't?"

TJ grinned. "Oh. Right. Thanks for that, by the way. You should give yourself a raise."

"I'll do that."

Sensing the tone, and perhaps the fact that Stone wasn't kidding, TJ looked at him. "Are you pissed at something?"

"No."

"You get shot down by the pretty Doc?"

"No." *Dammit.* "Yes, but that's not it."

"You hungry? You get cranky when you're hungry. I've got another sandwich—"

"Shut up, TJ." Stone sat up.

TJ did too, and looked at him for a long moment. "Annie smacked me around some this morning. She told me you've been putting in long hours at night in the office. You're overworked."

"Ya think?"

"I should have offered to help."

"You could offer now."

"Okay. You want some time off? You need to get the hell out for a while or something? You could take the first Alaskan trip, no problem."

Stone sighed. "It's not like I'm chomping at the bit to get out of here."

"But . . ."

"But . . ." He decided what the hell. "I want to do another renovation project."

TJ blinked. "So . . . you want to stop having fun all day in order to work your ass off?"

"I don't want to stop doing this. Jesus. You don't listen."

"I listen plenty, and what I'm hearing is that you need to get laid."

Stone let out a laugh. "Is that your answer to everything?"

"Yes," TJ said fervently.

Okay, true. Sex was an extremely nice fix to just about everything, but he knew he needed more than that this time. "Remember when I bought that house on the corner of Main and Sierra and fixed it up, then sold it to Old Man Pete?"

"Your first project. I remember. He turned it into the convenience store next to his gas station."

"Yeah."

"You nearly lost your ass on that project."

"That's because I was twenty-two and got screwed on the loan, but it worked out. It's not about the money, TJ. It's about doing something I love. This . . ." he gestured around him. "It's good. It gives Cam a purpose, and it's what *you* love, but I need more. I need something for *me*."

TJ just stared at him. "You're serious."

"Yes."

"Well, Christ, Stone. What'll we do without you?"

Now *he* stared up at the sky, feeling it weighing down on him. "I'm not leaving. I'm not asking to leave. I just want some time for me."

"Maybe you just need a distraction. Ask her out, man. It'll help."

Stone didn't have to ask which "her", he knew exactly. "No."

"Is it because she saw you buck ass naked on your first date? That could be construed as a romantic memory, you know."

Romantic? True, her hands had been all over him, but she'd been pulling gravel and chunks of rock out of his flesh, her fingers steady as a rock as he'd sworn the room blue.

Yeah, romantic as hell. "It wasn't a date, you ass. It was . . . an *encounter*. Then I brought her up a mountain to deliver a baby because you didn't notice that one of your clients was twenty-two months pregnant."

"Hey, that could have been romantic, too."

"How? How could that have been romantic?"

TJ thought about it for a minute and then shrugged. "Okay, maybe not."

Stone just shook his head.

"So what do you think you'll do for your next . . . *encounter*? Maybe tell her that the minor heart attack she thinks her father had was in fact a major one, and that if you hadn't been there he'd have died?"

"I thought I'd save that for some other time." Like, oh . . . never. Never worked for him. Emma wouldn't thank him for not telling her the truth, he knew that much. Nor would it matter to her that it hadn't been his truth to tell.

"Maybe you could try a new tactic."

"Like?"

"Like a date. Without the blood and guts and someone screaming in pain."

As the middle child, Stone was the talker, the peacemaker, the one who kept them all together, but as the oldest, TJ usually had the answers, at least when it came to women. "You don't think that would be a waste of my breath?"

"I think you've got a shot." TJ smiled. "I'll put your first-aid kit back so you have it handy. Knowing you, you'll need it." With a pat on the back, Stone's supposedly smarter, wiser, older brother got up and headed toward their clients.

The next morning, Emma woke up to her cell phone vibrating right off her nightstand. When she finally caught the thing, she saw Spence's number and felt herself smile.

Spencer did that for her, made her smile.

They'd become friends in an undergraduate freshman biology class at Columbia. They'd become friends-with-benefits their junior year when he'd been dumped by his long term girlfriend, and that tradition had continued on an as-needed basis throughout the years. When they were dating others—mostly Spencer, because Emma didn't often make time for dating, they saw each other less, but in between significant others—again, mostly Spencer's—they spent more time together. Whenever there were bad breakups, and for Spencer there was never any other kind, they'd occasionally knocked their feet together in bed.

It'd been a year since they'd last gotten naked, and that wasn't what Emma wanted from him now. She wanted the company of someone who knew her and accepted her, as is. "Tell me you're still getting on a plane tomorrow," she said.

"I'm already here. I got in late last night to surprise you."

"What?"

"Yeah, I've already been on a mountain bike ride this morning, in the rain, no less, which was *amazing*. I suppose your lazy ass is still in bed?"

"What do you mean, you're here? *Here* here?" Emma sat up and pushed her hair out of her face as she looked around her childhood bedroom, still so yellow and cheery and full of sweetness that she felt like she got a new cavity every night she slept here. God, she needed coffee. "I don't see you."

"I'm at a place called Wilder Adventures. You know it?"

She'd in fact been dreaming about Wilder Adventures for nearly two weeks now, or more correctly, of the men who ran it. One in particular.

Stone.

Naked.

Not muddy. Not bleeding. Not teasing her about her battery purchases. "Yes," she said weakly. "I know it. How do *you* know it?"

"My assistant looked up things to do in Wishful and found it. I'm only about four or five miles from you, and it's *sweet*. Did you know you can guide out *any* kind of trip you can imagine? It's amazing, and—"

"I know. I'm familiar with it," she said, closing her eyes tight. Her best friend and sometime casual lover had just slept at the place owned by the man she'd been fantasizing about. She didn't need a cup of caffeine, she needed an entire pot.

And possibly a shrink.

"Anyway, it's dumping rain, like buckets of rain, and supposedly the road out of here gets tricky without four wheel drive. Did your father leave you a vehicle that you can use to come get me?"

She got out of bed and padded to the window to open the shades.

Indeed, it was pouring rain, big fat drops that hit the ground and bounced back up like super balls. She eyed her father's ancient, massive Ford truck that he'd indeed left for her, and braced herself.

But just like anything else, she could handle it. "Yes, I have a truck. I'll be right there."

Chapter 7

The rain had let up as Stone came into the home stretch of a mountain bike race with Nick. He was winning too, when out of the corner of his eyes he saw Doc Sinclair's truck ambling up their driveway.

Only it wasn't Doc Sinclair behind the wheel, but his daughter, the one with the snooty 'tude and cool, steady hands, with the voice like sweet honey, and the bod to match. Surprised to see her, he pulled back, and Nick zipped right past him and over the finish line.

Emma parked the truck and hopped out, and pretty much leveled him with one flash of those baby blues.

Over the past few days he'd assured himself she wasn't as hot as he remembered.

But she was as hot as he remembered.

Maybe even more so as she made her way directly toward him, irritation blazing out of her pretty ears.

She wore another fancy pair of trousers, gray today, and a white top. No doctor's coat, which allowed him to see all those extremely pleasant curves she carried on her strong, lithe frame. She had real breasts and hips, the ones so often missing from the extreme athletes in his world. The last woman he'd dated had been so toned, she hadn't had an ounce of softness to her.

Dr. Emma Sinclair was soft.

At least on the outside.

Her fiery auburn hair was loose today, and it flew around her face in the light wind as she strode toward him with purpose, her face tense and not exactly friendly.

Which was a damn shame, as he was feeling quite friendly. "Hey, Doc," he said, getting off his bike, barely managing to control his wince from the pain his ribs gave him at the quick movement.

"What are you doing?"

He leaned his bike up against a tree. "Just enjoying the day." And the view. "How about you? What brings you out this way?"

She came toe to toe with Stone, in her very classy and expensive black heels which now had some mud on them, pressing up to his Nikes. Her eyes were stern and serious, conflicting with the scent of some exotic shampoo, and his brain got mixed signals. Sexy woman. Pissed woman.

"Are you stupid?" she asked. "Or just stubborn?"

"Uh, is there a third option?"

"You're still recovering. You have no business riding like that, getting air, risking crashing—" She went up on her tiptoes and ran a finger over his forehead.

Yeah, mixed signals, he thought dazedly as her voice brought to mind a teacher-to-errant-pupil sexual fantasy. His gaze ate her up as her fingers ran along his forehead. He couldn't help it, she was within the perfect eating up distance of about two inches. Hell, if he leaned in even a little bit, they'd be kissing.

Which would be nice. Really nice.

"It's okay," she said in relief. "You haven't ripped any stitches. You having pain?"

Yeah, in his ribs, but he was afraid of the black bag she had slung over her shoulder, so he smiled. "Aw, look at you. Caring about me."

Her eyes locked on his. "I care about all my patients."

"You make house calls for all of them?"

She narrowed her eyes and pursed those lips that were a little bit distracting for their fullness. "Delusional," she decided. "We should have that checked, too."

He grinned. "See? Falling for me."

"That would be a mistake. I don't make mistakes. You shouldn't be mountain biking, Stone." Without asking, she put her hand on his side, probing at his ribs. She was watching him carefully so he didn't dare grimace, but she shook her head, reading right through him. "You shouldn't be doing anything strenuous."

The image of him doing just that, being strenuous with her naked in his bed, wouldn't leave him alone. He wondered if she'd lose some of her tension if he got her out of those city clothes.

"Honest to God," she muttered. "Men." She dropped her hands from him and stepped back. "Racing when you're still in pain."

"You call that racing?" Nick asked, coming close with a laugh. "*Please*. I could have beaten him with both my hands tied behind my back if I'd wanted."

Stone shot Nick a *not helping* look, and smiled at Emma. "Honestly, I'm fine."

"You have seven stitches in your head, a cracked rib, and more road rash than a used car." She shoved up his shirt, revealing his abs. Her fingers brushed over his bruised skin, and he had an immediate reaction. So did she, given the way she dropped her hands as if he was a hot potato. "You have no business being on that bike, bouncing along on that rough terrain."

Well, actually, he did, but he didn't want to rile her up any more than absolutely necessary in case she was packing a shot of antibiotics in that bag.

"Rest, elevate, and ice, I told you. Why does no one listen?"

"I've elevated," he said. Hell, they were standing at 6,300 feet. That had to count.

"The other day, we flew a group of clients up to the Trinity Ice Flats," Nick interjected helpfully. "We climbed the ice dams and sat up there for a couple of hours. Stone was hurting so he lay down. On the ice."

Emma stared at Nick as if he'd sprouted horns. Without a word she turned on Stone, narrowing her eyes as she swept an angry gaze over him, lingering at his forehead and the stitches she'd put there herself. "You did end up on the climb?"

"Only a little."

"Do you have a death wish?"

"Only a little."

She tossed up her hands. "I give up." But instead of walking back to her truck, she headed toward the steps to the main lodge.

He exchanged a look with Nick, who shrugged. "Uh . . . can I help you?" Stone asked her.

"I'm picking up a guest you had last night." She didn't slow or look back. "Spencer Jenks. He's with me."

Stone had ridden earlier that morning with their New York guest. The polite doctor had been an outdoor enthusiast, but more importantly, outgoing, friendly, and adventurous. In other words, Dr. Emma's virtual opposite. "Spencer's with you?"

"That's right."

He watched her stride up the steps, her heels clicking with forceful purpose on the stone, his gut sinking.

"Is that the one who saw you naked?" Nick whispered.

Dr. Spencer Jenks was hers. "Yeah."

"I don't think you impressed her much."

When Emma got to the top step, TJ opened the door from the inside and he smiled at her. "Doc Sinclair."

She smiled back sweetly. "TJ."

"Did you come to check on my idiot brother?"

Still next to Stone, Nick snickered.

"Actually," Emma told him. "I came to pick up my friend Spencer."

"Oh. Here I thought maybe you came to kick Stone's ass for kayaking yesterday. With a cracked rib and all."

Emma turned and sent a slow, long, easily decipherable look in Stone's direction.

"Did you bring him another shot?" he heard TJ ask hopefully as he directed her inside.

The lodge door shut before Emma answered, and Stone looked at Nick. "You both suck, you know that?"

"Ah, don't be like that." Nick slung his arm over Stone's shoulder. "I think she likes you best."

Stone shoved him away and Nick laughed. "Hey, if you're worried about what happened in her office, you can always tell her you'd been swimming in some damn cold water before she made you take your pants off. Then she'd at least understand."

Ignoring him, Stone made his way up the stairs to the lodge.

"Don't do it, man," Nick called after him. "That one's Heartbreak City."

Like he didn't know, but when it came to Emma, apparently he was a glutton for punishment.

Stone found Emma sitting at the kitchen table with Dr. Spencer Jenks, both being served breakfast by Annie.

Spencer had an arm around Emma's shoulders and was grinning at her affectionately as Chuck wound around their ankles, mewing softly, waiting for crumbs to fall. "I'll get you on a mountain bike yet, babe."

"Too dangerous." She flung his arm off, but her body language was easy and comfortable, telling Stone that these two had a history. A long one.

Fine. She was taken. He should have assumed that. So she smelled good enough to eat and had eyes that saw beneath his bullshit, which had been a nice change. So he'd been momentarily distracted by her sharp wit and sweet curves. It didn't matter, because she wasn't sweet, at least not to him.

She was probably planning her and Spencer's reunion sex right now.

"Thanks again for the ride this morning," Spencer told Stone as he came into the room. "It was nice to have a day off. I don't get out of the hospital enough, that's for sure."

"Glad you enjoyed it." Stone looked at Emma, who oddly enough wasn't looking at Spencer with googly eyes, picturing their reunion sex. She was looking right at *him*.

"You're stressing your stitches," she said. "Stop frowning."

"I'm not frowning."

"Yeah, you are." This from Annie, who handed him a plate loaded with scrambled eggs, sausage and sour dough toast, his favorite. Over the plate, she waggled her brow in the direction of Emma. "You aren't going to catch anything with that scowl."

"I'm not trying to catch anything." Irritated now, he grabbed his plate and headed for the door.

"Where are you running off to?" Annie asked.

"I just thought our guest might appreciate some privacy. With his girlfriend."

Emma grabbed a piece of toast and slathered it with jelly. "Oh, I'm not his girlfriend."

"Nope." Spencer shook his head. "I date women who are much nicer."

Emma rolled her eyes and stole his coffee, while Stone tried not to acknowledge the relief rolling through him.

"See?" Spencer said to Stone, gesturing to Emma, now sipping his coffee. "Not nice."

Emma ignored him. "So," she said to Stone, innocently and daintily licking some jelly off her thumb. "Been to the bar lately? Where the three women jumped you? Because I brought you a shot of antibiotics. I wouldn't want you to catch anything."

His belly quivered, though he had no idea if it was from sheer lust of watching her tongue lick her thumb, or fear of her needles. "I'm good."

Annie barked out a laugh.

Spencer had stopped eating and was looking at Stone speculatively, probably wondering how three women had gotten the best of him, since he was by no stretch a small guy.

"Listen," Emma said. "*Three* women jumped you in a bar." She flashed him a look of mock sympathy. "They beat the crap out of you. That's got to be traumatizing to say the least."

"It's not so bad."

"Come on, Stone. You must feel violated."

Annie snickered. Stone shot her a look, and she tried to control herself.

"Anyway," Emma went on. "I've been worried about you, so I located a counselor in the area, someone you could talk to." Her mouth curved gently, only those razor sharp baby blues revealing her sharp wit.

Stone was well used to his brothers fucking with him. That's what brothers did, fuck with each other's head. But a woman? This was new for him. And oddly . . . stimulating. "I think I'm going to be okay."

She arched a brow. Daring him to admit the truth. "Annie told you," he said with a sigh.

"That you're on a volunteer search and rescue team and you were called out to save a guy who'd gone off a cliff on his rock climb? That said guy panicked once you had him halfway up the cliff to safety, knocking you down about fifty feet? Yeah, she told me. *You* might have told me."

He looked at Annie, who was suddenly very busy at the stove.

"Oh, and given the redness I see around some of your cuts and bruises, you do need the antibiotics."

"You said I looked good."

"That was a few days ago. You don't look good now."

She let him start sweating over that one for a beat, before she shook her head. "You fell off a cliff and you're scared of me?"

"Hell, yes."

She stood up and headed toward him, and he stumbled back a step, smacking right into the door.

Spencer winced.

Annie cackled.

"Careful," Emma said, still coming at him. "Your ribs." She reached her hand into her bag.

Oh, Christ. He pictured another needle and felt his skin go clammy. His stomach went queasy. This wasn't working for him, not one little bit. Not unless she was going to strip down for him again. "I don't need—"

Still looking at him, she pulled out . . . a prescription bottle. "Are you afraid of pills, too?" she asked innocently, when he was beginning to suspect there was nothing innocent about her at all.

Annie snickered again.

"I swear to God," he muttered in her direction.

Emma lightly smacked the bottle against his pecs, a fact he found interesting—was it his imagination, or did she touch him a lot?

More importantly, did she do it on purpose? It was worth finding out, and testing, he leaned into her, just a little.

Her pupils dilated.

Check.

Her nostrils flared.

Check, check.

If they'd been wild animals, their foreplay had just been conducted. Still testing, he lifted his hand and covered hers, still against his chest.

She stared down at their now entangled fingers around the pill bottle, then lifted her gaze to his. Her breathing had changed.

Quickened.

Test over, he decided, his own breathing changing as well. Because oh hell yeah, she was aware of him, every bit as much as he.

Which meant she was all bark and no bite.

That was *very* good to know.

"Twice a day for seven days," she murmured, her voice a little thick. "Come see me in two."

"For . . ?" He was imaging all sorts of things.

"I'll take out your stitches."

Okay, she had a little bite.

Actually, probably more than a little. "I can take them out myself."

"Come to me, or I'll come to you."

He liked the sound of that—her coming to him, on him, all over him, but he knew better. The woman was bloodthirsty. Plus he'd seen her steely, fierce determination up front and personal. Come to her? He'd love it, only it wasn't going to happen. "Sure thing," he said. "Two days."

Or never.

Chapter 8

To Emma, Spencer was cute in a Clark Kent sort of way; dark hair, dark eyes, and a helpless smile made all the more disarming for the simple sexy dimple that went with it. He had a lean runner's body that belied how much he ate, and a career in the surgical world that men twice his age would kill for.

But he had a fatal flaw. Emma called it Fickle-ality. He couldn't settle, on anything.

Period.

Still, as a best friend, it worked, and while she ran the clinic that day, he happily occupied himself in the great outdoors; kayaking, hiking . . .

That night, not content with the stack of casseroles to choose from, he cooked. Emma sat on the small kitchen counter and watched him throw some ingredients into a pan, from which came forth the most mouth watering scent. "What is that?"

"Roasted tomato mozzarella and eggplant pasta."

It never failed to amaze her—a professional water burner— that Spence was every bit as talented in the kitchen as he was in the operating room.

"Oh, Kate dumped me," he said, topping off their glasses.

Ah. That explained why he was here early. He'd gotten bored. "Didn't you date her only twice?" she asked. "That doesn't count as a dumping."

"Yes it does," he said. "Which also qualifies me for make-up sex."

"Kate's in the Sierras?"

"I meant you." He smiled, his dark eyes warm and affectionate. "I get another shot at you."

Yeah, right. He wasn't looking for another shot at her, he wasn't looking for anything but fun and they both knew it. It was why they made such good friends, because they didn't need anything from each other—perfect—as they didn't have anything to give each other. It was a selfish relationship on both sides, and also the only lasting relationship in *either* of their lives.

He came close and ran a finger over her jaw, rimming her ear.

"Let me save you some time on the foreplay action. We're not sleeping together, Spencer."

He merely topped off her wine with a small smile, clearly confident he'd change her mind.

After dinner, she showed him to the tiny spare bedroom. Spence caught her hand there in the hallway and flashed her a quick grin. "So what size bed do you have in your room?"

With a laugh, she looked him in the eyes. His thick hair was as unruly as his heart, dipping low over his forehead. He wore designer threads, and managed to look like he'd just thrown them on. He was rich, incredibly talented with a scalpel, and fun.

If she'd taken him inside her heart, he'd have broken it in half a long time ago.

Which was okay. She didn't have the urge to take him into

her heart. She didn't have the urge to take anyone in her heart. Her life was good as it was.

So good.

And she couldn't wait to get back to it. "A queen-size bed."

"*Nice.*"

"Perfect for one."

"Or two."

"Or one."

"Aw, Em." He stepped into her, pressing that runner's body to hers as he slid a hand up her side, gently squeezing her waist. "It's been awhile."

"Yes, since you were dumped on your sorry ass by Margarita."

"As I recall, you comforted me quite nicely."

"You don't need comforting, Spencer. Not tonight."

"Sure I do." Bending his head, he nuzzled her neck. "I'm in the big bad Sierras. I'm scared, Emma."

She laughed and pushed him away. "Stop it. You don't need me tonight. We both know it."

He cocked his head, studying her in the dimly lit hallway. "Actually, I think that's in reverse. You don't need me."

"Not in my bed, no." She took his roaming hands in hers and then hugged him. "But I needed you here, and you came."

With a sigh, he hugged her back. "I'll always come for you, Emma. Always."

The next day, Emma woke up to dark, wet skies, which fit her mood. She called to check on her dad, who was in the middle of fishing. She treated three thirteen-year-old boys, brought in by their scolding mothers. Seemed that the boys had been pretending to be the Wilder brothers, and had gone hiking in a gully near a river to catch crawdads, and instead had caught poison ivy.

One of the mothers paid with a chicken cheese casserole. Another paid with a check that couldn't be cashed until the first of the month. The third had a credit card and enough gossip to leave Emma's head spinning. She learned a whole host of things she didn't care about, but the one bit of supposed news that stuck with her was that Big Foot had made another sighting—Big Foot?!—but everyone was pretty sure it was just Old Man Pete terrorizing the tourists again.

Good to know.

When the stupid cow bell jangled midday, a woman came in and shook off her wet, lightweight jacket. Emma recognized her as the woman she'd seen in the frozen aisle of the grocery store, the one who'd told Stone she hoped that Cam got dumped by his new fiancé. She wore black jeans and a black t-shirt, with a white and black checkered apron that said Wishful Delights. She was carrying a matching black and white bag that smelled like heaven as she limped to the front desk. "I hope to God you and your big city airs can handle a toe infection."

Emma did her best to hide her irritation at the "big city airs" comment. "Toe infections welcome."

The woman, dark brunette, exotic and beautiful, laughed, a low husky sound that probably drew men like moths to a flame. "So it's true then, you did actually find yourself a sharp wit. Thank God."

When Emma just stared at her, her patient let out a breath. "You don't remember me."

"I remember you from the grocery store. You have a dislike for the Wilder brothers."

"Ha! No, that's actually not quite accurate. I had the great misfortune of loving one. But that's another story altogether. I'm Serena Salvo, from your first grade class. Class bitch," she clarified.

"The teacher's pet," Emma said, remembering now. "You were the one who always got to go out to recess first."

"Ah, now it's coming back to you." She grimaced. "Remember, it was all a long time ago, right?"

A rush of childhood memories hit her. Emma had been the quiet bookworm, a nerd in-the-making, in a town that prized athletics over brains. Her school life had been hell. "You sat behind me and cut my ponytail off."

"Okay now that was an accident," Serena said over her shoulder as she limped toward the exam rooms.

"You lifted it up like a trophy and laughed."

"Hello, first class bitch, remember? But if it helps, I'm extremely remorseful."

"Only because you got caught."

"Well that," Serena agreed, preceding Emma into the first room. "And because I lost dance lessons for a month."

"I looked like a boy for three months." Emma sat on the doctor's stool and began a new chart.

"Yeah." Serena winced as she sat on the table. "Jeez, I was thinking you'd be over it by now, but just in case, I brought incentive." She held up that delicious smelling bag. Wriggled it. "See? I've turned over a new leaf."

"What is it with people bringing food instead of cash?"

"Oh, I have a checkbook, too. Now aren't you glad to see me?"

Emma studied her face. She had been a beautiful little girl and that hadn't changed. She'd been mean-spirited, and Emma hoped like hell that *had* changed. "You once ratted me out for copying, when it was you who copied. I lost hall monitor privileges."

"Ah, so you still have the memory of an elephant. Excellent. Do you by any chance remember what happened to the pearl necklace I stole from my mother and lost right before Christmas vacation that year? She's never forgiven me."

Emma sighed again and guided Serena's foot up to the table. "Your father was mayor. He was a nice man."

"He had a heart attack and died when I was in fifth grade."

"I'm very sorry."

"He was screwing my teacher in the lunch room and the custodian found them. On second thought, *that* might be what my mother hasn't forgiven me for."

"How was that your fault?" Emma asked, horrified.

"My teacher." Emma shrugged. "Who knows. Listen, make this toe thing painless, and I'll keep you in brownies for the rest of the month."

Emma blinked. "No promises about being nice?"

"Trust me, you'd rather have my brownies."

"I don't intend to be here that long, but I'll do my best on the painless part."

Spencer stuck his head in the exam room door. "Hey, Em. I'm going into town, need anything?"

"Yes. More patients."

Spencer smiled, and looked at Serena. Predictably, he got that look in his eyes that all guys got in the presence of a gorgeous female who knew how gorgeous she was.

Serena waggled her fingers in his direction and he smiled. "See you later, Em."

When he was gone, Serena waggled a brow. "Who's the hottie?"

Emma looked at the closed door. "A friend."

"He looks like Jack from *Lost*, which is to say hot as hell."

"He's not your type."

"*All* men are my type. Is he yours?"

"That's really none of your business."

Serena grinned. "You know, I remember you being a sweet kid. You've grown claws. I like that."

Emma examined Serena's big toe. Classic ingrown toenail. "Yeah, well, you're not going to like this."

"Oh, shit. Okay, just do what you have to. I'll do what I always do when I'm nervous. I'll ramble. So. Did you miss this place? Is that why you're back?"

"I came to help out my father."

Serena hissed out a breath as Emma disinfected the toe and surrounding area. "So you didn't miss us then."

Actually, she had at first. Until her mother had given her all the things she hadn't been able to have here; ballet lessons, science camp . . .

See, darling. Getting out of here was a good thing. You can thank me later.

Emma sighed. Sandy had worked hard, so hard, for years. Eventually she'd remarried though; a brain surgeon, one on the way up to Places That Were Important, and they'd been happy, though he'd been gone so much—working—that Emma hadn't spent a lot of time with him. Or her real dad, for that matter.

"You were sweet to me," Serena said through her teeth as Emma worked. "One of the few. Which is why I'm not going to yell and scream but holy shit—"

"Done." Emma wrapped up the toe, gave Serena her instructions for care, and then was pleased to accept actual money.

And the brownies.

Yeah, she might have once been a sweet kid, but she'd changed. She'd changed greatly. Sweet didn't get the good jobs and sweet didn't always help her patients. And sweet would not help her father's practice.

That's why she was here, to help him. To run his business. She'd have liked to do more but he'd made it fairly clear that this was enough.

Fine.

She could understand and appreciate that. Sure they were blood related, but that was about it. Besides, she had a life, a great life.

A busy life that didn't include screwball romantic comedies and a different casserole every single night.

Her life.

Which she couldn't get back to until he was better. Dammit. At five o'clock she peered out the window, relieved that the rain had stopped and closed the Urgent Care. Spencer had come back with the truck and was happily cooking away in the kitchen. She went to the freezer and grabbed a stack of casseroles, the healthy ones she'd been saving over the past two days.

She got into the truck, eyed the sky, and gave herself a pep talk as she began driving. She knew in winter that these ten miles would be impassable without a snowmobile, and it boggled her mind, but her father actually liked it that way. Her great grandfather had built the cabin with his own two hands, her mother had told her so. It was how her father had talked her into living in it.

For a week, darling. For one week.

Right. At the one week mark, her mother had found a lone wolf spider in her bed the size of a man's fist, and she'd packed up and moved them into the upstairs of the Urgent Care. That had lasted until Emma had turned six.

Then Sandy had moved them to New York.

Emma was getting a little taste of how it'd gone down as she attempted to navigate the road, muddy from all the rains. She had to stop twice, once to let a group of deer finish crossing in front of her, and another to gather her courage to drive through a low running creek that was of questionable height.

She made it, barely. With a sigh of relief she finally pulled up to the cabin thirty minutes later.

And sat there in disbelief.

Just to the side of the cabin was a three-story tall rock that had been shoved here courtesy of the last ice age. Free-climbing the face was a group of teenagers, and her father. Not taking it easy. Not resting.

Climbing.

At his side, doing the leading was one soon-to-be-very-dead Stone Wilder.

Chapter 9

With that inexplicable and annoying awareness tickling up her spine, Emma got out of the truck and strode to the rock. Up close, it wasn't as tall as she'd first thought, maybe only twenty feet, and the kids were only about halfway, which meant that their feet were just about head level. Her father was slightly below the kids, Stone above them.

"Are you kidding me?" she asked, eyeing the kids on the rock and thinking of cracked skulls and broken bones, all of which would be utterly needless injuries. "Where are the safety ropes?"

Stone twisted around to look down at her, his jeans going taut across his butt.

It was quite the impressive butt.

In fact, everything about him was impressive. Arms and legs stretched out, muscles tight and strained, he was spread-eagle, holding onto what appeared to be nothing more than tiny crevices in the rock.

"We use ropes on the higher climbs," he said.

"It doesn't look safe." *Not the rock, and certainly not you.*

Her father began to work his way down toward her while Stone stayed with the kids. Stone's faded gray t-shirt was snug across his broad shoulders, loose around his waist, gaping out enough to reveal a tanned, sleek back. He was no longer wearing bandages over all the road rash, and she could see his injuries were healing quite fast and well as he moved along with easy grace.

Yeah, *that's* why she was staring at him, to make sure he'd healed properly.

Her father hopped to the ground. "Emma." He smiled at her, light and welcoming. "Nice surprise. Nobody needing you at the Urgent Care then?"

"No." With baited breath, she watched the group of five kids work the rock safely with Stone's quiet reassurances. "Who are they?"

"A group of local foster kids. Stone takes them out of their element and on mini-expeditions."

She'd already heard from Missy that he did this but it became real when she saw it firsthand. It was yet another layer of Stone revealed. Hard to keep picturing him as nothing but a mountain bum when he kept unraveling like a damn onion.

"He's big on making sure the kids don't fall through the cracks," her dad said. "Like he and his brothers did."

Tilting her head up, she watched Stone give each kid a fist bump as they got to the top. Hard to imagine him as a little boy, much less a vulnerable one.

"Anyway." Her father slid off his baseball cap. His gray hair was wild as always. "Today is rock climbing day, as you can see. We're rafting next week."

"We."

"I help with the kids when I can, which is more often now."

Ironic, she thought. He was there for those kids, when he'd never been there for his own.

The kids were preparing for their descent. She wanted to point out how dangerous this sort of thing was, but hell, the teens in New York faced their own daily dangers, and if there was someone to steer them through surviving out here, so much the better.

But that it was Stone . . . Yeah, it really put a dent in the whole ski bum rep.

"You're doing okay at the clinic?"

She looked at her father. "I accepted three more casseroles and two gossip sessions today. I had a case of poison ivy, a wicked toe infection, and . . . nothing. Nothing else. I'm not sure how I managed to handle it all."

He nodded sympathetically. "Different pace here, yeah?"

"You could say that. Dad . . ." She'd given up so much to be here, so damn much, and he was rock climbing. "What are you doing?"

"Well, Stone here and I will make dinner for the kids, and then—"

"I mean . . ." She pinched the bridge of her nose and took a deep breath. "How is it that you can rock climb and not work?"

"Oh." He moved toward his front porch with a surprising spryness for a sixty-one-year-old heart-attack victim, minor or otherwise. "Yeah. About that."

"You're improved enough to come back to work," she said.

Her father scratched his head. "Well . . ."

"Frankly, I think it's rude of you not to tell me so." They were on his porch now, separate enough from the others that they could have some privacy. "I've been asking to see your chart, to help you monitor your recovery, but you've chosen not to involve me. Fine, I get it, you have your life. But I have mine, too, Dad. A busy one, and I need to get back to it."

Her father's smile slipped some. "I didn't involve you in my care because it can be disconcerting to read the medical records of a close family member."

"As I buried mom only six months ago, I think I can handle it. Actually, I can handle anything. The bottom line is that I came to help you, and clearly you don't need it. I would have appreciated knowing that, as this hasn't exactly been a vacation for me."

"I didn't think so, Emma."

"Well, what did you think? That I'd appreciate, after all this time of no contact, having to drop everything and come do your work for you?"

He didn't say anything to that.

"I need to be in New York," she said quietly.

"Putting in eighty hour work weeks."

Minimum. With her mom gone, her stepdad gallivanting around the world, and nothing else going on, what did it matter? "I like the work."

"There's more to life than work."

"Dad." She rubbed a weary hand over her eyes. "It's a little late for the fatherisms, okay? If you're better, I just want to know."

He was quiet, and after looking at him, waiting, she turned away and nearly ran right smack into Stone, who'd climbed down the rock and come up onto the porch without a sound. The kids were in the yard, kicking a ball around. Stone's usual smile was nowhere in place. "He's not ready to go back to work, Emma. He's—"

But her father put his hand on Stone's arm, and whatever else he'd planned to say never left his lips.

Men. Stoic and silent and *stupid*. "I have three casseroles in the damn truck," she said, giving up. "I brought them to you so you'd have food." She stalked back to the vehicle; stacking the dishes up together when the skin at the nape of her neck did that prickle thing, a phenomenon which had never happened to her before Stone.

Not something she wanted to think about.

But damn him.

She whirled around and yep, there he was. Funny how fast the guy could move when he wanted to, like a cat, she thought, looking up, up, up into his eyes, which for the first time were closed off to her. A big, tough, wild *leopard*. Or a tiger. Something surprisingly silent and edgy and dangerous in worn jeans, his t-shirt molding to his broad shoulders and chest and abs. His wayward surfer hair was spiky today, as if he'd used his fingers instead of a comb. His face—"Hey." She ran her finger over his temple. "Your stitches."

"I took them out."

Yeah, he was most definitely dangerous, at least to her mental health. "You what?"

"Admit it, I did a good job."

The cut had healed, perfectly. "You should have let me."

"To be honest, I was never going to let you." He paused. "Emma—"

"No." She didn't want to hear it. She understood his role as protector, that he was there for her father. But she was pretty damn tired of everyone having someone at their back but her.

Damn tired. "I don't want to talk about it."

"Too bad, since I do." He turned to make sure no one could overhear. "He came to see you, Emma."

"What?"

"When you were young. He tried to see you, multiple times in fact. But your mother always caught wind of it and whisked you off on a trip somewhere."

"What are you talking about?"

"He sent letters and called too. He tried to be a part of your life, but she told him that it wasn't going to happen. That it couldn't happen, because she was aiming high with you, higher than him."

"No." Emma shook her head. "She wouldn't say that." But . . . but how many times had Sandy said those very words, that Emma was to aim high, far higher than her own roots. *Oh, God.* "I don't believe it."

"I know it must be hard, after being raised by her, to hear the other side."

No. No, it wasn't hard. She knew more than anyone that there were two sides to every story. But this, this couldn't be right.

Yet the look on his face, the utter empathy, the utter certainty . . . "Why?" she whispered. "Why did he let her tell him that he couldn't see me?"

"Because he owed her. He felt responsible for her losing those years of her life when she stayed out here, the years she blamed him for."

Sandy *had* resented those years, bitterly. Just as she'd bitterly resented every single wrinkle on her face, the ones she'd blamed on the high, harsh, Sierra sun. "He came to New York to see me."

His eyes softened, revealing his honesty. "Yes."

"And she turned him away."

"Yes."

Emma stared blindly at the granite rock, the rough, rugged pines. "She didn't want to share me."

"I imagine not, though it hurt him. And because he had time and love to give, he turned to other kids. Me, for one. And others." She heard him take a step toward her, his feet crunching on the fallen pine needles. "He's a good guy, Emma. A really good guy."

She closed her eyes at the emotion in his voice.

He cared about her dad. She absorbed that a moment, then went still at the feel of his hands pulling her around to face him. His arms slid along hers as he took the casseroles from her, his body warm and sinewy. "Stone?"

"Yeah?" He didn't shift away, remaining so close she could feel his breath warm on her temple.

"Thanks for telling me," she whispered.

He nodded, then shook his head. "He won't thank me." He set the casseroles on the hood of the truck, then stepped close again.

She'd never been so aware of a man's body.

Or her own.

Not good.

Yet she didn't move away. If anything, she shifted slightly closer.

"You look tense enough to shatter," he murmured, lifting a hand to touch her cheek.

Shocked at herself and her utter lack of control, she shifted into him. A mistake, because as she knew all too well, chemistry was basic.

And they had it in spades. "You might have noticed, I'm not good at relaxing."

His mouth quirked. "I can help."

Her mind went there, to how she'd let him relax her, and all it came up with was getting naked.

Oh good Lord. This was all his fault. He practically oozed sex appeal, and being this close wasn't helping. Nor was the hand he had on her arm. That and his eyes, on hers, weakened her defenses, tearing down a wall she'd put up a damn long time ago, leaving her feeling far too exposed.

"Yeah," he murmured, his thighs bumping hers. "It's definitely there."

Knowing what *it* was—that Chemistry 101 she was thinking about, all that sheer, bare, physical need—she lifted her chin. One thing at a time, and right now, she was concentrating on her self-righteous frustration over her dad. "This . . . this whatever it is between us, isn't going to be a problem."

"No?"

"*No.*" She firmed up her voice. "No way, no how."

"You trying to convince me?" he asked. "Or yourself?"

"I mean it. This would be a very bad idea."

"A bad idea, huh?" His voice was low and shockingly seductive as he dipped his head down slightly so that their mouths were disconcertingly close. "If that's what helps you sleep at night, Doc."

His eyes were smoldering with a dark and enticing knowledge, and her knees actually wobbled. Other reactions occurred too, reactions she wasn't ready to admit to. But she could admit this—for whatever reason, whether it was his sheer testosterone-fueled masculinity, or the fact that he was different from the men she usually let in her life—she was too vulnerable to him.

Far too vulnerable.

Turning, she picked the casserole dishes back up and shoved them into his arms. "You cook those at 350 degrees for about an hour."

His lips were curved slightly, and she drank in his closeness. He smelled a little woodsy, a little citrusy, and a whole lot male. His face was tanned, with fine lines fanning out from his eyes and the corners of his mouth, assuring her that he laughed, and often.

She had no idea why that was so damn attractive. Maybe because she'd always wondered what it was like not to be ruled by her work.

But her work was her life. She'd made sure of it.

Stone rubbed his jaw. He hadn't shaved that morning, maybe not yesterday either, and the stubble should have put her off.

Yeah. It so didn't.

She needed something to put her off. Maybe he wore holey socks. Maybe he snored. God, she hoped he snored.

"You going to talk to him before you go?"

"I think I said enough."

"You were pretty hard on him." The casual bluntness of the words struck a chord deep inside her, mostly because he was right. Which she hated.

"Maybe you could find something else to say. Something kind."

Ah, good, there it was, the putting off. Perfect.

But in the face of her silence, he just held her gaze, clear and steady, and she sighed. Just say it, Stone. Say the rest of what you want to say."

"Okay." He nodded. "I get that in your world, you can back up that badass city girl thing you've got going on, but things are different here."

"Yeah, I've noticed," she responded. "People around here tend to get all up in other people's business, for one." She shot him a meaningful look.

He smiled. "It's called caring."

"Oh. I thought it was called *nosy*."

He shook his head. "You're stubborn. You get that from him. He means something to me, Emma," he said softly, with steel underlying every syllable. "Maybe you could cut him some slack."

She wanted to promise him that she would, but that stubbornness reared its ugly head and she bit her tongue.

He looked at her for a long moment, then when she didn't speak, nodded his thanks at the casseroles in his arms and turned and walked away.

Chapter 10

Stone let out a low breath which diluted his odd and disconcerting lust for Emma not one little iota, and handed off the casserole dishes to Doc.

"Thanks." Doc got the door, then moved through his kitchen to the refrigerator, rustling through it for something to drink. As Stone had personally taken out all the caffeine, he knew Doc wasn't going to find what he was looking for—which was his beloved Pepsi.

"The kids!"

"The sun's peeking out. They're lying on the rocks," Stone said. "Why didn't you tell her?"

He was still rummaging for Pepsi. "Tell her what?"

Stone reached out, grabbed a bottle of water, and handed it to him. "Oh, I don't know, that you didn't ignore her on purpose when she was growing up. That you could have hired another doctor for your place but you wanted to see her. That you had a major heart attack not a minor one . . . pick one."

"Oh." Doc leaned back and stared at the bottle of water in his hand. "I think she knows."

"Really? Then why does she seem to blame you for the lack of relationship between you two?"

"Because her mother, well-meaning as she was, was a little distant. Her stepfather even more distant. In Emma's book, my actions—or lack of—put me in the same category as them. Emotionally, she raised herself. In doing so, she learned a painful lesson—that she could trust no one with her heart."

"That's a sucky lesson."

"Yes, and I take responsibility for that." Shaking his head at himself, he opened the water bottle and took a long drink. "We all know that *I* was the adult, that *I* should have tried harder. That *I* should have gotten over my broken heart and fought for my child. And she's right."

"So what now?"

Doc turned the water in his hands, as if he could turn it into the Pepsi he wanted. "If she asks me to, I'm going to sell the clinic."

"*What?*"

"Yeah." Doc nodded, looking unusually solemn. "I just wanted you to hear it from me before you catch wind of it."

"I don't understand."

"She isn't going to stay, Stone," he said very gently. "I can't *make* her admit that she belongs here—"

"She *does* belong here." Where the hell that came from, he had no idea.

"I can't keep the Urgent Care going by myself, we both know that. I can either hire doctors on a rotating schedule, or sell. If I sell, at least it isn't a burden to her, and maybe I can get into the rotation. A day a week would be right up my alley."

Stone stared at him. "You're sounding like you're okay with this idea already."

"Are you kidding? I hate it." Doc sighed. "If I thought anything or anyone could change her mind . . ."

Stone looked at Doc and saw the small light of hope. "Don't

look at me," he said quickly. "She wouldn't listen to me even if I tried. She has a bit of an attitude, in case you haven't noticed."

Doc laughed softly. "You're falling for her."

He *was* falling for her. "This is your deal."

"I'm just saying, if it came up . . ."

"Doc." Stone shook his head. "Listen, we've been through this. You need to talk to her yourself. You need to fight for her, as her father."

But Doc was shaking his head no. "Fighting for her, forcing her to divide herself between the west and east coast would be far more damaging than letting her go. I have to let go, Stone. I have to let her be. That's guilt speaking. I won't bring her any emotional strain. She's had enough."

Stone sighed. "You did the best you could."

Doc shoved back his unruly hair and smiled sadly. "You're making excuses for me. It's about accountability, which unfortunately I didn't learn until two months ago on an ER table. The truth is, I've been every bit as selfish as her mother. Emma knows it, and so do I." He opened the fridge one more time and sighed as he stared at the contents. "What I wouldn't give for a damn Pepsi."

"Accountability," Stone said dryly. "You needed a lifestyle change, which includes eating healthier, exercising more than lifting a fishing pole, and here's a new one—living until you've seen your grandchildren."

Doc's eyes, kind and sharp as they came, met his. "You should have been a doctor. You're a natural caretaker."

"As I'd have passed out at the first sight of a needle, I think it's fair to say I made a good choice."

"You're still taking care of people."

"Playing for a living," Stone corrected.

Doc smiled. "Now see, that's what makes you who you are,

Stone. Modesty. Because unlike myself, you've never acted selfishly in your life."

"Stop it."

"No, I mean it. You managed Cam when he was a world champion at such a young age. You helped TJ through his tragedy—"

"Both of those things were a long time ago."

"Yeah, and you're still there for them, keeping your family a unit. You invested Cam's pro earnings for him wisely, and now he's rich as sin. You helped TJ realize his dream by building that lodge. You keep both your brothers' dreams alive by running Wilder Adventures even though we both know you'd rather be wearing a tool belt and working with your hands. Face it, Stone. You're always, in one form or another, taking care of someone you care about, including trying to get between me and Emma to keep us both happy."

Uncomfortable with that, Stone turned away, looking out the window and automatically counting teenage heads to make sure they were all still out there. Last week two of the little geniuses had decided to take off on their own to smoke some weed. Today they were back at the lodge with Annie, cleaning toilets. His own unique form of punishment. "You make me sound like some sort of a saint."

"No." Doc tossed back more of his water. "A saint would have slipped me a soda."

Spencer had met a few doctors from South Shore and the next day was off with them for the day playing on Lake Tahoe. Emma didn't go because she had the clinic. In the hottest day of the year so far, she saw a total of four patients. She got one casserole, one IOU, and two checks.

Progress.

She treated a sprained elbow, two sore throats and one migraine. She'd say this—she was getting used to the lack of drama in her day.

Actually, it did make breathing easier. Not that she was ready to admit such a thing. Near closing time, Annie showed up. "Sorry to bother you," she said, holding Chuck in her arms. "But our vet is climbing Echo Summit." She set the cat on the reception counter.

Emma raised a brow.

"Yeah." Annie grimaced. "Seeing as you patched up our Stone so nicely, I was hoping you'd also—"

"There's a big difference between treating a man and a cat, Annie."

"Sure there is. My nephew's a big baby, and Chuck isn't."

Emma reached out to pet Chuck, laughing, and Annie smiled in approval. "Well there you are."

"Excuse me?"

"Oh, the rumors are that you're not as human as the rest of us mere mortals. But I see peeks of your father coming through."

"You do not."

Now Annie laughed. "That wasn't an insult. Your father's a good man." She patted Emma's arm. "And you're a good woman."

Chuck butted his head up against her hand, trying to get her to resume the petting. "How do you know that?"

"You flew out here to take care of his business, didn't you? That's what family does," Annie said confidently.

"You're close to your family."

"Extremely."

"How do you manage that?" Emma asked. "You're all so different."

"Oh, it's Stone. He does it. Ever since he was little, he's been the protector, the go-to guy. We joke that it's the middle child in him, but truthfully, his heart is bigger than the rest of ours." Annie nuzzled Chuck. "Aw, my poor boy."

"Stone?"

"No, Chuck. He's been through some rough times. Did you know when we first found him, he was skinny and missing patches of hair? He was the most pathetic thing you've ever seen. We fattened him up with food and love." She eyed the cat's belly. "I might have gone overboard on the food, but I couldn't stand to think of him hungry. Anyway, he's got a bellyache, and it's swollen. It's why we're here."

With a sigh, Emma reached for the cat, who rolled to its back, and exposed its belly.

"He's hoping you have bacon," Annie said while Emma probed and poked. "Or cheese. He's not picky. Which is probably why he has gas, right?"

"Yeah. Uh, he's not a he, Annie."

"What?"

"She's a she. I'm guessing she's about to pop out a litter of kittens."

"You have got to be shitting me." Annie stared at Emma for a beat, then Chuck, and burst out with laughter. "You know, I had a feeling, because we never really saw his—" She shook her head, her eyes lit with good humor. "I didn't want to be rude and look, and like I said, he came to us—*she* came to us." Annie scooped the cat up against her chest and kissed the thing right on the head. "Babies? Really?"

"*Kittens*," Emma corrected.

"Well better her than me." Annie lifted her gaze, laughing. "Unbelievable. But thanks. Thanks for taking me seriously, for not laughing at me for thinking my cat was a boy when I should have known better. I've been around long enough to spot another bitchy female when I see one, feline or not." She kissed Chuck on her head. "Nothing personal, Kitty." She turned to the door, then looked back. "Oh. You should know, I love your father. He's the best doctor Wishful could have ever asked for, but in his place? You're also the best we could ever ask for."

The door shut in tune to the ridiculous cowbells.

Calling himself all kinds of crazy, Stone pulled up outside the Urgent Care at five o'clock, hoping Emma would be done for the day. He turned off his truck just as the door of the clinic opened and a teenager stepped out. The kid was shirtless, wearing only cutoffs and flip-flops, and cradling his arm, which was splinted and held into place by a sling.

He was Tucker Adams, a local high school student, and one of the foster kids Stone worked with. Tucker had a nonexistent home life, a learning disability, and was a loner. By all counts, he should have been a rough, edgy kid, with a bad attitude to boot, but he wasn't. He was quiet but kind and unassuming, and did the best he could with what he'd been given.

Stone upped the ante in Tucker's favor whenever he could, having the kid work at Wilder on the weekends for extra cash, hauling wood for Annie's wood stove, serving the guests, whatever they had available, because it gave him and Annie the excuse to give Tucker some basic skills, and also the chance to feed him properly. "Tuck? What happened?"

"Nothing."

He didn't meet Stone's eyes, and Stone's gut took a hard twist. It'd either been Tucker's show-up-once-a-month father, or one of the assholes at school. "You come from class?"

"Yeah."

Okay, at least Stone didn't have to go beat up his father. "What happened?"

"I didn't start anything," he said quickly. "I busted up a

fight." He sounded proud, not pissed. "I got my wrist broke is all."

"And lost your shirt?"

He gave a quick shake of his head. "I gave it to someone."

"Someone?"

Tucker lifted a too-lean shoulder. "Shelly."

The girl he'd had a crush on all year. Like Tuck, she didn't exactly fit in, and Stone could absolutely see him standing up for her. Tucker was that kind of kid, even more so since he'd been hanging out at Wilder gaining confidence in himself. "She was hurt?"

"A couple of guys were teasing her after her swim practice. I made them stop."

And he'd given Shelly his shirt to put over her swimsuit, Stone guessed. He nodded, then watched Emma inside as she switched the sign from OPEN to CLOSED. She peeked out the window, saw him, and opened the front door. "Hey."

"Hey. You treated Tucker."

"I did." She smiled fondly at the kid, an uncalculated, honest, genuine gesture that had Stone's heart giving one hard kick.

"It's a clean, hairline fracture," she said, oblivious. "It won't give him too much trouble."

Stone nodded, relieved, and shrugged out of his button-down which he handed to Tucker. "Need a ride?"

"I've got my bike."

Stone would have liked to argue that Tucker shouldn't ride with a broken wrist, but the truth was, when he'd been that age, he'd have done the same thing. Annie would kill him, but he nodded. "With helmet?"

"The one you gave me."

"Take it easy then."

"I will."

When Tucker rode off down the road, Stone turned toward Emma. "Send his bill to me."

"I've got him covered."

"Thanks." Yeah, definitely he was in trouble here.

"I'm just closing," she said. "Spencer's not back yet, so I'm going to rustle up a casserole for dinner." She turned to go back in.

"Where's the fire?"

"The fire? Right here as a matter of fact." She fanned the steamy air in front of her face. "Does it always get this hot?"

He looked into her glowing face and nodded sympathetically. "We tend to get one really hot week a year. This is it."

"There's no air conditioning, which is crazy."

"We don't generally need a/c."

"I just wish it would cool off, I really need to go out for a run."

He shook his head. "Bad plan."

"I need to blow off some steam."

"I have a better way. You want to change into some casual clothes, maybe some shorts, first."

"Uh huh." She eyed him with exasperated amusement. "Tell me. How often does that sexy swagger and smile, and then the 'I have a better way to burn off steam' line get you laid?"

He laughed. "Look, I'm not trying to—" At her long look, he grinned. "Okay, I'm a guy, and therefore, by default, am *always* interested in getting laid, but that wasn't my ulterior motive."

"What was?"

"Getting rid of that stick up your ass."

"Excuse me?" She sputtered, then at a loss, laughed in disbelief.

"Look, you were saying you have an image problem here in Wishful, and I think I can help you."

"By loosening me up."

"By teaching you how to smell the roses. I'm a giver that way. Come on, Emma. Unless . . . you're too chicken?"

Chapter 11

Oh, wasn't he funny, Emma thought. And somehow . . . charming. And sharp. And he had a bad boy truck, and hell. Deep down, somewhere she didn't like to visit too often, she had a fantasy about a guy. Not another uptight doctor guy. Not a white-collared professional of any kind.

But a guy in a bad boy truck.

She wasn't proud of it, but there it was. "I'm not chicken." She swiped her damp forehead and looked at her watch. "You have thirty minutes."

"You can't put a time limit on relaxing."

"Try."

He smiled, promising no such thing, and drove her to Moody's.

Emma stared at the bar and grill. "You going to get me drunk?"

He shot her a look as he parked. "First of all, I never get a woman drunk on the first date."

"Why, because she doesn't remember you the next day?"

"No, because I don't like to clean up puke. And second, I was going to feed you food, not alcohol. Moody's has great burgers."

They got out of the truck and when he took her hand, she looked at him. "This isn't a first date."

"What is it?"

Since she wasn't quite sure, she didn't answer. They walked into the place, and immediately a handful of people waved at Stone. "You're popular," she said.

"Yes, and if you smile, you too can be one of the cool kids."

Okay, so she *was* holding herself tense, and she definitely wasn't smiling.

The place wasn't bad. It was done up Old Western style, with the bar itself a series of refurbished barn doors laid on their sides. The front room was filled with tables for dining, the back room held the pool tables, dart boards, and an area for dancing to the music blaring from the largest juke box she'd ever seen. There were huge antlers hanging on the wall, along with lassoes and brass light fixtures, casting an old-fashioned sort of glow over everyone.

They ordered burgers and fries, and by the time they were done, the place had filled. Stone brought her into the back, to a pool table where Annie, Nick and TJ were playing a rather intense game. Annie came around the table and shoved Stone very affectionately in the shoulder. He stumbled back a step, grinned, and kissed her on the cheek. She softened and hugged him tight.

TJ gave Stone a friendly shove as well, and nodded to Emma. "Hey, Doc. I'm kicking Nick's ass here. I can kick yours when I'm done if you'd like."

Stone turned to Emma. "He likes to think he's the best."

Emma smiled. "And is he?"

"Hell, no. That would be me."

"You wish, man." TJ turned to the bar. Serena was there with another woman, sipping something that looked cool and delicious, the two of them watching the pool game with inscrutable expressions. "Hey, Serena, Harley," TJ said. "You know Dr. Emma Sinclair?"

"Aw, look at that." Serena nudged the woman with her. "You said he didn't have any manners."

"No." Harley pulled off her knit cap, revealing short, spiky blond hair that framed a beautiful face that didn't quite go with the coveralls she wore. "I said he didn't have any *feelings*."

Annie laughed. "Good one," she said, and rubbed her husband's back when he looked at her with a raised brow. "Harley and the guys went to school together," she explained to Emma.

Emma was guessing that they'd more than gone to school together, at least in TJ's and Harley's case, and not a good one, as evidenced by the dirty look Harley gave TJ, and the way he pretended to ignore it. He leaned in with his pool cue and took a shot, sending the ball into a middle pocket.

Unimpressed, Harley made a sound that might have been a tire going flat.

TJ straightened and looked at her. "You have something to say?"

Harley's eyes were cool as ice as the air around them tightened with tension. "Maybe that's my question to you."

"Nope." He lifted a shoulder. "I have a clear conscience."

"A clear conscience is usually the sign of a bad memory."

"Okay, kids, off to your own corners." Stone smoothly stepped between them. "I'm thirsty. I'm having a beer, and then I'm going to show the good doctor how to play pool. Who else wants a drink?" He looked around, nodding with a question in his eyes at Emma.

"Whatever you're having," she said, and earned herself a warm, slow as molasses smile.

Just like that, the mood around them lightened again. Nick slung an arm around Annie. Annie patted the stool next to her for Emma.

Stone had done that, Emma realized. Gotten right in the middle of the people he cared about and easily, lightly, effortlessly, changed the entire atmosphere. She had little experience with this. At the hospital, which should have been a place ripe for conflict and tension, it never really happened. Mostly because they were all too busy, but if there was a problem, it was dealt with passive aggressive silence. Same with her family. When her mother and stepfather had fought, they'd done so civilly—behind closed doors.

Here, no one felt the need to hide their feelings. They talked, they laughed, they fought. They loved. Loudly, with no shame in any of it.

Annie had told her they had Stone to thank for that, that he was the central force, and he was good at it. He was good at a lot of things.

Unlike Emma, who was good at one thing, and that was work. She'd always been proud of that, but here in Wishful, she was beginning to realize that there was so much more to life than work.

Serena nudged a drink in Harley's direction, who took a deep breath and a deep sip, and TJ leaned over the table and took anther shot, putting the two ball in the top left pocket and the four in the middle right.

Nicely done.

He then put away the remaining four balls and pumped a fist in the air while both Annie and Nick rolled their eyes. "Four out of five," he declared, pointing at Nick. "You owe."

Serena turned to Harley. "Did you know that fifty percent of all statistics are made up on the spot?"

Harley let out a half laugh, tore her gaze off TJ and turned to the bartender. "I don't suppose you have a Xanax?"

"Finals?" the bartender asked in sympathy.

"Tomorrow."

The bartender poured her a double Scotch. "Consider me a

pharmacist with a limited inventory. But this should work."
He pushed the shot in her direction.

Stone handed Emma a beer and sank to a seat next to her,
smiling at her as she watched Annie take her turn at kicking
Nick's butt at pool. "Want to play?"

Her college apartment had been over a bar, and she and
Spencer had spent every single morning playing pool while
quizzing each other in chemistry and biology. Like everything
she put her mind to, she wasn't just good, she was great.

"Come on," he said at her hesitation. "I'll give you some
pointers."

"If you want pointers," TJ told Emma, "play me, seeing as
I kicked his ass last week. We bet all the paperwork at the
lodge for a week, and he's still at it."

"I do all the paperwork anyway, you ass." Stone smiled,
quite full of himself. "Besides, I let you win."

"Then maybe you'd like to make another bet."

"Sure."

"Okay, think about this, Stone," Annie said. "Remember,
you're already zero for ten this week alone."

Stone shook his head as everyone laughed. "It's a good
thing I'm not trying to impress the girl," he muttered.

The "girl" was looking at him, looking at the guy who ran
the business for his brothers, worked with foster kids, kept his
family together. Yeah, she was looking, and thinking there went
another layer off the mountain bum image. Even though he
looked the part; tall and built with that sun-kissed hair and
California surfer good looks, appearances were apparently de-
ceiving because he wasn't a slacker at all. Inside him beat the
fierce, loyal heart that would go to the ends of the earth for
those he loved.

"Aw." Annie patted Stone on the back. "If that's what you
were trying to do, honey, you probably shouldn't have brought
her here."

"True enough." He set down his drink, stood up and took Emma's hand. "A game?"

"Do it, Emma," Annie said. "Show 'em who's boss."

Everyone hooted and hollered at that, cheering for her. No one was looking at her like she was an alien, or politely but distantly calling her Dr. Sinclair. They were cheering, for her. She turned to look at Stone. "What would we play for?"

He arched a surprised brow. "You want to bet?"

Oh, yeah. She wanted to bet. "Unless you're afraid."

"Name it," he said, eyes lit with promised retribution as everyone let out a collective "oooh . . ."

"Well," Emma said. "If you're so good at paperwork, you could do all mine at the Urgent Care. I'd love to have a secretary." The crowd went nuts at this. "If I win," she added demurely. And she was going to win.

Still laughing, Annie started to say something to her but Stone put a hand in front of his aunt's face. Eyes still on Emma, he let out another slow smile. "And if I win?"

Everyone leaned forward eagerly to hear what he planned on claiming as his spoils.

"Maybe she could do *your* paperwork," Annie suggested.

Nick snorted and hugged his wife. "I'm pretty sure he could come up with something better than that, babe." He winked at Stone. "Maybe you ought to ask for free medical care for all your various injuries."

"Yes," Serena said slyly. "You can play doctor."

TJ chuckled and slung an arm over Stone's shoulders. "I'm not sure the boy knows how to play doctor."

Stone shoved him off and smiled at the good-natured ribbing. "I can pick my own winnings, thank you very much," and when everyone looked at him, waiting, he shook his head. "In private."

"Yes," Serena said. "Because nothing says romantic like kicking a woman's ass in pool and then demanding payment."

Harley took Serena's drink away. "Honey, your bitch is show-ing again."

"Whoops. Hate it when that happens. Especially since you're the one who has the right to be a bitch right now." She gave TJ a pointed look.

TJ's left eye twitched but he said nothing.

Harley said a loaded nothing as well, tossing back another shot, gesturing to the bartender for yet another.

Stone picked out a cue stick and turned to Emma.

Gorgeous.

And just a little cocky.

Bring it, she thought. "Ready?" she asked.

"Oh, yes."

Finally, something she could be better at than him.

Chapter 12

Stone racked the balls and gestured for Emma to take the break shot.

She gave him a slight bow and bent over the pool table, and he thought, oh yeah. Right there. *There's* the best reason on God's good earth to invite a woman to play pool. Who cared who won or lost when her pants tightened nice and snug across the sweetest ass on this side of the Sierras? Who cared who won or lost when—

She hit, hard and accurately, and three solid balls went in, the one, two and three balls consecutively.

A beautiful combo shot.

All eyes swiveled to him, accompanied by the low chorus of "oooooh."

Like he didn't know he was in trouble. He met her amused gaze.

"I'm solids," she said sweetly.

"You've played. A lot."

"I've played," she agreed. "A lot."

Oh, Christ, look at her, all cool and confident. It was the sexiest thing he'd ever seen. As was that fitted shirt she wore, only two buttons undone. Cerebral and hot at the same time, which was blowing the synapses in his mind at the speed of light.

Not good.

She bent over the table again and blew the rest of his brain completely out.

"But it's been awhile," she muttered demurely, rocketing the seven ball in the corner pocket before casually aiming at the five. And making it. She got the four ball in before she missed her last, the six, and he knew he should be at least worried, but goddamn if he wasn't smiling from ear to ear.

"You look like an idiot," Harley told him ever-so-helpfully. "Stop grinning and get in the game."

Right. He tore his gaze off Emma with much difficulty and did as Harley demanded. Luckily he really was good.

And lucky.

He hit every single striped ball in, until all he had left was the eight ball.

Emma was standing there, not so smug anymore. In fact, she now wore an "oh shit" expression. Yeah. She wasn't always the best at everything, which must be new for her. Plus he could practically read her thoughts. She was wondering what he was going to want. Good, let her worry, because he decided he liked her a little off her game, a little uncertain.

He finessed the shot and the eight ball sank right in, winning him the game and hopefully the girl.

Annie sighed. "I thought I taught you to always let the woman win."

"He can't," Nick told her. "He wants his spoils."

Stone looked at TJ, waiting for his smartass comment. He was certain his brother had one, his brother always had one. But TJ wasn't paying him the slightest bit of attention. He was leaning against the bar staring at Harley with a naked, love struck look on his face.

Great. So two out of three Wilder brothers were looking to get their hearts bashed in.

He tugged the cue stick out of Emma's hand.

She raised a brow.

He raised one back.

"Now?" she asked. "You're collecting your winnings now?"

Hell, yes, now. Though he had the oddest urge to toss her over his shoulder and take her back to his cave and pound his chest with his fists before sinking into her glorious body, he knew better.

She hadn't yet decided to sleep with him.

Which made them even. Oh, he *wanted* to sleep with her. Actually, he wanted to pull off her clothes with his teeth, lick every single inch of her soft skin, bury himself deep in her body and take them both straight to heaven.

Multiple times.

It'd been a long time since a woman had gotten stuck in his head and stayed there. Since he'd felt the long, slow, curl of heat deep in his gut that he felt now. A very long time.

But more than anything, he wanted to talk to her. Peel back a few layers, find out what made her tick. What made her so tough and edgy.

So competitive, so remote. So unwilling to connect. He stepped closer and she reacted with a hard swallow and the sudden fluttering of her pulse at the base of her throat.

She hadn't expected to lose.

He pulled her off the barstool and met her gaze, and in that beat at least, she was just a soft, gorgeous woman, suddenly looking at him as if maybe she wanted him as much as he wanted her.

Oh yeah, that worked for him.

She followed him outside into the tangible heat. It was only six thirty. They still had hours of daylight left.

Perfect for what he had in mind. "Trust me?" he asked her. "Hell, no."

He grinned and pulled out his keys. "You reneging then?"

She put a hand on her hip and gave him a long, even look that stirred him up. "On what exactly?"

"It's a surprise."

She stared at him, then laughed. "You are unbelievable."

"So you *are* reneging."

"My word is my word." She eyed his truck, sighed heavily, and hopped into the passenger seat.

Unable to believe his luck, he stared at her for a beat, then jogged around to his door before she could change her mind.

Emma swiped her forehead on her arm. Lord, it was hot. Very hot. She looked around the cab of the bad boy truck. It wasn't for show, the thing had dents and wear and tear, and was clearly well-loved and well-used.

And it had a/c.

Her secret fantasy upped a notch.

Stone started the engine, made her his friend forever when he cranked the air, and within five minutes they were out of Wishful. They made a quick stop at the lodge, where he vanished for a minute, then came back and loaded two bikes in the back.

"I'm not a mountain biker," she said.

"You will be."

He took them up a narrow dirt road that she'd never been on before. The going was rough, and she was grateful for her seatbelt as she was knocked side to side. The landscape was thick here, overgrown and wooded, and with the late afternoon sun making shadows, she couldn't tell much about where they were going except that they were climbing.

And climbing.

"How about a hint about where we're going?" she asked.

"It'll take your breath," was all he said.

Well at sixty-three hundred feet, that she could believe. She looked over at him, driving the nearly nonexistent road with ease in his loose and battered jeans and a t-shirt. His Nike's looked as old and comfortable as his jeans. Once again, his hair was finger-disheveled and he hadn't shaved.

Another secret fantasy, a man who wasn't a slave to his razor. She wanted to know what that stubble felt like rubbing against her skin.

He glanced over at her. "What?"

"Nothing."

"Oh, it was something. You looked . . . I don't know. Hot."

"That's because it's a million degrees." She'd rather work at the Urgent Care for the rest of the year than admit she'd been picturing him running his face all over her body. "You're not really a ski and bike bum, are you?"

He slid her another glance. "Is that what you were thinking about?"

"Sort of." Indirectly. "You *run* Wilder Adventures. You lead treks by day, and by night you work on the business end; the reservations, the books, the scheduling. Annie seems to think you're the glue that keeps your family together."

He seemed amused by his aunt's assessment. "That's because I'm her favorite."

She slid him a look. "She said Cam was."

He laughed, and she couldn't take her eyes off him. He was at ease, confident. *Happy.*

God, that was attractive. "You're a close family."

He slid her another look. "We are." He pulled into a clearing and turned off the truck. "But we're not exclusive."

"What does that mean?"

He got out of the truck and came around for her, opening

her door, waiting until she leaned forward to get out before stepping between the opened door and where she sat.

Her legs bumped his. She liked the feeling.

Slowly he crouched until they were at eye level. "It means I know you're feeling alone. That you don't think you fit in here. But you're wrong about both. You're not alone, and you can fit in."

It was a nice thought. A comforting thought. It put others into her head, which meant her brain got a little fuzzy, what with the hot guy hunkered in front of her and his hot truck at her back. Anticipation hummed through her, and more shocking, a hunger.

Not the usual hunger to be busy, or the thrill of a new medical case.

But a hunger for a man.

For him.

Needing some space, she nudged him with a hand to his chest, and for one beat, he nudged back, his broad torso filling her vision, his eyes suddenly somber and filled with a hunger of his own, his heat and strength tantalizingly close. Just when her fingers were beginning to fist into his shirt, he backed off and held out his hand.

She followed him around the back of the truck. He pulled out the two mountain bikes and handed her a helmet, and when she just stared at it, he put it on for her, his fingers brushing her throat as he clicked her in.

"I don't know about this," she said. "It's so damn hot."

"It'll cool down soon."

"Is this the bet then? You want me to ride with you?"

"No." He eyed her for a moment, scrubbing a hand over his jaw, which made an oddly erotic scraping noise. "You don't like to do new things."

She looked at the trailhead. It seemed narrow. Scary. "I do so."

"No you don't. And I know why."

She turned back to him and put her hands on her hips. "Okay, Mr. Know It All, why don't I like to do new things?"

"Because you only like to do the stuff you're good at."

She blinked, and he laughed at her softly. "Have you ever really had to try at something, Emma? Something important? Or does it all come naturally to you in your world?"

Okay, she resented that. "I worked my ass off to get through medical school."

"Really?"

She stared at him, then deflated. "No. It came. . . . easy, and I loved it." He couldn't be right, could he? "But residency was hard and exhausting," she came up with triumphantly. It'd been hard and exhausting and . . . and exhilarating. "Oh, shut up."

He grinned. "Can you ride a bike?"

"Well now's a fine time to ask, but yes."

"Are you better at riding than driving?"

Okay, *that* lit a fire under her competitive nature. "I drive just fine."

"Well as I've seen you, we're going to have to respectfully agree to disagree there."

"Funny."

He waggled a brow. "So how about a little race?"

"Is *that* the bet?"

"Sure." He smiled. "That's the bet. Think you can take me?"

She let her gaze slide over his leanly muscled, incredibly fit body. Nice. But *she* was in shape, too. Sure she'd been eating cheese casseroles for weeks now, all in the name of saving her father's health, but she was the most determined, stubborn person she knew. Plus surely he didn't plan to kick her butt twice in a row. He was a man on a mission to get laid so she figured he'd let her have this one. "I do think I can take you."

He sent her a long, slow grin. "Care to make a little wager?"

"Another bet?"

"Uh huh. Unless you're afraid of losing. Again."

Oh, that was it. "If I win," she said, pointing at him. "You're taking me to find Thai take-out. I don't care if we have to fly to Thailand to get it."

"Deal. And if I win . . ." His smile turned bad boy wicked. "You'll go swimming with me."

"I didn't bring my bathing suit."

His smile spread, and her belly fluttered. "I am *not* going skinny-dipping with you in some lake or river, Stone."

"So you think you'll lose then."

Oh, he was good. She threw her leg over the bike. "You know what? Bring it on."

"I'll even give you a head start."

She'd take that.

"Start slow," he told her in an easy, comforting voice that shouldn't have sparked her competitive nature even more, but it did because he didn't think she could win.

And she was *so* going to win. She was getting Thai, come hell or high water. "You just want to watch my ass."

"Well, it is a sweet ass."

She laughed, then prepared to take off, stopping as something occurred to her. "Okay, maybe you should tell me the difference between street riding and trail riding."

"Comply with all signs and barriers."

"That's just common sense." Which, not to be egotistical, but she happened to have boatloads of common sense. "Tell me something I don't know."

"Okay, you need to maintain a distance between the bikes."

"Again," she said. "Common sense." The trail was thick with ruts and mud from the previous day's rain. Distance was a safety issue. "If that's all there is to this, prepare for your ass kicking."

He put a hand on her handlebars, stopping her from taking off. "We're going to try to avoid the trails that are too wet or muddy."

"Good. I don't like wet and muddy."

"I'd like to assure you that wet and muddy have their place, but not with newcomers." He turned her bike toward another trail that she hadn't seen, a slightly wider one, that hadn't been as damaged by the rains. "Ride in the middle and try to avoid side-slipping, which can lead to erosion."

She stared up at him, her eyes going directly to that face she couldn't stop looking at. The men in her world might be more refined, more attached to their razors, but she really liked how he looked.

She liked the rugged arrangement of his features, the way his mouth curved so generously—

"Ready?"

"Ready." She pushed off into the heat and found her sea legs fairly quickly.

"Change gears," he called out from behind her. "You want comfortable momentum but traction so you don't slip—"

"I'm fine—oh, shit," she gasped as she slipped, and quickly changed gears. Not good. If she was going to win this thing, and she planned to, she'd need to concentrate. She wiped her damp brow and did just that.

The trail turned sharply, then went on a decline, and on instinct, she hit her brakes.

"Careful," he warned. "Don't lock 'em up."

"So as not to gouge the trail?" she asked.

"Or die."

Good to know. She eased off the brakes. The ride wasn't anything like she'd imagined. For one thing, it was a whole lot harder than she'd expected it to be. They were on a rocky trail and it was bumpy. She had to concentrate on not pitching her-

self over the handlebars. For another, as the trail widened and
Stone came up alongside, she had to concentrate on not staring at him, at all those lean, hard muscles working, at the way
his legs churned, how his hands held the grips as if he'd been
born to it.

Oh man was she out of her league, *so* far out of her league,
but luckily, he was just as enthralled watching her. He eyed her
legs, her arms, her face, and smiled. "Damn if you're not harder
to beat than I thought you'd be," he murmured.

Good. She planned on taking advantage of that. Finally, far
up ahead, through the tree about a hundred yards ahead, she
could see where the trail ended, and after half an hour on this
seat, she was ready for it to be done. So she dug deep and sped
up, taking the lead.

He let her.

When she stood up to pedal harder, she heard his low breath
of appreciation at the view she was giving him, and knew she
had the win in the bag. She smiled, because God she loved to
win—

Suddenly something whizzed by her, and Stone came to a
skidding stop on a dime.

Dammit. "You won," she gasped, barely able to talk through
her wheezing for air.

He modestly lifted a shoulder and got off his bike. "If it
helps, you very nearly kicked my ass."

Very nearly wasn't going to get her out of swimming. She
got off her bike as well, too, still huffing and puffing. Sweating. She couldn't catch her breath, and sounding like a broken
locomotive, she turned and looked at the view.

And went still.

Just ahead was an alpine lake, about a mile across, slightly
wider than that. It was completely surrounded by towering
mountain peaks lined with thick, lush growth. "Oh my God."

"Hidden Lakes. We passed two others, hidden in the growth. This one's the furthest, and the hardest to get to."

She stepped closer to the water lapping at the coarse mountain sand, taking in the cattails lining the edge, the lily ponds in the shallow water, and shook her head. It was so beautiful she could hardly speak.

They were completely isolated, surrounded by three-hundred-feet-tall sequoias and pines.

And alone.

Stone dropped the small backpack he'd worn on the ride. Something inside squawked, and he crouched down, pulling out a radio. "Go ahead, TJ, over."

"Where are you? Over."

"Third Hidden Lake. Over."

"That group going down Cascade Falls tomorrow showed up two days early. Annie and I rushed back to the lodge and they're pissed. The schedule's fucked up, and Annie's bitching because her pies didn't get delivered, and now I'm double-booked for tomorrow. When the hell are you getting back? Over."

"If the schedule's fucked up," Stone replied, "it's because you put your grimy fingers on it." Sitting on his haunches, he sighed and shook his head. "Leave it alone. I'll fix it when I get back. The two clients yelling at you can wait for me as well. You'll just piss them off more. Send Nick for the pies. And you're not double-booked for tomorrow. I'm taking the Alpine trip. Over."

"You still didn't say when you'd be back. Over."

Stone glanced up at Emma and smiled. "I'll be back when you stop yelling at me. Over." With that, he tossed the radio to the ground.

"He sounded desperate," Emma said. "You're just going to leave him hanging?"

"Sure. He's done it to me plenty of times. You okay?" he asked when she sank to the coarse sand.

"Just shaking. I think it's the altitude."

He opened the backpack and pulled out two bottled waters and a Ziploc bag full of cookies, which he handed over. "Some sugar should help. Try 'em. They're my specialty."

She took a bite and moaned in sheer bliss. "Oh. My. God. This is better than the scenery, and that's pretty darn amazing." She couldn't get the rest of the cookie in fast enough. "Seriously. You made these?"

"Yeah."

"They're the best cookies I've ever had."

He looked amused. "They're just basic chocolate chip."

Yes, but when she wanted cookies, or any food for that matter, she went to the store. She used her oven as storage for the pots and pans she'd never used. "I burn water."

"Well, it's a good thing I'm not asking you to cook for me then, isn't it."

She looked up, caught the teasing light in his eyes and smiled. It was true. He hadn't asked her to cook for him. He hadn't asked anything of her.

Which should have made him the perfect man.

Did make him the perfect man.

Except for the fact that she didn't want or need one. She didn't want or need anyone in her life, thank you very much, she thought as she licked the last bit of chocolate from her fingers. "Omigod, these are better than . . . everything."

He followed the movement of her tongue with his eyes, but smiled easily. "Life isn't all about food."

"True. It's all about take-out."

He laughed.

"Hey, I'm not kidding. After twenty hours on your feet and

only a few coffees in your system, you wouldn't snub your nose at Taco Bell, I can promise you."

"You must work some crazy hours."

"Yeah."

"You miss it."

"Yeah." She sighed. "I do."

"What do you miss the most?"

"Oh, that's easy. I miss . . ." She blinked, shocked to find herself drawing a blank.

He arched a brow. "You miss . . . ?"

So much. But suddenly, there in the last of a gorgeous, hot day, surrounded *not* by the smell of antiseptic and the nagging beat of her pager and cell phone, instead looking into a set of deep jade eyes which were smiling at her with affection and heat, she couldn't think of a single thing.

How odd was that? "I miss . . . Thai food," she said triumphantly.

There. She'd thought of something. A lame something, but still.

Looking amused, he slowly shook his head. "That's reaching."

Yeah. It was. Then, still looking at her, he stood up, tall and lean and damp with sweat, and her heart skipped a beat. "What are you doing?"

"Relaxing. Swimming." He kicked off a shoe. "You remember who won, right?"

Oh, God. "Yes, but . . . but your brother sounded pissed. Maybe we should go back."

"Serves him right. You didn't answer my question."

"Um," she said brilliantly as he kicked off his other shoe.

"You lost," he pointed out gently.

"Oh, that silly bet?" She swallowed hard as he lifted his T-shirt off over his head and tossed it aside. *Sweet Jesus.* She stared at his mouth watering chest as his fingers went to the button on his jeans. "Stone?"

"Yeah?"

"Are you wearing a bathing suit?"

"Nope."

Chapter 13

Stone's eyes were full of mischief and a wicked intent, both of which had the same effect on Emma's insides as his bad boy truck. "Stone. You can't just—"

He could, and did.

He toed off his socks.

"Yeah, now see—"

Ignoring her stammering, he unbuttoned his Levi's, and she nearly swallowed her tongue. She'd seen him without a shirt before. On her examination table up close and personal, though of course this time he was void of all the dirt and blood. He still had some scrapes and bruises, which in no way marred the utter perfection of his broad shoulders, chest, and six-pack abs that she suddenly and inexplicably, desperately wanted to lap up like she'd lapped up the last of the chocolate.

His jeans were low-slung and loose enough that they pulled away from him, leaving a tantalizing gap that a woman could stick her entire hand down and—

"Your turn," he said, pausing from his stripping down.

"I am *not* going skinny dipping with you."

"Now here's one thing I don't get about women. They always make blanket statements like that, and then change their mind. Wouldn't it be easier to say nothing at all?"

He wasn't wearing a belt, so when he finished unbuttoning his jeans, they sank even lower, nearly to indecent levels, and she stared at what he was slowly revealing. "I don't make blanket statements as a rule, and I always mean what I say."

"See?" He smiled. "Another blanket statement."

"I *do* mean what I say. Look, it's . . . late. I need to go back."

"It's seven thirty."

"Almost my bedtime."

"You said you were hot," he pointed out reasonably.

Yes. Yes she was hot. Holy smokes . . .

He added one of those panty-melting smiles. Oh God, she was in trouble.

"I'm simply offering you the solution to your problem," he said.

"Yes," she managed. "While creating a whole new one."

"Which would be?" he asked innocently.

Ha! "You. *Naked.*"

He shoved off his jeans and kicked them aside, leaving him in a pair of dark blue knit boxers that clung to his tough thighs and lean hips. When she managed to lift her gaze to meet his, she found his eyes both hot and amused.

If she thought she'd been sweating before . . .

Then, without a word, he turned from her, stepped a few feet into the lake water and dove in.

Vanishing beneath the smooth surface with hardly a splash.

A few drops hit her and they were so deliciously, deliriously cool, she actually moaned. *Goddammit.*

He surfaced facing her, just his perfect chest, shoulders, and head popping out of the water. He shook his head, and water went flying. He looked at her, hair crazy, face streaming water, smile so contagious she had to work to keep solemn. "Stone—"

"You lost."

"Yes, but—"

Still smiling sweetly, he pushed his hand through the water, and splashed her.

Right in the face.

"*Hey!*"

He arched a brow.

She let out a breath, torn between indignation and utter bliss—because God, the water felt amazing. "What if I'd straightened my hair and didn't want it wet? What if I was wearing makeup?"

"Did you? Are you?"

"No. But still—"

He splashed her again, and that was it. He was going down. She yanked off her shirt and tossed it to the ground while she kicked off her shoes at the same time. "You are so going to get it."

"Promises, promises."

Leaving her plain black cotton bra in place, she shoved down her trousers. Her equally plain cotton bikini panties weren't any prettier than the bra, but she didn't happen to care much about lingerie. She cared about comfort. Right now she was uncomfortably hot and uncomfortably worked up. She stalked toward the water, ready to rumble.

His gaze had all but glued itself to her body. His mouth had fallen open a little, as if he needed it that way just to breathe. His eyes were eating her up, caressing her body as if she was the best thing he'd ever seen, and if she hadn't been so over-heated, with adrenaline pumping through her instead of blood, she might have been flattered. "Prepare to die."

He lifted his gaze to hers. At the look on her face, he backed up, further into the water.

"Get over here and take your medicine like a man." She stood at the edge and let the water lap at her feet. Oh, God, it was so *cold*. She kicked it and splashed him, but it wasn't enough.

So she dove in. Not nearly as gracefully as he had, but she hadn't been in the water much since high school, where she'd been on the swim team. It came right back to her, and as the gloriously cold water closed over her head, she pushed down, swimming underwater up to a pair of long, masculine, still scraped up legs. Her plan was to swim past him, out as far as she could get, hopefully ridding herself of as much of her restless energy as possible, and only when she could be sure to keep in control, would she turn back.

She got maybe a stroke past him when she felt a big, warm hand close around her ankle. She kicked, but he was far stronger than she, and pulled her back against him.

She fought, but he merely wrapped two long, hard arms around her and lifted her to the surface for air.

The air was shimmering hot, the water icy cold, his body a perfect mix of hard sinew and warm skin. A paradox, because her instincts were at odds.

Fight him.

Hold onto him.

Kiss him.

Splash him.

God. She wanted to do all of it, and all that heated, strong, sleek flesh was pressed up against hers. In fact, staring into his stark green eyes, eyes that didn't attempt to hide a thing from her, she was having a hard time remembering that she was supposed to be fighting him at all, or why she even wanted to.

Then he smiled; a soft, sweet, sexy smile, and she was lost. She smiled back, and let her fingers play in his hair. Just for a minute, she told herself. Then he dipped his head close to hers, kissing her cheek, letting his mouth skim the edge of her jaw, and she sighed in pleasure, closing her eyes, melting into him, all resistance gone, and—

And he dunked her.

Dunked.

Her.

Sputtering and wriggling, she nearly got away but once again he caught her, slowly tugging her back like a fish on a line. As much as she tried to get away, she was held tight, her back to his chest, her butt to his crotch, which she only realized because the more she fought, the harder he got. "You should know," she said through her teeth. "I'm pretty good at this."

"Swimming?"

"Kicking ass." But though she struggled and fought, she couldn't get free. "Let me go!"

"Say the magic word."

"Let me go or you'll be walking funny tomorrow."

With a low chuckle, he put his hand on the top of her head and pushed, dunking her again.

His mistake.

Because beneath the water, she whirled to face him, then sank even lower, where she grabbed his ankles and lifted, tumbling him backwards under the water. Without waiting to see how he took that, she whipped around and started swimming away, laughing in sheer triumph. She got two strokes this time before she was once again dragged back against his hard, wet body.

He turned her to face him, but she wasn't falling for those sweet, sexy eyes again. Oh, no. She *learned* from her mistakes, and she twisted free, sinking back down and around him. Opening her eyes, she placed her hands on the backs of his knees and pushed.

When his legs obligingly collapsed, she laughed beneath the water and nearly drowned herself. She managed to swim away, and she kept at it, going as hard and fast as she could while laughing out loud.

He caught her, disturbingly easily, so easily in fact that she had to wonder if she'd meant him to. Hands on her waist, he yanked her under with him. They wrestled beneath the surface, and though she had little wrestling experience and he apparently had plenty, she did have one advantage. When he pulled her up against him and held her in so that her arms were completely ineffective, she brought her knee slowly up between his, stopping just short of her mark.

He went instantly still. His eyes met hers.

She arched a brow.

"Uncle," he cracked, and loosened his arms enough that she could drop down through.

But she hadn't thought it all the way through, because she felt every inch of his chest and belly and thighs, every single hard, perfect inch, and here she was, free to swim away, and she didn't want to.

"You think you're all that," he said, his mouth to hers, his voice low and husky and full of laughter as he completely supported her.

"I *am* all that."

He laughed again, and looked into her eyes.

And she had one thought. *Send a life vest, I'm going down.* The last of the sun beat down on them as the water lapped at their entangled bodies. His arms were hard around her, her breasts mashed up against his bare chest, her belly plastered to his.

He was still hard, and she could feel him, pressing up against the soft core of her. She looked into his face. The cut over his eye was still healing, but that wasn't what made her breathless. Her legs bumped into his, and she actually physically had to fight the urge to wrap them around his waist, further opening herself to him.

As if he could read her thoughts, his smiled faded. His eyes flamed.

She flamed too, from the inside out, and when he leaned in close she had to bite back a moan.

"You feel . . . amazing," he whispered huskily, and without her permission, her hands glided up his sleek, strong back, over those amazingly reassuringly wide shoulders, to sink into his wet hair. "Same goes," she whispered back.

"Yeah?"

"Yeah."

"Good." Then he slowly lowered his mouth and finally, oh God, *finally* kissed her.

She met him halfway, loving the feel of his warm hands on her body in the cool water, gliding everywhere, her waist, her back, her breasts, as if he couldn't get enough of her.

She couldn't get enough either, responding the same way, running her hands all over him, opening her mouth for his tongue, letting her legs do as they'd wanted and wrap around him so that he could nestle his erection against her core. And rock.

God. God, it felt so good she could actually feel her insides quiver. Her toes curled, and—

He tore his mouth from her. She gasped in denial, and eyes closed, body humming, she tried to bring him back to her, even as she heard him swear roughly against her cheek.

Then came TJ's voice. *"Are you fucking kidding me?"*

TJ stood on the shore next to his Yamaha dirt bike, hands on his hips, looking pissed off.

Well, hell, Stone thought. The guy had always had some pretty shitaceous timing, but this topped the cake. Stone tightened his arms around a squirming Emma and lowered the both of them further down into the water so that it lapped against their chins. Not that he wanted to cover the gorgeous, wet, mouth-watering body of the very hot woman in his arms, but she was for his viewing pleasure only.

He intended to view. Then touch.

Then taste.

And he thought, given how she'd watched him strip, how her eyes had eaten him up in the water, how she'd been pressed up against him, panting for breath when he'd touched her, that maybe she'd had similar plans for him. *Thanks TJ.*

Emma dropped her head to his shoulder. "I'm going to kill you," she muttered beneath her breath.

Gorgeous, wet, hot, *and* furious, and he sighed. How he'd not even heard TJ's approach or the bike's motor, he had no idea. "What are you doing here?" he asked his brother.

"Your radio called me with your distress call."

"What?"

"Oh, and when you're alive? Answer your goddamn radio!"

Still holding Emma, a little sidetracked by the way her breasts were pressed against his chest, nipples hard, Stone shook his head. "What the hell are you talking about?"

"The radio? The thing we use to communicate? If you're not dead or dying, you answer it after you send a distress call."

"I didn't hear it."

"I can see that, but you've been sending out a distress call to me for the past twenty minutes. I raced my ass up here to save yours."

Emma, apparently having enough of this, jerked free of Stone and straightened. When she realized they stood in only waist deep waters and that she was in nothing but her bra and panties, she squeaked, slipping back down against him, sending blasphemous, black looks his way.

Yeah, he probably deserved that. But he hadn't expected to be interrupted, and by his own brother, no less. "I don't know what you're talking about," he told TJ, playing a silent tug-of-war with Emma beneath the water. He had no idea where she thought she was going, but the only place to go to was straight toward his brother, who he intended to get rid of so Emma could try to kick his ass in private. "I'm nowhere near the radio, as you can see."

"It was going off like mad." TJ pulled his radio from his pocket. "It's still going off."

Huh? In the silence that followed Stone could hear it, the beep-beep-beeping of the receiver.

TJ turned to their discarded clothes. Specifically Emma's. He nudged aside her shirt, and then her shoes, both of which had been dropped . . .

On top of the radio.

Specifically the talk button.

The radio stopped beeping.

Emma looked up at Stone, horrified. "I did that?"

"Mystery solved," TJ said. "I can't believe you were fucking around on duty. You wrote the book on protocol for us, remember? You made Cam and I swear not to—"

"Excuse me," Emma said stiffly. Both men looked at her. "For the record, he wasn't 'fucking around'. Not literally anyway," she muttered, and stormed out of the water, a glorious, furious goddess in her underwear.

TJ shot Stone a holy-shit look.

In return, Stone shot him a get-the-hell-out-of-here look, which he knew damn well TJ received and understood, and yet the dumbass just stood there.

With a sigh, Stone followed Emma out of the water. "So you drove all the way up here to chew my ass out?"

"I drove all the way up here because I thought you'd fallen off a cliff. I thought you needed my help."

"I don't fall off cliffs."

TJ gave him a droll look.

"Okay, one time!" Jesus. "And that wasn't even my fault. Look, we're both fine, as you can see for yourself." Stone lifted his hands to prove it. "Now go away." He wanted to pull Emma back up against him—

She stared at him in disbelief, her fiery temperament matching her fiery hair shining in the sun. "It's our fault he's here!"

"Yes, but now he's leaving."

TJ, not leaving, smiled, and when she stomped her way toward her clothes with her head held high, he picked up Stone's shirt, and held it out to her.

"Thank you," she said loftily, snatching the shirt and pulling it on over the body Stone had been dreaming about for weeks. She wrapped her arms around herself and sent Stone another glacial stare.

With a sigh, Stone glanced at TJ. "Thanks, man."

Emma picked up her pants, realized both men were looking at her, and snapped, "Turn your backs!"

TJ obligingly closed his eyes.

She looked at Stone, who looked right back. "Close 'em."

With a sigh, he did, then peeked. She was gathering up all the clothes including his, shoving them into the backpack, and then she got on her bike.

With his stuff.

"Uh," he said, lifting a hand toward her. "Maybe we could—"

She put on her helmet and rode off.

TJ looked at Stone in his wet underwear and grinned. "Going to be a fun ride back." He patted Stone's shoulder, and whistling now, took off as well.

Chapter 14

The next day, Emma was over what had happened.

Okay, not quite. She kept reliving the night before. Basically, she'd stripped down to her underwear with Stone.

She'd wrestled in said underwear with Stone.

She'd laughed. Hard.

She'd lusted. Harder.

If TJ hadn't shown up, they'd have had sex right there in the water. She knew it. And worse, she knew that Stone knew it as well.

He'd dropped her off with a promise that next time he'd tie up TJ before they set out for their fun, but she'd told him she'd decided fun should be off the menu, that she should really concentrate on what she was here to do.

The end.

He hadn't argued with her but neither had he agreed, and she had the uncomfortable feeling they weren't done discussing the issue.

She'd gotten out of his truck—still in his shirt—and left him in nothing but his underwear, an image that was going to keep her warm all night.

After a full day in the clinic, Emma stood upstairs in the living room, looking at her mother's picture over the fireplace, and voiced the question that had been bothering her all day. "So is it really true that I've never really had to try at anything?"

"You talking to yourself again?" Spence asked from the kitchen, where he was making dinner.

She looked into her mom's eyes and sighed. "Yes," she said. Because that was far less revealing an admission than the fact that she'd been hearing her dead mother's voice in her head since she came to California. She joined Spence in the kitchen, hopping up onto the counter. "Do I never have to try hard at anything?"

"Never." He handed her a plate filled with the peppered steak he'd whipped up while singing along to her father's old boom box. "Taste."

She did. "Oh, yeah, baby."

He smiled. "Right?"

"I've died and gone to steak heaven. I'm going to need you to stay here with me until I can blow this popsicle stand."

He grinned. "I have something you can blow—"

"*Spence.*"

"Just saying."

She took a sip of the wine he'd brought, and then nearly spilled it when he tugged her off the counter and to her feet.

"Good song," he said. "Dance with me."

It was an Alicia Key power ballad, and right there in the kitchen, he pulled her in close, dancing like a pro, singing in her ear while he was at it—not like a pro—making her both laugh and sigh at the same time. He smelled good, felt good, and he rubbed his jaw to hers. He was like a security blanket. Familiar. Easy. "I'm glad you came," she whispered.

"Are you?"

She pulled back and looked at him. "Of course I am."

"Then why are you keeping me at arm's length?"

"I'm not." But she dropped her gaze to his chest, suddenly aware that she was doing that very thing, holding her arms a little rigid to keep him from pressing too close.

"Emma," he said gently, and tipped up her face.

She met his eyes with hers, then let out a breath. "I don't know."

"Is it me? Or you?"

"Neither. *Me*," she amended. "I don't know."

"Emma." He ran a finger over her cheekbones. "I've been trying to figure out how to tell you that I didn't come here for purely altruistic reasons. I came to see if we could combine the friendship with more."

"Oh, Spence." He made her heart hurt. And her stomach, because suddenly she was afraid she'd lose him. "We've been there, done that."

"Never seriously."

Her breath caught, and she backed out of his arms, turning off the music. Through the window and the glass in the upper half of the back door, it was pitch black dark, the way only a Sierra night could get. Needing to busy her hands, she flipped on the porch lights. "Spence—"

"I know." He leaned back against the counter, watching her carefully. "It wouldn't work. I'm getting that. It's just that all this time I thought it was *me* holding us up, but I can see now that it's you."

"What?"

"Yeah. You like having me in your life but not having me. I liked it too." His gaze, dark and solemn, met hers. "Past tense."

"What changed?"

"Thirtieth birthday." He shrugged. "Cliché, I know, but it's true. I want more, but you still don't do more. It's not in your nature."

"Wait." She shook her head. "*I* don't give more? You mean *you* don't do more."

"No, I give plenty, usually to too many women at one time, who then get pissed and dump me. You, you don't give anything of yourself."

She was still just staring at him when he smiled and leaned in, kissing her temple. "Don't look so stricken, Emma. We all have our faults."

"Yeah." She let out a breath, not exactly sure he'd gotten hers right. She gave plenty. Ask any of the patients she saw. Ask any of her bosses. "It's damn California," she decided. "It's being here."

"Well, if that's true, then hopefully you won't be staying here too much longer."

"I wish I knew. My dad's being . . . elusive."

Spence nodded. "And while you're here, you're very . . . preoccupied."

"Yes, I know. I actually think business is starting to pick up."

"Yeah, actually, I meant with the expedition guide." He paused. "Stone Wilder."

"What?" She laughed, but it sounded forced. "Don't be ridiculous."

"Face it, Emma. There's something there."

"Yes, it's called irritation."

He looked doubtful. "Uh huh."

"It's true. We . . ." *Turn each other on.* "Irritate each other."

"And . . . ?" He sipped his wine and watched her over the glass.

"And nothing else is important."

"Really."

"Really."

"Huh." Spence set down his drink and pushed away from the counter. "It used to be, Emma, that I could do this . . ." Leaning in, he kissed her on the lips. "And we'd end up in bed."

Her heart panged a little. *Dammit.* "Oh, Spence. I—"

"No." He set his finger against her lips. "It's okay. You're thinking of someone else now. I've certainly done it to you plenty of times."

"I'm not—"

"No?" His smile was just a little sad. "Then tell me if you feel anything when I do this—" He kissed her again, not softly and definitely not sweet, and she went still, utterly still, willing herself to feel the same shiver of excitement she'd felt the night before with Stone.

Nothing.

She opened her eyes and lifted her head, and met the sharp green gaze of the man she'd been thinking about, who just happened to be standing on the other side of the door, visible through the glass. "Stone?"

"See?" Spencer's eyes were still closed when he sighed. "You're thinking of him even as I kiss you."

"No. I mean Stone. Here." She pulled out of Spencer's arms and opened the door, but Stone had already turned away and was halfway down the back stairs. "Hey."

He wore a baseball cap, sweats, a torn t-shirt and a scowl. The material was damp and plastered against his torso. He stopped and faced her, the air between them heavy and awkward. "You're busy," he said.

"Not in the way you think, no."

"Look, it's no big deal. I was just coming back through town and thought I'd stop by for Band-Aids. I'll get them when I get home. Carry on."

"*Stone.*"

He jogged down the rest of the stairs and was gone.

"Well, that went over well," Spence said from the open doorway when they'd heard his truck start and take off.

"Dammit." She sighed. "He must be just off a hike or something. He wanted Band-Aids. Which means he's hurt." And hot and sweaty. And sexy. "*Dammit.*"

"You said that already." Spence watched her grab her black medical bag. "So you're really doing this."

"Doing what?"

"Falling for a big, tough, outdoorsy guy with more testosterone in his pinky finger than most guys have in their entire body."

She shook her head. "I'm just going to take him Band-Aids, Spence. And see how badly he's hurt." With that, she walked out the door, Spencer's knowing gaze following her.

She didn't catch up with Stone until she pulled into the driveway at the Wilder Lodge. As she hopped out of her dad's truck and moved toward his, she found him leaning back against his driver's door, arms and legs casually crossed. Eyes inscrutable. Expression closed.

She looked him over carefully, her heart stopping at the napkin wadded in one of his hands.

There was blood on it.

She took another closer look, then eyes narrowed, stepped right up to him so that they were toe to toe and pulled off his baseball cap.

Bingo.

The wound on his head was bleeding, and she went up on tiptoe to study it closely. "Dammit, Stone."

"It's nothing."

"Can we go inside?"

"It's nothing," he repeated.

"Inside."

"Fine." He straightened, shoving his hands into his pockets. Gesturing with a jerk of one shoulder in the direction of a trail next to the lodge, he started walking. She followed him past two small cabins and up to the front of a third. He opened the door, then gestured her in ahead of him.

His place, she realized. He flicked on the mudroom light. The entry opened to a living room which was dimly lit by the single light by the front door, but she could see exposed wood beam ceilings and gorgeous distressed oak wood floors. There was a large comfy looking couch and several chairs facing the biggest TV she'd ever seen, and beyond that, a huge sliding glass door leading out to the black night.

Using only the mudroom light, he moved to the couch and plopped down, kicking his booted feet up onto the coffee table next to an SLR camera and a tool belt.

A study in contradictions. "I can't figure you out," she said.

"Ditto."

She took her bag off her shoulder, set it at her feet, then crouched down to open it up.

"Don't bother, I'm not letting you re-stitch."

Glancing up along the length of him—*and up*, because damn, the man was tall—she wished he'd turn on another light. Especially since his broad shoulders blocked out the glow from the mudroom, casting his face in shadows. "I'm just going to disinfect and put on one of your standard medical go-to's—a Band-Aid. Okay?"

He said nothing, so she flipped on a lamp herself, then pulled out antiseptic and a gauze. Bending over him, she wiped away the now drying blood. "You know, you ought to think about buying stock in Band-Aids."

He said more of his loaded nothing. She put on a steri-strip, then straightened and sighed. "Okay, listen. There's nothing going on between me and Spencer. At least not in the way you're thinking."

His eyes cut to hers. "Not that it matters, but your definition of nothing is interesting, considering I saw you playing tonsil hockey with him."

"You saw him kissing me. He was proving a point." At his raised brow, she raised one of her own. "That our chemistry is no longer there. How did you get hurt?"

He lifted a shoulder.

"Let me guess. You went to Moody's and once again got beat up by three women?"

A corner of his mouth quirked, and he let out a breath. "I helped TJ on a climb, and as it turns out, our client is an idiot."

"You should probably try harder to weed those out in the selection process."

"We do try, but sometimes they get past us."

"Huh."

He slid her a look. "Hey, even you have to treat the assholes of the world."

"Yes, but I don't have to put my life into their hands. What happened?"

"We were roped together and he screwed up on a grip. Kicked me in the head as he fell. He's lucky that I have fast reflexes and caught him anyway, or we'd both be bleeding. Or dead."

She stared at him. With those surfer boy good looks and that throwaway charm he exuded in spades, she kept forgetting how easy it was to underestimate him.

She'd underestimated him.

Because no matter how much he looked like a slacker, he was nowhere close. "I'm really not sleeping with Spencer, Stone."

"Anymore."

"Anymore," she agreed. "I'm not sure why I feel the need to tell you this, but it's the truth. And, as long as I'm opening a vein, I'll tell you I haven't had sex in nine months."

"Long time."

"At about the six month mark I stopped missing it."

"How is that even possible?"

"I'm a girl. We aren't programmed to think about sex 24/7 like guys do."

"We don't think about it 24/7. It's 20/7, max."

She smiled wryly. "I keep telling myself it's not nearly as good as I remember it."

He tugged her down to the couch with him. Those broad shoulders of his blocked out most of the light. His eyes were very dark. "It would be with me."

Oh boy.

He shifted closer, then closer still. "Tell me one more time why you were kissing Spencer."

"To see if there was a spark."

His hands settled on her arms as he slowly but inexorably pulled her up against him.

He looked at her mouth, his eyes heavy and sleepy, and she shivered, anticipation racing down her spine, branching out into all her good parts, of which there were many more than she remembered.

Way more.

She could feel his hard chest against hers, the easy strength in him as he held her. He was still looking at her mouth as he dragged his teeth over his bottom lip, like it was taking no effort at all to hold her, but plenty of effort to hold himself back. "Do you feel a spark now?" he asked silkily.

If she felt any more sparks, she'd burst into flame.

Chapter 15

Stone absorbed the bone-melting sensation of Emma's arms winding their way around his neck. "Do you, Emma? Feel a spark?"

She pressed even closer, letting out a hum of desire that went straight to his head. And parts south. *Far* south.

"It's too soon to tell," she murmured in his ear.

"Liar."

"Okay, fair enough." Her lips were brushing his earlobe with every word, and he was hard as a rock. "I think . . . I think I feel an entire set of fireworks."

"Good." He nodded, definitely feeling the same fireworks. He'd nearly made those fireworks work for him the last time they'd been alone together, when she'd nearly given it all up for him. Nearly . . . nearly . . . and then TJ had shown up and he'd been shit out of luck. Suddenly, he had hopes that tonight would end better. "Let's make sure."

"How—"

Which is all he let her get out before he leaned over her, pressing her back down, down, down to the couch. Towering over her, he looked into those fathomless eyes, letting the anticipation drum between them before bending low to kiss her.

Together they sank further into his comfortably worn couch as she opened her mouth for him, gently sliding her tongue to his. Oh, God, yeah, that worked, and he tightened his hands on her, apparently the universal sign for more, please, because with a little gasp of breath, she made room for him between her legs and arched up to rock against him. "You sure yet?" he asked as the both of them panted for more.

She blinked up at him, lips wet, eyes wide. "I'm sorry. I lost all track of our conversation."

With a ragged exhale, he pressed his forehead to hers. Pressed up against him, she undulated her hips against the hard-on he'd had since she'd driven up to the lodge. "Okay, it's definitely safe to say I'm sure I feel *something*," she murmured.

With a low laugh, he pressed the "something" up against her. "Not what I meant, Em."

"I feel it." She cupped his face. "It's been so long that I almost didn't recognize it, but I feel it." She touched his hair, his jaw, nothing but a touch, and he nearly melted on the spot. It'd been awhile for him too, at least awhile since he'd felt so moved. As in earth rocking, foundation slipping, dizzy from the emotions *moved*. He was still trying to gather his wits when she whispered his name in a low, shaky voice that said she was with him on this. Unnerved, unsure, but with him.

Slowly, he lowered his head and kissed her again; a deep, long, wet kiss that shut down what little brain power he had left. She tasted warm and sweet and innately female. She tasted like the solution to his restless loneliness. She tasted like she was . . . his. "I want more than Spencer got," he murmured. "I want more than the kiss. Tell me right now if you don't, before this goes any further."

"That elusive word *more* again . . ." she whispered, staring at him as she pulled his head back down. "Kiss me, Stone. Take what you want."

He would. He did, taking what he wanted without apology,

showing her what he was beginning to realize he felt. A fact
that amped up both his heartbeat and the mood, which went
from calm and lazily aroused to hot-as-hell wild frenzied as
they went at it, their hands fighting for purchase, tangling in
each other. She was letting out those helpless little pants as
she tried to get under his clothes, the sexiest breathy sounds
he'd ever heard, which were going to make him go off so he
grabbed her hands and pressed them high above her head.
This brought his entire weight down on her, which she wel-
comed by spreading her legs even further and wrapping them
around him, bringing him in tighter against her. "God," he
murmured, his mouth on her throat now. "God, Emma."

"I know," she gasped, latching her mouth onto his shoulder.
It was crazy how fast the air changed, how fast it sparked, and
lit fire.

Crazy. *Take what he wanted?* He wanted it all.

"Stone—"

"Tell me."

"You. I want *you.*"

The words were no sooner out of Emma's mouth before he
ripped off his shirt, and then hers, both following the same air
path over his shoulder and across the room.

He popped open her bra and bent his head, kissing her jaw,
her throat, her shoulder, and then a breast, gently pulling it
into his mouth and sucking, a motion so perfect that it arched
her right off the couch and further into his mouth. An inarticulate sound left her, one that conveyed shocking need and hunger,
which might have horrified her if she'd been alone in this.

But she wasn't. For once, she wasn't alone at all, and given
the sound that escaped his throat—one of equal need and hunger,
and also of thrilling impatience, he felt it too as he lifted up
enough to unhook and unzip her pants. Still teasing her nip-

ples with his tongue, he slid a hand down her leg, bending it
so he could reach to yank off her shoe.

She went to work on his clothes, and had his sweats opened
and her hands inside when he twisted to get at her other shoe.
Tangled up in each other, they lost their balance and together
fell off the couch and onto the small space on the floor between the couch and the coffee table.

"Jesus." He arched up to slide his hands beneath her head
as she dissolved into laughter. "Are you okay?" he demanded.

"Yes." She held onto him when he would have pulled away.
Her bra was caught on her elbow, her pants half on and half
off, both hampering her movements. He lay over her, no shirt,
his sweats halfway down. His chest was warm and deliciously
hard against her. She realized he had a leg thrust between
hers, one hand still cradling her head in a protective gesture
that melted her as his other hand, low on her back, moved
lower to cup her bottom. "Very okay. You?"

His eyes were lit with heat and humor as his mouth curved.
"I could be better."

"You have a nearly naked woman in your arms and you
could be better?"

"I could be inside you."

His words liquefied her bones. "I suggest rectifying the situation. Stat."

"I love it when you get bossy." He pushed with his thigh,
just a little, which opened her legs to him further, and then he
settled into the spot as if he'd been made for it as his fingers
slid between her legs and stroked.

She cried out, she couldn't help it. She'd never been amused
and excited at the same time before, never, and it confused her
brain, flipped a switch somewhere deep inside, making it feel
so intense she almost couldn't take it. "Not to criticize your
technique," she panted. "But what's taking so long?"

With a grin, he lowered his head and licked her nipple, rasping his tongue over the tip, and then again, while she sucked in a breath. "I've never been a fast mover," he said against her flesh.

As if to prove the point, he slid his way down her body, kissing her ribs, her belly button, her hip. His fingers idly, almost lazily, hooked in her pants. He lifted his head and watched her as he tugged.

But since he'd only gotten one of her shoes off, they got stuck on her leg. He didn't seem concerned as he dropped his gaze to see what he was doing, and ran a finger over the elastic on her bikini panties. "Pretty," he said of the navy blue and white sailor stripes. He slid them down, sucking in a breath at all he'd revealed. "God. Look at you."

"Stone—"

"Open." Accompanying this gentle demand, he settled a hand on her thigh and nudged it, wedging his shoulders between her legs, giving him quite the front row view.

"Um." Trapped, she lay there on the floor between the couch and the table, her legs held open by his wide shoulders, with nowhere to escape. She could have pushed him away, could have sat up, could have stopped him in a hundred different ways, but instead, when he leaned forward and lapped at her like she was a bowl of cream, she sank her fingers into his hair and held on for the ride.

She cried out again. And then again when he added his fingers. She was burning up, from the inside out, trembling with strain, her every muscle taut and seeking release as she clutched at him with a horrifying desperation.

It'd been so long. So damn long, and even so, she honestly had to admit, she'd never felt like *this*. Like she was going to die if he didn't finish her off, like she didn't have to struggle to get to the edge, didn't have to *try* to orgasm because she was there on the very brink already. He held her there, damn him, held her there for an interminably long beat before he let her take the plunge.

She very nearly came right out of her own skin. Cradled by him, she shuddered and trembled, and shuddered some more, *shocked* at how easily it had barreled through her.

Stone lifted his head and lazily kissed his way up her body as if totally relaxed—except for the erection pressing against her hip.

She reached for him, managing to stroke him once before a rough rumble escaped his throat and he staggered to his feet. The light fell over him, revealing just how incredibly made he was. His chest was perfectly sculptured, his belly flat and six-packed, his thighs hard and powerful.

And between . . . God, between them he was just as glorious, but that was as far she got before he scooped her up against him and carried her through the living room, down a hall to his bedroom. He set her on the bed, then flicked on a lamp, which gave her a moment of self-awareness she could have done without. But then he moved into her line of view and she blessed the light because he was so beautifully made she could hardly stand it.

He had a condom, and she stared at it thinking good God, she'd have actually forgotten. For the first time in her life, she would have forgotten to have responsible sex.

Good thing *he* could think, because she was apparently beyond it, as proven when he ran a hand down her body, over her breasts, her belly, to between her thighs, where she was wet and beyond ready. Apparently agreeing, he let out a heartfelt groan, knelt between her spread thighs and entered her.

With an arch of her back, she gave him entry, and when he pushed all the way into her, their twin gasps of pleasure echoed in her ears. She'd have thought she was finished after that last orgasm, but he began to move and she clutched at him, rocking to meet his every thrust, shocked at how good she felt, how high, how utterly filled.

He whispered her name, cupped her head in his big hands and kissed her as deeply as he was within her body, and when he lost himself and came with her name on his lips, she followed him over.

It took her a long time to come back to herself, but he didn't seem to be in any hurry for her to. His mouth was against her throat, nuzzling. His muscles were still quaking faintly as he pressed his pelvis to hers, relishing the last of his pleasure.

And there'd been such pleasure. As she slowly came back to herself, she realized she was clutching him tight, digging her fingers into him. Yes, she was gripping his ass like a vice while still gasping for breath like she'd just run the marathon. With a sound of embarrassed regret, she started to pull free, but in what was perhaps the nicest moment of all, he didn't move away from her, instead seemed content to stay and just kiss her neck, his hands slowly sweeping over her as if to help calm her.

Cuddling. They were cuddling. That's when she remembered. She didn't do the cuddle, never had, and she gave him a little push.

He obliged her by rolling off, but he didn't go far. On his side now, he propped up his head with his hand. His other went to her hip, covering nearly the whole thing with just one warm, callused palm. An easy touch. A familiar touch.

Which, given what he'd just done to her—that being completely shattering her—he probably *was* feeling pretty damn familiar. Utterly unconcerned with his nudity, he smiled.

"Hey."

"Hey." Good Lord, how had one guy gotten so sexy and cute at the same time? It seemed like an unfair disbursement of the goods, and if she ever stood in the line at the Pearly Gates, that would be the first thing she'd ask about.

But for now, she had places to go, people to see, things to do.

And a hot, sexy guy that threatened her very soul to get away from. Making her move, she shifted, getting to her belly before he slid a leg over her, holding her down. She turned her head and looked at him.

"Question," he said lightly.

Seeing as she was pinned like a bug, she blew her hair from her face and did her best not to give herself away. "What?"

"Are you relaxed?"

Ha. "Let me go."

"Because you were feeling pretty damn relaxed until about two seconds ago, when you realized you were hugging me for all you were worth. That's when you got all uptight again."

Okay, true. As was something else—she'd finally answered her own question on how his stubble would feel against her skin.

Like heaven. "Let me up now."

His leg slid from her immediately. "My apologies."

Fine. He was insulted. She'd deal with that later. She got out of the bed and realized her clothes were in the living room. Which was why she liked her affairs simple and in the dark.

He'd rolled to his back, hands behind his head, and was watching her from beneath lowered lashes, giving nothing of himself away.

Except, of course, the fact that he was sprawled out naked as the day he'd been born, revealing everything, anything she wanted to see.

Damn. To be that open. She whirled around, found one of his shirts and shoved it over her head, forgoing both panties and bra. On the other side of the country, her mother was rolling over in her grave.

Goodness, darling, you could have had Spencer. That boy's a surgeon, and he'd have left the light off.

Rolling her eyes, she headed toward the door. But suddenly, the man lounging so lazily on the bed beat her to it, and put a hand on the handle. Before she could say a word, he'd opened it for her, not attempting to hold her in.

She looked up into his eyes.

He flashed a smile that didn't quite make it to his usual full potential. "I take it we're done here tonight."

"Yeah, I have to—"

He put a finger over her lips. "Don't make up an excuse to run away. I don't need a pretty lie."

Fair enough. "I just have to go."

"Did I scare you?"

Yes. He scared her by showing her the very depths of his soul, and reflecting hers right back at her. He scared her by making her feel. Her initial reaction was to offer a denial but he'd just asked for no pretty lies, so she just looked up at him.

He pretty much gave her the opposite reaction she expected. Standing there, naked, he chuckled. "Tough question, huh?"

"Yes." There. The truth. "Care to try an easier one?"

"All right." He stroked a strand of hair from her face. "You going to steal another of my shirts?"

"It appears so."

"Go out with me, Emma."

Tempted beyond belief, she looked at his mouth, wishing it was back on hers. "You should know. I'm unusually slow to get on board when it comes to these things."

"What just happened between us didn't feel slow. It felt like a freight train slamming into my heart."

Hers skipped a beat at that. "You should also know that men don't tend to hold on to me for long. I only tell you this to save you some time and effort. Give you a short cut to the exit."

A slight smile tipped his mouth upward at her somber tone. "I don't tend to take short cuts. I also tend to jump right in."

"Well we both did that today."

"Yeah, but I meant more, too."

There was that more thing again. "I definitely don't do more."

"Has that ever worked out for you, the not doing more thing?" he asked.

"No."

He just smiled, both sweet and challenging at the same time. And sexy.

So damn sexy.

"I get that you're a thinker," he said gently. "You need to think, process. Analyze."

"I do."

"Premeditated thinking doesn't work for me."

"Because you jump right in."

"That's right. So I'm already on the page. The *us* page."

"Oh, God."

"It's okay. You go home and think. Process and analyze. Whatever you have to do."

Whatever she had to do? Hell, she had to run far and fast. Only she couldn't, she was stuck here in Wishful.

Yeah. She was in big trouble.

Emma dreamt about Stone, about his couch, his floor . . . his bed. About what he wanted from her. And she woke up hot and bothered.

Cost of processing and analyzing: two hours of sleep.

Cost of thinking: two more hours of sleep.

Cost of giving the elusive more to the insanely sexy Stone Wilder: *priceless*.

And something she couldn't face, not and function properly. Already exhausted before she even began her day, she heated up one of the casseroles labeled breakfast for her and Spencer, who was embarking on a long day hike.

By himself.

"Don't worry," he told her, scooping more cholesterol into

his bowl. "TJ mapped out the trek for me. They said I couldn't get lost if I stayed on the trail. I'm looking forward to being by myself."

They hadn't talked about the fact that she'd chosen Stone over him. Nor that she'd taken two hours to come back the night before. "You won't be by yourself," she said. "There'll be spiders and bears and coyotes, oh my."

Spencer grinned. "Then come with me. Protect me."

"Ha. Maybe if it was spa day." She was still pining for Starbucks and Thai take-out, still missing the crowded, noisy, bustling streets, where the scents came from sidewalk vendors and exhaust, where wide open spaces were to be mistrusted.

Missing all of it.

Wasn't she?

She wasn't sure. The truth was, the air here was amazing, clean and fresh, and she'd saved a fortune by not buying from a menu every time she ate. Plus, she'd gotten damn good at making her own coffee.

Interesting.

She drove Spencer up to Wilder Adventures, the starting point for his trek, holding her breath on the narrow road between town and the lodge. "Damn roads out here are barbaric."

"It's the rains," he said. "You're doing much better these days."

Better was relative, but they made it without incident. It'd rained heavily all night long, but though it'd momentarily tapered off to a light drizzle, the skies were still dark and threatening. "Are you sure about this?"

Not appearing at all bothered by the prospect that he'd likely be wet all day long, he nodded, "It's going to be good."

At Wilder Lodge, he got out of the truck and went to the back for his gear. Emma got out, too, looked up at the dark sky again, and shook her head. "Not too late to change your mind."

"Not too late to come."

"Like I said, let me know when it's spa day, with good food service and no bears." She pulled him in for a hug, closing her eyes when he tightened his grip. "Spence—" She didn't want to lose him. "About you and me. I—"

"Em." He smiled, tugging at a strand of her hair. "I'm okay. Really."

"Are *we* okay?"

"Very okay."

"Really?"

"Yes, why?"

"It's just that you got over me pretty darn quick."

He laughed, and patted his chest. "Fickle heart, remember?"

God, she loved him. She cupped his face. "Be safe."

"And you take it easy on yourself. As in try to get into the slower pace or something."

"Yeah. Right."

"Don't worry. Soon enough you'll be back in your big, crazy city, and this will all be just a bad dream."

A bad dream. And a *good* one . . . She watched him go, heading off into the wild forest willingly. Happily.

Darling, what's YOUR day long trek?

At her mom's words in her head, she sighed. The question was valid. What was there in her life that made her as at peace as Spencer had looked just now?

That the answer was a big, fat *nothing* didn't help.

God, she was tired of herself. "And you too, mom." She got back into the truck, taking a quick glance at the lodge as she drove off, wondering what Stone was doing.

Was he still in bed? The bed she'd been in last night, panting his name, leaving nail imprints in his ass—

Above her, the sky opened up with a bright burst of lightning, accompanied by a sonic boom that had her nearly leaping out of her skin. Startled, she jerked to a stop right in the middle of the road. The rain started up again, pummeling the truck in tune to her pounding heart.

She looked out the windshield.

There was nothing on this stretch of road, just trees, trees, and more trees. Oh, and two ditches running alongside.

Her gut clenched but she put the truck back into gear. This weather wouldn't have stopped Stone, and it wouldn't stop her either. She hit the gas, but in the past few minutes, the road seemed to have turned into an instant muddy swamp.

Not good.

Tightening both hands on the wheel, she concentrated on staying on the road and not sliding off into either ditch. She was doing good too, but then something hopped out of the driving rain and bounced across the road right in front of her truck. A deer. She hit the brake as the thing vanished into the trees, and the truck's wheels lost their tenuous grip in the muddy road, slipping, hitting a rut and jerking her off the road—

Right where she didn't want to be—into one of the ditches.

Chapter 16

Stone drove like a bat out of hell, hoping it wasn't bad.

"Jesus, man." TJ tightened his seatbelt. "Slow down. She didn't say there was a three alarm fire. She said she'd driven into a ditch."

Stone tried to peer ahead through the fog and rain but visibility was nonexistent. He and TJ had been talking to Cam on iChat, having a grand old time, laughing at Cam's recollection of him taking Katie zip-lining across the rain forest, and how she'd screamed her way through it.

Then they'd heard Harley on the radio say she was responding to a truck in the ditch between Wishful and the lodge, and Stone had hung up on Cam.

Because there'd only been one truck on that road today—Emma's. And so no, regardless of the fact that the level headed TJ had a point, Stone didn't slow down. A mile later, he was glad as he came to a stop just behind Harley, who had pulled up just in front of them.

Emma had indeed gone into the ditch. The truck was grounded on its belly, the front wheels firmly in the muddy ditch, the back wheels no longer touching the ground. Emma stood to one side, out in the driving rain, an arm wrapped around her middle, the other shoving her wet hair out of her eyes

Harley moved toward Emma. "Good one."

Emma turned and looked at her. "You're roadside assistance?"

Harley, in a ski cap and coveralls, nodded. "Until I pass my finals," she said proudly, then turned to look at the truck. "So you've introduced yourself to the ditch, up close and personal. Let's un-introduce you."

"It got the better of me."

"Happens to all of us at least once. You hurt?"

"I—" That's when she noticed Stone and TJ and closed her mouth. Harley turned and looked, caught sight of TJ, and swore. "She called for roadside assistance, not an audience."

TJ's usual smile was nowhere in sight. In fact, his scowl matched Harley's. "We heard the radio call go out and thought maybe you could use some help muscling the truck out of the ditch. We thought maybe you'd appreciate the help."

"This is *my* job, Wilder." Harley accompanied the statement with a finger in TJ's chest. She was a full foot shorter than him, yet somehow managed to look down her nose at him. "So back off and let me do it."

TJ lifted his hands in surrender, and looking unaccustomedly irritated, stepped back.

Stone left those two to their tempers and looked at Emma. "Are you really okay?"

"Yeah."

Behind them, small but mighty, Harley didn't appear at all daunted by the task ahead of her as she went around to the back of her truck and began to pull out a large set of chains. "If you want to you can wait in the cab of my truck," she said to Emma. "It's dry, at least."

"I'll help."

Harley looked over Emma's pinstriped trousers, silk blouse, and light cashmere sweater. "That would be great, except I think your outfit probably cost more than all of my clothes put together. I've got this." Harley's sharp eyes narrowed in on what Stone had also narrowed in on—Emma holding her ribs. "Really. You go sit."

"I'm fine." She swiped the rain out of her eyes and appeared to gnash her back teeth together. She was soaking wet, and looked cold, miserable, and mad at the world, including Stone. "I was trying to avoid Bambi."

Harley shook her head as she wrapped the chains around the Sinclair truck. "First rule of the Sierras. Never swerve to avoid an animal. It's survival of the fittest out here." She struggled with a clamp on the chains, and TJ moved in.

When their hands touched, Harley jerked back and shot him a glare, which TJ ignored, muscling her out of the way to do her job.

With temper making her ears red, Harley jumped into her truck and the two of them worked silently together to pull Emma's truck out of the ditch. It was like watching an old silent movie, no words necessary since the seething tension between the two of them spoke for itself.

"They go way back," Stone said to a shivering Emma.

She looked up at him. "I'm sorry, what?"

Hiding his concern, he shrugged out of his denim jacket and wrapped it around her shoulders. "Take it," he insisted when she opened her mouth to protest, pulling the fleece lined hood up and over her head, using the excuse to touch her. He'd come to see her again, since he hated how she'd left last night, but now he was very glad he had because she needed him.

And she didn't need easily. "You're shivering."

"No, I'm not."

"Yeah, you are. Come here," he said, and pulled her in his arms to try to warm her up.

Emma hadn't even noticed how cold she was until Stone had pointed it out, and then she'd realized that she was shaking rather violently. And there was a funny pain in her chest—not funny good but funny bad. "I'm fine," she repeated as he hugged her very carefully, as if she were a fine piece of china. "I'm just annoyed that you've caught the stupid city girl getting stuck." Annoyed and embarrassed.

"It's okay to be stupid once in a while."

"Really? Does this ever happen to you?"

'Well, no."

She was still shivering like crazy, and that made her mad too, just as it also made her want to burrow even closer, which didn't help. Not one little bit. "Everything's so easy for you." She told herself to let go of him but she didn't listen. "Well, here's a memo for you, life isn't easy."

"No," he agreed, sweeping a hand up her back, his smile gone. "Life sure as hell isn't. But you make of it what you can, and you do your best to enjoy the hell out of it, because it's the only life you get." He turned her toward the truck, which was out of the ditch now—thanks to Harley and TJ.

Not saying another word, Stone reached across her to open the door for her.

There was no reason for her to feel like a complete ass, yet she did. With as much dignity as she could manage, she thanked Harley, arranged to go by the shop later to pay her, and then hopped up into the truck, the movement giving her a bad moment. Her ribs were killing her.

Her own fault.

Just as she put the truck in gear, the passenger door opened and Stone got in, as drenched as she. His hair was plastered to his head, little rivulets of water raining down his jaw. His eyes seemed darker, the lashes inky black and spiky with rain water. "What are you doing?" she asked.

"I had a choice." He plopped his big, wet body into the seat. Having given her his jacket, his t-shirt was sculpted to his chest. His jeans were plastered to him as well, the soft, worn, drenched denim lovingly molding to his hips, his thighs, the intriguing bulge behind his button fly—

She jerked her gaze up to his eyes, and met his wry ones. "Choice?"

"Between being a referee for TJ and Harley, or . . ." Leaning forward, he flicked the heater on high. "Figuring out how badly you're really hurt."

She hugged herself and her aching ribs. She was having trouble keeping her eyes off him, which was odd since she'd seen all there was to see last night. "I'm not."

"Do you want me to drive?"

Yes. More than she could say, but that would be admitting defeat, and she never admitted defeat.

"I swear I won't write the feminist police," he said dryly.

She sighed. "It's not that. If I let you drive, I'll never be able to face this road again."

He looked at her, something new coming into his eyes in addition to the irritation—approval.

It was unexpected, and washed over her like a welcome balm, whether she liked it not. For the record, she didn't. She didn't like it at all. She swiped at the water running out of her hair and into her eyes, a movement which hurt, dammit. "Can I ask you something?"

"Anything," he said.

That was another difference between them. She would never

have left herself so wide open. What if she wanted to know how many lovers he'd had, or the last time he'd cried? "You were right about what you said before. How we only get one life, how we need to handle it right. So I guess what I want to know is . . ." She paused. Talk about putting herself out there, but it was too late to go back now. "Are you happy? Here? With what you do for a living?"

He let out a low sound that might have been a laugh, and scrubbed a hand over his face before he leaned back and looked at her. Water was running down his face too, in little rivulets. "I guess I thought whatever question you could possibly have for me might be a whole lot easier to answer than that one."

"So you're not? Happy?"

"Oh, I am. I get to work with my brothers, when they're around. I'm my own boss, which actually isn't quite as fun as it should be. I get to do the outdoor stuff I love to do, but . . ." He breathed out heavily and leaned forward to crank the heater up. "Sometimes I'd like to also do something else as well, not for Cam or TJ, but for me."

"Like?"

"Come on. Do you really want to know this?"

"Actually, yes. Maybe I like knowing I'm not the only one who wishes things were different. Misery and company and all that."

He arched a brow. "I almost thought you cared there for a minute."

"Maybe I do care."

"You have a lot of maybes going on." His eyes were steady on hers. "I used to do some renovating and I want to get back to it. I want to restore one of the historical buildings in town, top to bottom."

"Yourself?"

"I like the work, like using my hands to fix things up."

Besides the fact that she had firsthand knowledge that he was excellent with his hands, she worked with her hands and she got it. "I can understand the appeal of that."

His smile was small, but warmed her nevertheless. "Thought you might."

She thrust the truck into drive, took a deep breath, which tweaked her ribs and gave her a jolt of pain as she eased back onto the road. The rain was still coming down in droves. Every bump was agony on her ribs, not that she'd admit it to the man sitting next to her.

For his part, Stone didn't say a word, just sat there filling up the passenger seat of the cab with his big, tough, rangy body, until about a mile down the road when she hit another bump and just about died.

"Okay, stop."

Instincts had her doing just that. "What?" She whipped her head from one side of the road to the other, looking for trouble. "Another deer?"

"Scoot over, toward me." Before she could move, he shifted closer on the bench seat, his hands going to her hips, lifting her as he slid beneath her to switch positions without getting out into the rain. There was one breathless heartbeat at the halfway point, with him under her and her straining above him, when her bottom ground into his crotch.

She didn't mean for it to happen, she sincerely doubted *he* meant for it to happen, but it did, and the two of them went utterly still.

She had no idea what he was thinking in the moment, but she knew what she was thinking.

Sweet Jesus.

The small, inarticulate sound that escaped her seemed to

galvanize him into action and he lifted her over to the passenger seat, as he landed in the driver's seat. For a minute, he stared straight ahead, hands on the wheel. The inside of the cab was warm and humid from their wet bodies. The windows were closed and a little fogged up.

It felt close. Intimate.

With fingers that weren't quite steady, Stone shoved his wet hair out of his face and let out a very long, low breath. "That keeps happening."

She didn't ask what. She knew exactly what. The bolt of sexual awareness between them that packed a punch of, oh about a million watts. She let out a shaky breath of her own. "I thought we'd be over it after last night."

"Yeah." He shook his head. "No."

"Maybe . . . maybe it's just the altitude."

He let out a mirthless laugh and drove the rough roads with a smooth ease that didn't escape her. She was good at being a doctor, she'd made sure of that. But as she kept noticing, he was good at all the life stuff. The important stuff.

She could admit that when she'd first come to Wishful, she might have imagined herself just a little above it all. Above them. But both the town and the people in it had proven her wrong.

On every score.

"You can stop blaming yourself," he said quietly without looking at her. "This road is really hard to handle in the heavy rain or snow."

She turned to face him, watching as a lone drop of rain slid down his temple. "You read minds?"

"I read yours easily enough, apparently. You're mad at yourself."

"And you. Let's not forget that."

"Why me?"

"Because you make the drive look easy."

"I've been driving it since I was fourteen."

That effectively took her mind off being cold, wet and hurting like hell. "You're not supposed to drive until you're sixteen."

He shrugged. "Didn't have a lot of supervision in those days."

She'd left Wishful far too young to remember him or his brothers, or to even know their story. "Where was your mother?"

"Gone." Keeping his eyes on the road, he lifted a shoulder. "She had three little boys, then decided life was too hard out here." He glanced over, his eyes reflecting the knowledge that they had that in common.

But her mother had at least taken Emma with her.

His mother had walked away from him and his brothers. She couldn't even imagine how incredibly devastating that must have been. "That's just so wrong."

"Agreed."

"What about your father?"

"He was a mean drunk who only paid attention to us when we were bad—which we were a lot. We were as wild as they came."

"Which explains how it is that you were driving so young."

He flashed a short smile. "Yeah. So do you drive in New York?"

"No."

"Why am I not surprised?"

"I have my license," she said a little defensively. "I made sure to get that when I was eighteen."

"I'm sure you did."

She narrowed her eyes. "What does that mean?"

"It means you're a thorough woman, Emma. You like to cover all your bases. You probably studied hard for your test, passed it with flying colors, and keep your license renewed even though you don't drive."

"Yes," she said, not liking how amused he sounded. "I don't see why that's funny. It doesn't hurt to be careful, to be organized and on top of things."

"Thing is, Emma, as you pointed out, life isn't easy. And it's sure as hell not black and white. Being on top of things doesn't always count. Your father would be the first to tell you that."

Well if that didn't make her feel even more defensive. "My father isn't big on telling me anything."

"Everyone makes mistakes."

"He's trying to fix his by having me out here. I know that." She thought of her mom, and more than physical pain stabbed through her. "I just don't think that he gets that it's not the right way, not for me. I don't want to resent being here, but . . ."

"But you do. You're tired of treating the flu, and wayward cats. Who, by the way," he added with a smile, "gave birth to four adorable, wayward kittens last night. Annie named the first one Emma. She has your eyes."

She snorted and put her head back against the headrest, casually setting her hands on her aching ribs for support. "That's nice."

His gaze cut to her hands, though he didn't say a word about her ribs. "But you still don't want to be here."

"I can't seem to help it. Being here reminds me of my mom." She hated that her voice cracked.

"You miss her," he said very softly, taking his gaze off the road for a beat, offering her the sympathy that tripled her pain.

It took her a minute to speak. "So much."

Reaching out, he squeezed her hand, and she cleared her throat. "I just want to go back to my world," she told him. "Where I'm in control. My mom liked to be in control. I guess I got that from her."

"How's your stepfather taking it?"

She shrugged, which shot pain through her. *Note to self: stop moving.* "He left on a world cruise after the funeral. He needed to get away. It must be working because he hasn't been back."

"So you've been by yourself?"

"I'm a big girl, you know," she said wryly. "I've lived on my own from the day I went off to college."

"Sure, but it's nice to have family around. You've been without."

"I manage to keep busy enough."

"That's not what I mean. Everyone needs a support system, Emma. People they can count on."

"I have friends."

"Spencer."

Again their gazes met as he pulled into the Urgent Care's lot. "Yes," she agreed. "Spencer. And others."

Stone turned off the truck, handed her the keys, then surprised her by getting out into the rain with her. She started to run through the downpour to the building, but the small movement sent fire along her torso and slowed her down. When she came to a stop on the top step, she pressed her hands to her chest as spots swam in her vision. *Dammit.*

With a low oath, he took her keys from her hands. "Easy," he murmured, and unlocking the door for her, very gently nudged her inside.

They entered the reception area together, dripping water all over the floor as she realized he was now stuck here without a way home, which showed her just how little she'd been thinking in the past half hour. "I'm sorry. I'll drive you—"

"I'll call TJ for a ride." But instead of doing that, he came at her. "In a minute."

He was big and tall and wet, and not looking nearly as laid-back and easygoing as she was used to as he reached behind her and locked them in.

"What—"

"Let's go." He took her hand and pulled her down the hall to the first examination room, nudging her up against one of the tables. "Let's see," he murmured. "How did you get started with me? Oh, yeah." He smiled grimly. "*Strip*."

Chapter 17

Emma let out a laugh that sounded jittery and nervous to her own ears, but that was bound to happen when a gorgeous, wet guy looked at her from amazing green eyes and murmured "strip." "Okay," she said, lifting a hand. "I can appreciate both the irony and your sense of humor on this but this is really completely different from when you were hurt."

"No, it's not." Clearly knowing his way around, he opened the drawer and pulled out a cotton gown, dangling it from his fingers.

She laughed, and crossed her arms over her chest. "I am not going to play doctor with you."

"Ah, come on." He waggled a brow. "I'll let you hold the stethoscope. It'll be fun."

"You know, it just occurred to me to wonder why you're not married or at least taken. But I think I'm getting why."

He laughed. "Hey, I've been occasionally taken. It's just that nothing's stuck." He set his hands on the jacket he'd put on her, spreading it open.

"Hey—"

He gently tugged it off. "I know why *you're* not married," he said. "You're too mean."

"I'm not married because I'm unusually hard to hold on to. As I've mentioned."

"Yeah. Handy excuse."

"What?"

"You're easy enough to hold on to, Emma." Evidenced by the way he was holding onto her. "You just get restless and anal and uptight, and scare them all off."

"Stone—"

"Emma," he said, mocking her fierce tone. He reached for her drenched and very clingy sweater. She slapped his hands away, but that didn't stop him from unbuttoning the three small pearl buttons.

"Okay," she said shakily, crossing her arms over her breasts. "This has gone far enough."

"It most definitely has." His eyes met hers, filled with humor and determination, and a surprising affection. "Though I'm starting to see past the usual chilly Dr. Evil exterior."

She choked out a laugh. "Dr. Evil?"

"Dr. Fiercely Determined, then. Better?"

She looked into his eyes again and saw something else, to go with all the other things that had already overwhelmed her, and this one stopped her heart because it brought the night before to the forefront of her mind—as if it'd ever left!— Heat.

God, so much heat.

He stepped closer, his voice a husky murmur. "I don't care that you scare men away, Emma. Or that I'm too laid-back for you. I don't care that we tend to annoy the shit out of each other, and that while we're at it, we also make each other hotter than a bonfire in July. You're hurt. You know it, and I see it, and I'm not leaving here until I know how bad."

She stared into his eyes for one more beat, saw the mulish stubbornness that matched her own, and let out a breath. *Fine.*

Lifting her fingers to her sweater, she shrugged out of it herself, biting her lower lip at the pain in her ribs as she did so.

His gaze dropped, and though he didn't say a word or move a muscle, she nearly slipped to the floor in a boneless heap from the sheer heat that blazed from him.

She looked down as well.

Her silky white top was wet and was plastered to her like Saran Wrap. It was also sheer, as was the white bra beneath it, leaving her pretty much completely exposed.

Letting out a low breath, he lifted his hands and set them on her waist, fingers spread wide, his touch light and almost unbearably gentle. "So how do we check to see if you broke a rib?"

"I don't think I did."

"So I suppose all you need is a Band-Aid."

She met his smiling eyes. "At least you won't have to give me a shot. I wouldn't want you to pass out."

"Ha ha." His hands slid to the buttons and began to flick them open. "Let's see what you did."

The room was entirely silent except for her suddenly accelerated breathing, which she couldn't seem to control.

His breathing wasn't any too steady either as the backs of his fingers brushed her skin, or as he then peeled the top from her shoulders. With a soft hiss of a breath, he traced a long, work-callused finger over first one collar bone, then the other, where already a blossoming bruise was developing in the shape of the top half of the steering wheel. "Jesus, Emma."

He crouched to look lower at her ribs and abs. He had a hand on her thigh, an innocent hand, bracing himself, but her mind went back to the last time he'd been in this position. How his hand had glided up her thigh, followed by his mouth—

"You got yourself good." He straightened to his full height again, his finger running over her shoulder, catching on her narrow bra strap.

Which obediently slipped off her shoulder. "Stone."

"You took care of me when I was hurt—"

"Yes," she agreed. "Even though you lied about how you got hurt."

"Admit it, you enjoyed thinking of me as a lazy ski bum."

True enough. "So you thought you'd perpetuate the image?"

He smiled. "You sound so snooty when you're pissy. I think it's the New York accent."

"I'm from *here*."

His smile faded. "Yeah. You are."

"For the record, I took care of you, because that's what I do."

"I know, but it's what I do, too. Take care of people."

She stared into his jade eyes, so clear, so utterly calm and steady, in a way she admired far too much.

"You're already bruising," he said quietly. "Let's just do this."

"It's not as bad as it looks." Her arms were trapped at her sides by the top that was hanging off her elbows, and she was glad because she had the oddest urge to wrap them around his shoulders. He'd touched her, put his warm hands on her, reminding her of what they could do. It didn't matter that the touch wasn't supposed to be a sexual one. Her body didn't seem to get the memo.

Leaving one hand on her shoulder, he spread his other hand over her belly, which was rising and falling way too fast. "The bruising isn't as bad here."

Good to know. Not that she was feeling any pain, not with his hands still on her, his face so close to her breasts he could have put his mouth on them.

"X-rays," he said in a thick voice into the crackling silence. "You need them."

Shrugging her shirt back on, she pushed him back a step and headed to x-ray at the end of the hall. She flipped on the machine and set up an x-ray tray. "I've got this," she said when he stood far too close in the small room.

"You'll need me to hit the button."

True enough. She showed him what to do, then turning her back to him, pulled off her shirt again, because what the hell, he'd already seen her. In fact, he'd tasted every inch of her.

They were both wet and chilled, but she didn't feel the cold, not one little bit, not with his eyes heating her up from the inside out, and her memories stoking the fire. She positioned herself in front of the machine, extremely aware of the fact that she stood there half bare while he was fully dressed.

Five minutes later they were standing side by side studying her x-ray. Stone didn't know what she was thinking but he was thinking that he loved how warm he felt next to her, how that warmth seeped into him, how much warmer they'd be without their wet clothes, sharing body heat—

"Nothing broken," she said, her voice husky enough to tell him she wasn't thinking only about her ribs either.

"So your treatment?"

"Ice and rest."

He waited until she turned off the x-ray light before putting his hands on her hips and turning her to face him.

"What?" she asked a little breathlessly, and just the slightest bit defensively.

Poor baby. She didn't know what to do about him, how to feel, what to think. He knew the feeling. "I can't help but notice that we have the same treatment plan, you and me."

A smile touched her lips. "You didn't pay the slightest bit of attention to your treatment plan."

"Sure I did. I just didn't have time to rest and ice. I do now." He took her hand and led her into the small kitchen, where he headed directly to the freezer and pulled out a small ice wrap.

Holding it up, he stepped toward her, and with a low laugh, she took one back. "Oh, no."

Stone liked the sound of her laugh, a whole lot. It softened her face, it softened everything about her, and he liked her soft. He liked her tough, too. Bottom line, he liked her every which way. He lifted the ice pack and waggled a brow.

"I can ice myself," she said.

"Ah, but I have experience with icing yourself. Trust me, it's never as fun." He stepped closer.

She took one back and came up against the vee of the counter. Perfect. He put one hand on the tile. "Open up," he said, gesturing to her shirt.

"You've gotten a good enough look already."

He braced his other hand on the tile as well, trapping her between the counter and his body. "Honey, I have a good enough look right now."

She looked down.

Standing as close as he was, the top of her head brushed his chest as she took in what he meant. Her blouse, still wet, still sheer, revealed her as perfectly as if she'd been nude; delicate collarbone, perfect breasts tipped with perfect rose colored nipples, and gently curved belly, moving in and out with her quickened breathing.

Rolling her eyes at herself, probably at him too, she grabbed the ice pack, set it across her collarbone, just above her breasts, and sucked in a breath.

He smiled.

"Are you enjoying this?"

His gaze dipped low again, watching as her nipples hardened even further, and let out a heartfelt sigh. "Most definitely."

"I didn't enjoy the sight of you when you were on the examination table."

"Maybe not then, when I was muddy and bloody, but I bet you thought of me later."

She pulled her lower lip in between her teeth, trying to maintain a somber attitude.

"Come on, admit it. You did."

She rolled her eyes, as good an admission as he was going to get. They were standing close, eyes locked together, and she smiled, and then so did he. And then, just as suddenly, his amusement faded.

Zero to sixty . . .

Emma let the ice pack fall. Their thighs bumped. His hands went to her waist. Hers slid up his chest, and they were staring at each other.

Not smiling.

Not even breathing.

His hands tightened on her, then glided up her slim spine, one fisting in her wet blouse, the other sinking into her hair. She shivered, but he knew it wasn't from the cold.

"Are we still playing doctor?" she murmured.

"I'm game. I think I should check you out much more thoroughly."

"You've done that."

"A second opinion never hurts." When her breath caught audibly, he pulled her up against him, careful of her ribs. "I'll start with your mouth."

The mouth in question fell open and she licked her lips, that quick little gesture she sometimes did when she was nervous.

Oh yeah, he liked her that way. She let down her guard, and he definitely loved watching her with her guard down. She didn't quite know what to do with herself when she stepped out of her element.

She fidgeted, shifted her weight, nibbled on that lower lip in a way that made him very, very hard. "Come closer," he murmured.

"Any closer, and I'll be breathing your air."

"Exactly what the doctor ordered." And with that, he made the move and kissed her.

Ah, yeah. *That* was what he'd been craving since she'd left his cabin the night before. Hell, since the first time he'd seen her.

Unlike her wit, her brain, her eyes, which were all sharp as a razor, her mouth was soft.

Warm.

Sweet.

Giving.

For one blissful moment she sank into him.

Just like that, the discomfort of being wet and cold vanished, since between them they were generating enough heat to supply a small third world country with electricity for a year.

Her fingers tightened in the material of his wet t-shirt, then slid up his chest, until her arms were wrapped around his neck, holding on as if maybe he was giving her something she hadn't been able to get from anyone else, something she really needed.

Something he was so willing to give.

Then she pushed free, and walked out of the room.

Chapter 18

He followed her. Of course he followed, Emma thought. She could hear the squeak of his wet boots on the floor behind her as she moved into the small office and opened the closet door. The closet was almost larger than the office, and she blindly reached out for the set of sweats she kept there.

Because that was why she was covered in goose bumps. She was cold.

Yeah, and she was also the Tooth Fairy.

When the small single overhead light bulb flicked on, she turned.

Stone stood in the doorway of the closet, one hand still raised, holding the chain to the light. She'd intended to dress in the dark, but what the hell, he'd already seen everything she had to show. She tugged off her blouse, and met his gaze, surprised to see not just blazing heat, but also a baffled affection, one that really plowed into her, staggering her back a step until she came up against the wall and the large storage bin that held God knew what.

He came toward her, gently pushing a stack of boxes out of his way, making the rather large closet seem small with his presence.

And getting smaller.

He took the sweats from her hands and set them aside. "Hey," she protested. "Changing here."

He unhooked her bra, took in what he'd uncovered, and let out a breath of appreciation as he dipped his head.

"Stone—"

"You're hurt. I wanted to kiss it better." His mouth covered a breast, his fingers danced down her quivering belly as his tongue flicked a nipple. Without missing a beat in teasing her into an instant puddle of need and desire, he opened her pants and let them fall.

"I'm not hurt there."

"I don't know that for sure." His fingers hooked her bikini panties and slid them down, an action that wrenched another moan of appreciation from him. "God, look at you."

"I—"

She broke off as he very gently lifted her onto the storage bin.

"I need to check you out more thoroughly."

She was completely naked. He wasn't. "The damn thing is cold."

He smiled. "I'll warm you up." Making good on his word, he dropped to his knees between hers and slid his warm hands beneath her bottom, cupping her as he pressed his mouth to an inner thigh. "Looking good so far . . ."

Oh, God. She whispered his name, sounding a little frantic to her own ears. She had no idea how she could want him like this— in a closet!—but she did. Even her pain was gone, though he seemed very aware of her injury, and took great care to make sure she stayed still and that he didn't jar her. When he kissed her other thigh, she let out a needy little whimper, watching as he pulled her to him so that his mouth could have its merry way with her.

With one languorous stroke of his tongue after another, he wound her up, tighter and tighter. Her hands were in his hair now, her only anchor in a spinning world as he dragged her into a pool of sheer sensation. "*Stone*—"

"Yeah, you're going to be okay. Did you know you taste like heaven?" he murmured against her wet flesh, his talented, greedy mouth very busily driving her to the edge and holding her there with nothing more than his velvety hot tongue. In less than two minutes, she was gasping for breath, panting his name. "Stone, I'm going to—"

"Yes. I want you to."

She couldn't have stopped it to save her life. It started in her toes. They curled, and her body tightened like an arrow, and just as he sucked her into his mouth, she exploded. He held her through the most intense orgasm of her life, coaxing her down slowly. Gently.

When her muscles stopped shuddering and finally went still, he raised his head and looked at her with a fierce pleasure and intensity that nearly had her coming again.

He pulled a condom from his pocket and stripped off his shirt. As he unzipped and shucked, she blessed the light because he was so magnificently made, she could have stared at his body all day.

She took his condom and rolled it on him, prompting a few low, roughly moaned oaths from him and a shiver of anticipation from her. He wrapped her legs around his waist and stood up with her in his arms. Pressing her back against the closet wall, where she was cushioned by several hanging coats, he sank into her with one mind-blowing, soul-searing thrust that had them both gasping, swearing, *dying*.

She was in a closet, closed off from the world except for Stone, and it was the most sensual, erotic thing she'd ever done.

He began to move and it rocked her world. He rocked her world, and she set her head back against the wall, arching to meet him as he pushed into her again.

And again.

He was so deep inside her that she could feel his heart pounding in tune with hers, and still she couldn't get enough. His mouth claimed hers, hard and deep, and she gave him everything she had, which was new and more than a little terrifying but in that moment she didn't care. From day one he'd been there for her, always, strong and solid and on her side like no one else ever had. From day one, there'd been a bond, one that had only grown stronger, and she clutched at him, needing him, needing this. She was breathing crazily, and he was too, harsh and rough in her ear as his body moved within hers. "God, Stone."

"I know."

"You—I—" She broke off, closing her eyes to better absorb it all. "Again. I'm going to again."

Apparently the words were all he'd needed. His mouth skimmed her jaw as he tightened his grip on her, pressing his face in the crook of her neck with a low, unintelligible groan as he stiffened, giving himself up to her. He took her with him, and she surrendered everything, every bit of her, heart and soul right there in the closet.

They stayed like that for long moments, him cradling her against him, her muscles still spasming around him, until finally he stirred, pressing a kiss to her jaw. "You okay?"

"Yes." She let go of him, but his arms tightened on her as he lightly ran his mouth along her throat. "Mmm. You always smell good."

That was nice, this was all incredibly nice, and it was almost too much for her. If she stayed like this with him, she'd start thinking, and thinking about this, about him, could only lead to hurt. Not wanting that, not wanting to do or say anything to that dark, deep look in his eyes, the one sending warning signals to her still out-to-lunch brain, she stirred.

"Don't move," he protested huskily. "Not yet."

She had to. Had. To. "I have a hanger poking me in the back and my bare ass is against the wall. It's time to move."

"In a sec." His mouth lazily skimmed over her shoulder, making his way toward a nipple that, unbelievably, hardened for him.

Even more unbelievably, her eyes rolled in the back of her head, and of its own accord, her body arched, giving him the access he needed. Even her face lifted, rising up for another kiss.

Good God. Someone send her a raft, she was going down . . .

Stone was melting in pleasure. Emma's tongue was warm and sweet, and danced to his, and he was still buried deep inside her. He was loving all of it, until suddenly she put her hand on his chest and started to disentangle herself. He tried to hold onto her but she gave him the look, the one that said back off, and with a sigh, he let her go.

She immediately turned from him, which gave him a fantastic view of her world-class ass as she began looking for her clothing. "This," she muttered, "is becoming ridiculous. I have got to start taking my clothes off in a more civilized nature."

"Civilized?"

"Yes." She shook out her wrinkled, wet blouse. "And hanging things up would be good too."

"You think you should be able to stop and hang up each piece of clothing as it comes off." He nodded even though he thought it was the stupidest idea he'd ever heard.

"It would be helpful."

He laughed at her, at himself, then bent with her when she

went for her pants. He put his hands on her arms and kissed her, kissed her long and deep and wet, and when he pulled back, they were both breathing hard again. It would have been pretty damn ego-boosting at how fast he could get her all worked up except she didn't want to be worked up to begin with. "Tell me how the hell we're supposed to do *that*," he demanded softly, "and think rationally at the same time."

She blinked, as if surprised at the question. "Well, I've never actually had this particular problem before. I've always been able to maintain some composure."

He stared at her, then shook his head. "Who have you been sleeping with? Robots?"

Not the right thing to ask, given the way her eyes cooled. She turned away from him. "Not robots, no."

He stared at her stiff, proud shoulders and sighed. She hadn't given herself to anyone else in a long time, and when she had, it'd been Spencer, who while an excellent friend, apparently hadn't inspired any wild passion. Before that, maybe another doctor, someone fancy and important, maybe someone on a schedule similar to hers. They'd probably booked their sex on their Blackberries, maybe even had their assistants book it, all "civilized." "Emma."

She didn't look at him as she pulled on the dry sweats and hung up her wet things, so he put on his wet clothes with a wince. There was nothing worse than putting on wet clothes after very satisfying sex, except for maybe putting on wet clothes after *not* having very satisfying sex. "Emma."

Nothing.

He turned her to face him. Her cheeks were pink, her eyes unhappy, and his stomach clenched as he tried to pull her in.

"Okay, whoa." She pointed at him. "No more of that."

"The hugging?"

"The looking at me like I mean something to you. The soft,

sexy voice that makes it so I can't think. The touching. The kissing. The . . . rest. Most definitely the rest." She exited the closet, heading to the reception area, where she pulled open the door for him, setting off the ceramic cowbells.

It'd stopped raining, but water still dripped off the eaves. He walked to where she stood in the doorway, purposely crowding her. "Can't help the looking at you like you mean something, because you do."

"Stop."

"Because . . . ?"

"Because it's a mistake. And because I don't like to make mistakes. Look," she said on a sigh, searching for words. "Starting something with you wouldn't be right. I've already got one foot out the door. I'm only here for my father. That's it."

"Sure about that?"

"What does that mean?"

"Well, seems to me that you could have told him no. You could have hired another doctor to run the place. But you didn't. You came. I think you did because you wanted to connect."

"I connect plenty. I'm connected to work. I'm connected to Spencer. I was connected with my mom."

"Your mom is gone," he said very gently, taking her hand when she whirled away. "Spencer is a man who by your own admissions is someone who doesn't stick. And—"

"I've heard enough."

"And," he went on anyway, "work doesn't count. So the question stands, Emma. How exactly are you connected right now?"

"You think you have me all figured out." She yanked free. "But you don't. You don't know me."

"I'm starting to know you plenty. I know, for instance, that you swim like a fish, that you're insanely competitive, a crappy driver, and that you're amused by people afraid of needles."

She met his gaze. "That's all superficial stuff."

"I'd know more, but you're pretty careful of yourself."

"Yeah." She let out a low breath and looked away. "I guess it's hard to be insulted by the truth."

"Look, I know you like challenges," he said very quietly, stepping close again because he liked being close, lifting her face because he liked to see her eyes. "So here's a big one for you."

"I'm not making another bet. I keep losing."

"You'll win this one. Let me know you. Let me in."

"Stone."

"Try connecting, Emma, with me. Come on, what could it hurt? Unless, of course, you're afraid."

Her gaze hit his, inadvertently revealing to him the truth, that she wasn't afraid of much, but she most definitely was of this.

Them.

"Is that it?" he pressed. "Did I find something the tough, badass New York doc fears?"

"Oh, you want to mock my fears now?" she asked, clearly trying to throw him off the track with her ironic tone. "Really?"

Willing to laugh at himself, he grinned. "Okay, but at least I know mine."

She made a soft disparaging sound. "This is ridiculous."

"Uh huh. Because you're afraid."

"Say that one more time, say it to my face and see what happens."

"You're afraid," he taunted softly.

"You are impossible."

"See? You're getting to know me already." He smiled when she laughed. "Come on, Emma. Give me a try."

Staring up at him, she shook her head.

"You might like it. You might like me."

"Awfully sure of yourself, aren't you?"

"Sometimes." He was also smart enough to know when to back off and let a woman think. With a steady purpose, he leaned in and kissed her once, slowly, with just a hint of heat, and walked away.

He hoped like hell the gamble paid off.

Chapter 19

Emma was still in an odd and conflicting state of arousal and confusion that night when Spencer got back, dropped off by TJ, not Stone, which she knew because she found herself pressing her face to the upstairs living room window to peek.

Give me a try, he'd said. Connect, with me.

And she'd scoffed. She didn't need to give him a try, she didn't need to give anyone a try. And connecting? *Please.* She was only here for a very limited time, and then she was going home, where things were great and nothing was missing from her life.

Nothing.

Except someone to connect with.

Damn him for pointing that out. Damn him for being right.

"Hi honey, I'm home!" Spencer came in the door and tossed down his backpack, opening his arms in great exaggeration for a welcome hug and kiss.

She lifted a brow. "I see a bear didn't get you."

"Nope. Miss me?" He was smiling, but it slowly faded, to be replaced by a questioning curiosity. "What's that look on your face?"

"I don't know. Nothing."

"You have a mix of . . . I'm not sure if it's a glow, or a temper."

She covered her cheeks with her hands, knowing it was the damn closet. "I don't know what you're talking about."

"TJ told me about the truck and the ditch. You okay?"

"Completely fine."

"So what's wrong?"

"Nothing. Nothing's wrong."

"Emma, it's me. The master of deception when it comes to feelings, remember?"

"Well then, I certainly wouldn't want to burden you with mine."

"Nice try." He pulled off his sweatshirt and tossed it aside. "Look, we could do the whole dance around it thing, but I'm hungry and tired, and don't have the patience."

She laughed. "Honestly, it's touching how into me you are."

"I'll drive all the way to South Shore and buy you that Thai if you tell me."

She'd have done a whole hell of a lot more for Thai, so she caved like a cheap suitcase. "It's Stone."

"Ah. You still crushing on the big, bad boy of the mountain?"

"Yes. No. I don't know. How's that for a straight answer?"

He tugged affectionately on a strand of her hair. "We've always been close."

"No. Actually, we've remained such good friends because we *aren't* too close, right?"

He lifted a shoulder in acknowledgment of that. "Fine. But one thing we have always been with each other, is honest. Brutally so."

"True."

"So." He offered her a half smile. "Be honest now. You slept with him. You slept with him and instead of being done as you usually are, you want more."

She stared at him, stunned at that quick and horrifyingly accurate assessment. "Yes."

"Well that sucks." He let out a breath and turned away so she couldn't see his eyes. "I'm hungry. I don't suppose you cooked?" He sighed again at the empty kitchen. "Yeah. Didn't think so."

"Spence—"

"It's okay, Emma. I'm a big boy and I asked." At the unexpected knock on the door, he moved toward it. "Hey, maybe it's a miraculous Thai food delivery from heaven."

Instead, it was Serena, wrapped in a wind breaker and a black mini skirt. "I'm looking for the doc," she said to Spence. "Is she here?"

Emma moved into view. "Right here, Serena. Is there something wrong?"

"Well, I guess you could say it's that I wasn't the dweeb and didn't waste the best years of my life in medical school like you did."

Spencer leaned against the doorjamb, amused. "So you're a close friend of Emma's then."

Serena sighed, closing her eyes. "Dammit. Was that snippy, because I was actually going for nice. I'm not very good at it." She opened her eyes, which were just a little glazed over. "I'll stick with my bitchy self. I need a doc, Sexy Man. So move out of my way."

Spencer didn't. "I'm a doctor, too."

"Wow, God really gave with both hands when it came to you, didn't he." She narrowed her eyes as she took him in. "Quick, what are your faults?"

"I leave the toilet seat up and don't bother with the cap on the toothpaste."

"Sharp wits, too. Very nice. How are you with the bedside manner?"

He grinned. "Better than Emma."

From behind him, Emma rolled her eyes, but Serena laughed. "And confident. Okay, I pick you."

Spencer looked intrigued. "For . . . ?"

She pulled her hands from beneath her coat. One was cradling the other, wrapped in a towel.

Spence immediately reached for her. "What happened?"

"A new knife and a stubborn piece of chocolate."

Emma grabbed her keys for downstairs. "Let's go take a look."

"No, I pick Dr. McHottie," Serena said.

"Sorry. I'm the doctor on call," Emma told her lightly, trying to save Spencer. At the very least, Serena would walk all over him. At the most, she'd eat him up and spit him out.

But Spencer smiled. "I'd love to earn my keep. I'll be happy to take this one."

Emma swiveled to look at him. "Earn your keep?"

"Seeing as you've put up with me all week." He slid an arm around Serena's waist and guided her down the stairs as if she was an invalid.

Not that Serena seemed to mind.

Emma followed. *Earn his keep, her ass.* Inside the clinic, she flipped on the lights and prepared a tray, but when she moved to wash her hands, Spencer was already ahead of her, washed up and unwrapping Serena's hand to examine it. "Ouch," he murmured sympathetically.

"Yeah." Serena held her breath as he touched. "Bad?"

"No." He smiled into her face. "Just a couple of stitches. Probably only two."

"Oh boy." Serena nibbled on her lower lip. "I don't like needles."

Must be a Wishful thing, Emma thought, and opened her mouth to say something, like consider it Karma with a capital K, but Spencer spoke first.

"Don't you worry about a thing," he told Serena. "I'll make sure you're comfortable."

"Really?" Serena's eyes locked on his. "Can you do that?"

"I specialize in it." He glanced at Emma with the unspoken question, and with a shrug, she gestured him to go ahead.

The bedside manner he'd mentioned didn't escape her notice. He was good at that, making a patient forget their pain, putting them at ease. He could read a person like no other, and know what they needed in any given moment.

In Serena's case, a little harmless flirting had taken her mind off her pain, and Serena would never forget him. As Emma brought him the tray with everything he'd need, she thought of her last needle-phobic patient.

She'd treated Stone to a textbook T. Yep. She'd fixed up his body and he'd heal quickly and wouldn't scar.

But she'd ignored his other needs.

As much as she hated to admit being second best at anything, her very lack of "bedside manner" is what made Spencer a better doctor than her.

She watched him continue to keep Serena at ease and wished she'd learned the art of it. Why hadn't she?

Because she was focused.

Because she tended to be concerned first and foremost with a patient's physical well-being.

In Stone's case, because she'd been unnerved by him and her reaction to him.

There.

That was the bottom line, the truth.

And it shamed her. She'd always prided herself on being the best she could be, on giving the best care she could, and in doing so, she'd actually concentrated on herself more than her patients.

By now, Spencer had Serena leaned back and was making her comfortable, distracting her with an easy smile and quiet voice.

"So are you Emma's?" Serena asked him.

"Nah," Spence said easily. "She wouldn't have me."

"She always was shortsighted."

Spence grinned.

"We're just friends," Emma said a little tightly. "Though sometimes I wonder why . . ."

Spencer kept on grinning, thoroughly enjoying himself.

"Are you from New York, too?" Serena asked him.

"Yep. Dr. Spencer Jenks, but any friend of Emma's can call me Spence."

"Oh, we're not friends," Serena told him, still studying his face. "I used to torture her in first grade. But I did try to make it up with brownies the other day. Double fudge, warm, soft, out-of-this-world brownies . . ."

Spencer groaned appreciatively. "Now you're just teasing me."

Serena smiled. "I have a fresh batch . . . I could share."

"I like the sound of that," Spence assured her. He had the syringe in his hand, low at his hip where Serena couldn't see.

Emma had always scoffed at that practice. In her opinion, assuming the patient wasn't a kid, she believed they wanted things upfront and honest.

"What else do you make?" he asked Serena.

"Name it."

"Really? God, I love a woman with talent in the kitchen."

Serena smiled. "Honey, I've got talents in every room of the house, trust me."

He laughed again, clearly enjoying the unmistakable hum of attraction between them. "Not fair," he said. "I hiked all day and I'm *starving*. Tell me what you have in your front case," he directed, "and I'll pretend it's right here in front of me."

"Oh, you should see today's pies." Serena's eyes were closed and she smiled dreamily. "I love pies. They're my specialty." Her lips curved. "Amongst other things, of course."

"Of course. But what's your favorite?"

"Pumpkin. My pumpkin pie is completely and totally out of this world."

"I bet. A quick prick now," he murmured. "That's it, that's all there is. Keep breathing. So do you use whipped cream on that . . . ?"

Much later that night, Emma lay in bed staring at the ceiling trying to figure things out. Why she suddenly felt so restless. So out of place in her own skin.

So . . . alone.

She didn't have to be. Stone had made that clear. What she hadn't told him was exactly how tempted she was to go to his cabin and take him up on his offer.

He could alleviate all her restlessness, and leave her humming with pleasure while he was at it. But . . .

But.

Something about his challenge to connect with him scared her, because she knew that she *could* connect with him, big time.

And then she'd leave.

It was in the cards, the plan all laid out—as soon as her dad was better, she was gone.

Even she couldn't repair a broken heart.

Chapter 20

Emma dreamed about Stone and woke up wishing he was in bed with her. What was up with that? She got up and showered, and thought about how it'd feel to have him soaping her up.

Okay, this Stone obsession she had? It had to stop. In fact, she wasn't going to think about him again.

For at least five minutes.

Helping with that, Spencer made an extravagant breakfast, waiting until she took her first bite and moaned in amazed culinary pleasure before he leaned in. "Em."

"Ohmigod." The perfect way to put Stone out of her head—with food. "This is fantastic."

"Of course it is. Listen, you know I'm leaving in two days. I have a little favor."

"Anything," she murmured, shoveling in more food. "Name it."

"I want to ask Serena out."

She slid her gaze to his. "Serena, bitchy Serena?"

"She's not all bitch."

"Don't fool yourself. She's purebred bitch."

"I can handle myself. Now take me out of my misery. Yes or no?"

She set down her fork. "You're serious."

"Yes."

"You won't let her skin you and eat you alive?"

"Not on the first date," he promised.

Emma picked her fork back up. The food was too good to let it go cold just because he wanted to get his heart kicked. "Will you still cook for me?"

He grinned. "Always."

Later that morning, Missy Thorton came by the clinic carrying a casserole dish and Emma sighed. "What's wrong today, Missy?"

"Nothing. Just wanted to bring you this."

Emma peeked inside the casserole dish and went still.

"It's *tom yum goong*. Hot and sour soup with shrimp."

"Homemade Thai food?" she asked in disbelief.

"Stone mentioned you were lonely for it. My nephew's niece spent a summer in Thailand. She has the most amazing recipes." She tapped the dish. "I'll need this back of course."

With that, she turned and walked away.

Emma was still staring down at the dish in stunned amazement when Harley stopped by for a tetanus shot because she'd sliced her finger on a rusty nail. In return, she fixed all the squeaky doors and gave the truck a tune-up.

Emma had three other patients that morning, and not one person asked for a real doctor, or suggested she confer with her dad. As a bonus, each paid with a check or cash.

This damn town. It'd sneaked up and snatched her damn heart when she hadn't been looking. Not good. Not good at all.

She needed out.

At lunch, she drove to see her dad. She wanted his damn

medical records and an ETA for his return to work, and the subsequent return to *her* life—a life that did not include nice but busy-body patients who knew all her business, a life that didn't include one certain tall, sexy Wilder brother who was starting to haunt her every waking—and sleeping—moment.

She found her father in front of his cabin, tending to a fire pit and cleaning the trout he'd just caught in the lake. He still wore his vest and hat, and the distinct smell of fish.

"Perfect timing," he said with a smile. "I'm going to barbeque these up for lunch right now. State your preference; medium or well-done?"

"I'm sorry, I don't really have time for lunch. I was hoping to see those medical records of yours, and get an ETA for your return."

"Ah."

That was all he said, just "ah". She looked at him for a long moment, finding herself asking a question she hadn't meant to ask at all. "Why didn't you ever tell me that you came to see me in New York?"

He froze, then looked down at his fish. "Medium. No one likes well-done fish."

"Dad."

"Hey, that's good." He poked at his low burning fire. "You do remember what to call me." He nudged a chair in her direction. "That's a great start. Now why don't you take it another step and have a seat."

She gave him a long look, walked past him and into his cabin. On his square wood kitchen table sat two thick files. She opened the top one, saw that it was indeed his medical records and grabbed them, going back outside, where she sat in the chair next to him.

He began preparing the fish to be cooked, but as she opened and flipped through the first file, his hands fell still. As she read, she felt him looking at her.

After less than a moment, she knew why. She raised her head, unable to keep the accusation out of her voice. "You said it was a minor heart attack. As in *minor*."

"I don't believe I ever used the word minor, no."

"You were hiking. You called TJ for help, but he was out of town. Stone came." Her voice shook on her next line. "By the time he got to you, you weren't breathing. He gave you C.P.R." Why Stone had never mentioned it, she couldn't imagine. "You were air lifted to South Shore. They'd resuscitated you twice."

"Yes."

"You almost died."

"Yes."

She closed the file. "You're not going back to work any time soon."

He hesitated while she held her breath, literally and figuratively. God. God, she didn't want to hear his answer because it was going to change her life and she knew it.

"No," he admitted, very quietly. "I'm not going to be going back any time soon."

She surged to her feet and paced the length of the porch, the wood creaking beneath her feet. "You should have told me."

"Should've, yes."

"Dad." She pressed her fingers to her eyes, then dropped her hands to her sides. "What was your plan? That I'd just stay? Forever?"

"Well . . ." His smile was self-deprecating and pretty damn irresistible, except she couldn't—wouldn't—be charmed.

"A man could hope his only offspring would want to take over his business."

Oh, no. No, no, no . . . This was so much worse than she'd thought. She stared at him, stunned. "*Dad*." At a loss for words, she turned in a slow circle. It was quiet. No traffic sounds, not even the hum of anything electronic, nothing but a light wind and the occasional bird cry.

So different from home. "I never intended to move here."

"I realize that now."

He was disappointed, and sad, and pretty much ripping out her heart because she could only imagine the pain of his realization—that he wasn't going to go back to work, at least not fulltime, not for a while anyway. "Dad, have you thought about selling?"

He didn't say anything to that and her gut sank. "I could make sure you get a great price for it," she assured him. "You could fish the rest of your life, or *whatever* you wanted."

"I know. Listen, Emma, it's okay. Don't you worry about it. I'll figure it out."

"Not to rush you, but how? How will you figure it out?"

"Well, I don't know exactly."

"It'll just come to you? You have to make plans, Dad, and figure it all out."

"No," he said very gently. "That's you. *You* like plans, *you* like to have everything all figured out."

"Okay, fair enough. But do you expect me to continue to stay here until you come up with something?"

He turned from her, giving himself away. "Of course not." He shoved his hands in his pockets and stared out at the sparkling lake. "As you've mentioned a time or a thousand, you have a life. I don't wish to keep you from it. Let's just both cut our losses now."

Goddammit. "*Dad.*"

He turned and looked at her, and for the first time, he looked his age. Worse, he looked sad, which just about killed her. "It was wrong of me to bring you out here like this, and even more wrong to try to keep you. I just thought I'd try to do things differently with you this time." He smiled, though it was a heartbreaking one. "It'll be okay, Emma, you can stop looking at me like that. I appreciate what you've done. It means so much to me that you were willing to come out here and spend so much time, but reality has set in and it's over now. I understand, I really do. It's time to sell." He moved to the small fire and set a grate over it for the barbeque.

She stared at him, torn. She'd been given her freedom. And yet . . . and yet she wasn't running for her suitcases. "You're really okay with that, with selling?"

"I think that's best, yes."

"Let me at least help you find a buyer."

He stabbed at the flames with a poker and sparks rose, cutting into the still air. "You have the second file? The one beneath my medical records?"

She opened it, and stared down in astonishment. "You have a stack of offers on the Urgent Care."

"The vultures began picking at me once the word got out that I was out of commission for a while. I know it's hard for you to imagine, but there are doctors who would sell their soul to work out here. I'll take one of those offers. It'll free you up to go home."

She was released from her ties here. Free. She should be jumping over the moon. Instead she set the file aside and crouched at his side. "I'm not running out of here. I'm not going anywhere until you're settled."

"It won't take but a few days."

"Dad. I want you to have a full physical."

"Will that make you feel better about going?"

Not even close. "Is it so weird that I worry about you?"

His smile warmed and he reached out to squeeze her hand. "Same goes."

"So will you?"

"If I say yes, will you sit and have lunch?"

She gave him a half smile. "We don't do lunch."

"We don't do a lot of things. Many of them my fault. But it

turns out an old dog can learn new tricks. Question is . . ." His eyes sparkled with a dare. "Can a new dog accept them and give more as well?"

She blew out a low breath. "People keep telling me I'm falling short in the giving more department."

He raised a brow. "I hit a nerve."

"Apparently so." She looked at the fish and her stomach rumbled hungrily. "Can you really cook?"

"Of course. Can't you?"

She had to laugh. "Not even a little."

"Ah," he said, looking amused. "So maybe this old dog can teach you something after all."

Stone spent the next two days working his ass off. He took a group rock climbing at Mile High Lakes, and then that night led another group on a moonlight hike along Thigh-Breaker trail, named Thigh-Breaker for a damn good reason. The next day he taught wake boarding to a group of local kids, then looked at a property for sale in town. It was boarded up, and he managed to get a handful of splinters getting back out, which pissed him off, especially as the place was so overpriced he couldn't even seriously consider it. Halfway back to the lodge, he got called in to volunteer at Search and Rescue to help locate a missing hiker. After a very long night of searching, they found the guy sleeping off his twelve-pack on the north shore of Jackson Lake.

Idiot.

Irritated, tired, hungry, hand hurting from the last splinter he hadn't been able to get out, Stone once again headed for home. "I have a massive splinter and a headache," he told TJ on the phone.

"Hey, you're the one working yourself to the bone."

"Well, someone has to."

"You don't have to do it all, Stone. No one ever asked you

to. In fact, you need to do as you're always telling everyone else, you need to relax. Go get laid. Call the pretty doctor. I promise not to show up this time."

Stone opened his mouth, then shut it, and at his silence, TJ gleefully pounced. "So you closed the deal, nice. Why didn't it relax you? You doing it right?"

Stone shut his phone, cutting his brother off.

He'd done it right.

They'd done it so right that it was pretty much all he could think about. He wanted to do it again.

And again. But he wanted something deeper than just sex this time.

And he didn't care that that made him sound like a cheesy movie.

When he stepped into the lodge kitchen, he found Annie and Nick entwined together, kissing as if they hadn't been together for twenty years already. "Isn't that getting old yet?"

Annie separated her lips from Nick's and smiled. "Nope."

"Definitely not," Nick said.

With a grin, Annie pulled on an apron that read: DOES NOT COOK WELL WITH OTHERS, and made breakfast burritos.

Starving and exhausted, Stone sat to stuff one in his mouth. Annie poured him some orange juice, then pushed back his hair to look at the healing cut on his forehead.

See, he didn't need love. He had his family. He didn't need more than what he had right here. Except . . . except he did. Catching her hand, he looked into her eyes. "I'm okay."

"Are you really?"

"What is that supposed to mean?"

"It means that you're working too hard around here. We all know there's other things you'd rather be working hard at."

"You too? Jesus, my entire life isn't about Emma."

Annie looked at Nick, then carefully stuck her tongue in

her cheek and turned back to Stone. "Honey, I was talking about the renovating."

Ah, shit. He downed the juice.

"So . . ." Annie sat at his side. "Do you want to talk about Emma?"

"Hell, no. As far as the renovating, I'm looking at properties to buy, but I still want to be here. Okay?"

"Okay. Good. Just go after your heart, Stone." She smiled at Nick over her shoulder. "No matter what it is. Or who."

"Annie."

"It's just everyone needs someone once in awhile, Stone. That's all I'm saying."

"Thanks for the newsflash." Stone stood up to go, but Nick stopped him by gently nudging Annie. "Tell him."

"Oh." Annie's hands went to her belly as she once again looked at her husband. "I haven't said it out loud yet. I don't know if I'm ready."

"You have nine months to get ready," Nick said, eyes bright, mouth curved. "I'm just thinking that Stone's going to need that long as well."

"Oh my God." Stone divided a look between the two of them, Nick nearly bursting with pride, Annie seeming torn between sheer joy and sheer terror. "He knocked you up."

"Hey." She smacked Stone upside the back of the head. "True, but hey." She spread her fingers over her belly, her eyes going misty. "It's weird, right?"

"Yeah." Feeling suddenly a little misty himself, he pulled her in for a hug. "But good weird."

Annie's breath caught as she pulled back to cup his face, her smile soft and warm and happy, so happy it almost hurt to look at her. "Yeah?" she whispered.

"Yeah," he whispered back. "Now you'll have someone new to boss around. No one does that as good as you."

"Aw, that's the sweetest thing you've ever said to me. Now." She moved to the kitchen window. "Back to you."

"I don't want to talk about me."

"Even if the woman you think you don't want to talk about, the one who's leaving soon, just drove up?

He stood up, watching as Emma parked her father's truck out front. "What do you mean, leaving soon?"

"They found a buyer for the clinic," Nick said.

Goddammit.

He walked outside as she got out of the truck, and though he'd just eaten and satisfied his belly, his gut still took one hard kick at just the sight of her.

Chapter 21

Stone watched Emma stride toward him, her legs eating up the ground. He wondered if she was going to mention that she was leaving.

He'd have guessed that the thought of leaving would make her happy. Yeah, he'd really thought that, except the look on her face didn't say happy. It said frustration.

It said tension.

It said unhappiness. "Dr. Sinclair," he said with mock formality, hoping to coax out a smile.

It didn't. She stopped before him on the steps of the lodge, and when he reached for her, she jabbed him in the chest with a finger. "You should have told me."

Okay, he'd play. He grabbed her finger. "Told you what?" That when she looked a little hot under the collar like she did right now, *he* got hot?

She yanked her hand free. "I know you saved my dad."

Ah, shit. That.

She let out a breath and lost some of her tension as she met his gaze, her own shiny, deep, and real. Very real. "Thank you for that, by the way," she whispered. "I'm really glad you were able to get there as fast as you did."

"I'd have done it for anyone, Emma," he said, watching her turn and walk away a few steps. "And so would you. Thanks aren't necessary."

"You saved his life, Stone."

"Yes. How many lives have you saved?"

She shrugged in acknowledgment of that. "Why didn't you tell me? Why did you let me think his heart attack was minor?"

He sighed. "If you'd known, would you have agreed to stay?"

She turned back. Her eyes were cool now. "That question bites."

"Yeah, it does." But he needed the answer.

Shaking her head, she took in the sharp, craggy mountains behind her. "I'm scared to death for him," she whispered, hugging herself.

At that, he let out the breath he'd been holding. Okay, he hadn't been wrong about her. She cared, deeply. Question was, did she care for *him* as deeply? "Of course you're scared for him. We all are. But he's doing great."

"I just wish I'd known. If we'd had the relationship he wanted," she said quietly, "he'd have told me sooner. That's my fault."

"No, Emma, it's not." He pulled her around to face him. "He's stubborn as a mule. A trait, I'm beginning to see is a family thing.

She shook her head as a small smile escaped. "You have this way of cutting right to the chase."

"Saves time."

"I just wish someone would have told me, that *you* would have told me. I thought—" She broke off, then shrugged. "I thought we might have had something."

"Yeah?" He tried to get past the stab of the past tense of that statement. "I thought so too. You're leaving."

"I was always leaving."

"Sooner than later."

"Yes. Spence is leaving today and I'll be a few days after him."

"A few days?"

"By next week, certainly."

While he tried to adjust to that, she said, "We have offers on the clinic."

He closed his eyes. "He's actually going to sell?"

"With the option of a contract for his services part-time so he doesn't have to retire."

"You're worried about him, but you're still going to leave?"

With a sigh, she started walking. "You don't understand. After this week, he won't need me full time." She didn't turn back to the truck, but walked across the wild grass in front of the lodge, and he followed.

"So you're on the part-time daughter plan, is that it?"

"Yes, actually. I am." She stopped and faced him. "That's what our relationship's always been, Stone. Part-time. If I could figure out how to do it differently, I would. But the truth is, the clinic is beyond him right now, and unlike what you seem to be implying, I'm not just walking away. I'm going to have him all set up before I go. I just wish I'd known about his condition sooner."

Yeah. No way around it, he felt like a jerk for that. "Emma—"

"No, don't." There was a light breeze ruffling her hair and she shoved it out of her face. "You care about him. It's good. It's good that I know your loyalties are with him. It makes you trustworthy."

He stared at her, not liking where this was going either. "But not trustworthy for you?"

"Honestly? I don't know."

Damn, if that one didn't hit home. "You know what I think? That you're using this as an excuse to run scared from whatever the hell it is we're doing."

"First of all, we're not *doing* anything. We're both geographically unavailable, remember? And second, you really think I'd use my father's health as an excuse?"

"I think you'd do anything to get out of here. Away from the emotional roller coaster this place has presented. Compared to us, New York must feel like a dead zone. No personal emotions required."

"Don't," she said tightly. "Don't get me started. I came here for him. God, don't you understand that? He needed me and I came."

"And in return, you don't need him at all? Is that what you're saying?"

She let out a frustrated breath and then turned to walk again. "I'm a lot of things, Stone. Anal, obsessive, obnoxiously competitive . . ."

"Obstinate . . ."

Her lips quirked. "That, too." She stopped and let out a breath. Closed her eyes. "You're right. I'm looking for an excuse to blame you when the truth is, I'm so grateful that you were there that day that I don't even care why you didn't tell me. I'm picking a fight because . . . because I'm a coward."

"What are you afraid of?"

"Leaving you."

He let out a breath and stepped closer. "So don't go."

"I have to. I am leaving, Stone. I am. I want us both to know that."

Feeling like he'd swallowed sand paper, he nodded. "I know it, and I want you to know that I didn't tell you because it was *his* story to tell, not mine. I didn't mean to hurt you. I care about him, and I care about you. Very much."

"Even though I'm going."

"Even though you're going." He forced a smile. "You think if you say it enough times we'll get used to it?"

"Yes."

Fair enough. He reached for her, so over fighting with her. They didn't have enough time left to fight. "Let's be done rumbling in the parking lot."

She tried to remain stoic and utterly failed as a small smile crossed her face. "I don't know. I like to rumble."

God, he loved her smile. "Let's kiss and make up instead." Reaching up, he set his palm on her jaw, then winced.

She pulled his hand down and looked at it. "You have a splinter."

"It's no big deal"

"It's already getting infected."

"Later." He tried to lean and kiss her but she slapped a hand to his chest. "Wait here." She grabbed her bag out of the truck. "Come here. Unless," she said with a raised brow. "You just want to use a Band-aid or super glue on this too?"

"Ha ha. I'm fine."

"You will be. I have everything I need right here." She patted her bag and smiled reassuringly. "And there's not a needle in the mix, I can promise you." Without waiting for him, she took his hand again, pulling it closer, turning it to get better light. It also blocked his view of the tweezers she'd pulled from her bag, which amused him. "You think I'm a pansy-ass."

"No, I know you're not." She paused. "I've been thinking about what you said last night."

He felt a very slight tug in his palm. "About . . . ?"

"The letting me inside you thing." Her gaze lifted from his hand to his eyes. "Specifically the part where I don't connect."

"Oh. I like the letting me inside you thing better."

She laughed, and he felt another slight tug, but then she was leaning in so close that her breast brushed his arm, and he ceased to think at all.

"Did you know when you say it that way?" she murmured. "It sounds . . ."

Another slight tug, which didn't bother him in the least

since another part of him altogether was once again stirring. "Sounds . . . ?"

"Dirty."

"You think sex is dirty?"

One more tug and then she ran her thumb over his palm, her gaze direct and intent on what she was looking at. "You heal fast."

He grabbed her wrist when she would have turned away. "Nice change of subject."

She smiled. "I'm the master at it." She pulled her hand free. "Your splinter's out."

"Thank you."

"And no." She squirmed. "By the way. I don't think sex is dirty. Although, we had our moments, didn't we."

He grinned. "Yeah." He looked at his palm, while his heart thudded heavily with the weight of pretending that her leaving wasn't going to destroy him. "Nice bedside manner, Dr. Emma."

"Working on it."

He cocked his head and studied her. "Is that what that was? Flirting, to distract me from what you were doing?"

"I didn't intend for it to be *flirting* necessarily. But yes, I was trying to distract you."

"Nicely played. Sex is always distracting. But why the change of tactic?"

She sighed. "I watched Spencer deal with a patient who needed stitches, and he did it better than me."

"Ah." Now it all made perfect sense. "It's a competition thing."

She winced. "I liked the look on the patient's face. She . . . she *liked* him. She *connected* with him, because he made her feel better. I wanted that too, wanted to make you feel better."

Touched, he took her hand. "You know, I like this new you."

Clearly uncomfortable with that, she looked away. "It's the same old me."

"Well whoever it is, I like her. So . . . back to that connecting thing."

"Yeah, about that." She closed up her bag, then looked at him. "Look, we all know that I didn't want to be here in Wishful. But it takes a lot of energy to hold onto that much resentment. I had no idea." She shook her head. "I must be burning calories left and right with it, because do you have any idea how many casseroles I've eaten in the past few months, and I haven't gained an ounce. But I can't do it anymore. No more resentment. Instead, I want to . . ."

"Connect."

She smiled, looking relieved that he was following her. "Yeah."

"Before you leave."

"Yes." She took a step into him and set her hand on his chest. "I want to go knowing I learned to fit in. That I learned to be . . . softer, kinder. More relaxed and laid-back, easygoing. Like you, Stone."

She hadn't taken her hand off his chest, which he considered fair game, so he put his hands on her as well, gently squeezing her hips, pulling her in, feeling the tension in her. "You're not there yet."

She looked down at their bodies now touching from chest to belly to thighs and everything in between, then back up at him, her eyes heating. "I know. That's because when I'm with you like this, I don't feel relaxed so much as . . . revved up."

"Is that right?" He slid his hands up her back slowly, past her still slightly aching ribs, letting his fingers dig into her muscles just a little in a massaging pressure. "How about now?"

Her pulse kicked. Her nipples hardened, pressing against her silk top.

"Feel nice?" he murmured.

"Nice makes me think of kittens and flowers." Her pulse was fluttering like crazy, which he liked. A lot. "I'm not thinking kittens and flowers, Stone." She pressed into him, and he knew the exact moment she felt how hard he was because her eyes locked on his.

"Yeah," he said huskily. "My body thinks you're hot."

"And your brain?"

"Oh, my brain knows it." He tilted her head up so that their mouths were only a whisper apart. "Let's forget everything else, Emma, and connect."

"And the rest."

"Right. Let's teach you to be laid-back. Easygoing. I've got just the thing."

"Well . . . in the name of personal growth then," she whispered, letting her fingers play with his hair at the nape of his neck.

"In the name of personal growth." They kissed, long and deep and so hot he nearly melted.

Chapter 22

Eyes still closed, Emma pulled back, breathing hard. "Okay, it's not working." When she opened her eyes and met Stone's dark, heated gaze, she felt . . . flummoxed. When he looked at her like that, she felt other reactions as well; in her throat, in her belly, in her upper chest, which she told herself was a purely physical response to a gorgeous man, but she knew the truth.

It was her heart, something she wasn't quite ready to admit. "I'm the opposite of relaxed."

"We're getting to it."

At the sexy confidence in his voice, a shiver of desire shot through her. "We should be over this by now."

"I don't feel over it." Slipping his hand around the back of her neck, he let his fingers play on the delicate skin as he kissed her again, opening his mouth on hers, letting her know how much he wanted her, which was the most amazing thing to her.

He wanted her.

Slowly, he broke off the kiss, taking his damn sweet time about it too, leaving their lips still touching for a long beat before finally pulling away. "Do you?"

She looked into his eyes. Dammit. She'd had lovers. Maybe not a lot of them, but certainly enough. And not one, not a single one, had ever made her feel like Stone did, like if she didn't have him, nothing was ever going to be right again. "You're not taking my problem seriously."

"You know what I think?"

"That sex is the answer to all the planet's problems?"

He grinned. "Well, yes. I also think you're trying too hard."

She stared at him, lifting her hand to touch her still wet, slightly swollen lips. "How do you stop trying to relax?"

"Stop thinking."

"Yes, but . . . with us, everything's so . . . hot. So wild."

Looking quite proud of that assessment, he smiled.

"It makes my brain race."

All she could think about was him, the way his body moved against hers, how he was made of pure corded sinew, how warm his smooth, tanned flesh felt against hers. And then there were his eyes.

And his mouth.

God, his mouth. "How? You're pretty potent, you know."

"Same goes, Emma. Come on, I have an idea." Taking her hand, he tugged her around the side of the big lodge to the first of two equipment garages. Opening the first door, he led her inside, where there was a large snowcat, several quads, a snowmobile, and a whole bunch of other outdoor equipment she couldn't quite catch because he turned her toward the small office to the right.

"Nick's," he said, and opened the door. The room had a metal desk and an old, beat-up couch. Skis, poles, boots, bikes and other various parts were scattered everywhere except the one spot where a large basket sat next to the couch. In it was a watchful Chuck, and her four soft, fuzzy, wiggly kittens.

"*Oh*," Emma murmured, her heart melting in a puddle as she dropped to her knees by the basket. "Oh, look at them."

"Their eyes just opened this morning. See that soft gray one?" Stone crouched just behind her, speaking softly, pointing to the one kitten she'd already spotted, the one that was just a little bit separate from the others. "She's the youngest."

"The runt."

"No, she's not weak. She's a fighter. Look at those eyes. She's fierce, intense, and just a little bit pissy." His voice was full of both amusement and pride, and Emma turned her head to meet his gaze.

"She reminds me of you."

"Hey," she said with a laugh. "*Pissy?*"

He smiled, and she sighed. "Okay, so we share a few traits. Are you sure she's a she? Because Chuck surprised all of you."

"She's a she." His gaze ran over the features of Emma's face, which felt like a caress, and her entire body reacted.

"You know," she said unevenly. "It's a pretty cheesy move on your part to use kittens to soften the female into having sex with you."

"So it's working then?"

"No," she said on a laugh.

He lifted a kitten and nuzzled it to his jaw, and every hormone in her body stood up and tap-danced. Apparently in agreement, the kitten "mewed" softly, let out a huge yawn, and cuddled against him.

Emma's heart, already melted, twisted hard. *Dammit.* "It's hard to think too much when you're holding one of those."

"Okay." Shifting, he set the kitten in her arms, who happily snuggled in, and Emma sighed, definitely falling for the sweet little thing.

And maybe, just a little, for the man as well.

Or a lot . . .

As she thought it, as she leaned over the kitten to kiss Stone, to crawl into his arms and burrow in much like the kitten had, the door behind them opened.

*   *   *

Stone sighed and looked up at Nick, standing there holding the door open for Spencer and Serena.

Nick lifted a brow at the sight of Stone holding Emma, who was holding the kitten. "Bad timing, huh?"

"No, not at all," Emma said, backing out of Stone's arms, who turned and gave Nick a long, thanks-a-lot look.

"Sorry," Nick said lightly. "Spence's leaving today, and he wanted to see the kittens before he left. But apparently he's not the only one who hoped to use the adorable factor to his benefit."

Spencer and Stone winced in unison.

"Hey," Emma said, slipping the kitten back in the basket with reluctance. "Give the women some credit. We recognize the tactic."

"Definitely," Serena agreed, but then turned to look at Spencer speculatively. "Is that what you were doing, using the kittens to seduce me?"

"No. Absolutely not. I was using the kittens to make you *want* to be seduced, so that on my next visit—"

"I'd be all buttered up." She gave him a long look. "I haven't yet decided on you, Dr. Spencer Jenks."

Spencer's dark eyes and dimple flashed. "Which is why I'm hedging my bets."

"Well I'll tell you," Serena said. "It's going to backfire on you, because kittens make a woman want to be seduced now, not later."

Stone looked at Emma, who laughed and shook her head.

He sighed, rose to his feet and pulled Emma to hers. "Excuse us," he said to the room. When he had her outside in the hot sun, he looked at her. "I thought I'd give Spencer a second chance with Serena."

"And you a second chance as well?"

"Most definitely."

She laughed, and he loved the soft, musical sound. They walked the trail back around the side of the lodge. It was a beautiful day, and he pulled her around, backing her to the wall of the lodge.

"What?"

"Back to that relaxing thing." He slid his fingers into her hair.

Her lips quirked as he leaned into her. "I'm going back to the clinic now, Stone." Belying the words, she put her hand to his jaw and he turned into her touch. "You have to admit," she said quietly. "This is unexpected, this thing with us. Unexpected, and surprisingly persistent."

"Surprisingly." He looked a little amused. "So what do you do in New York with surprises?"

"Work them into my schedule."

He laughed and shook his head, cupping his hand over hers, bringing her palm to his mouth.

"We're awfully different, Stone."

"Yes, and you happen to like those differences, remember? You wanted me to help you bridge those differences." He put his mouth to her ear. "Run back to the clinic. But go out with me tonight. We'll finish what we started here. I'll show you how to relax."

"I'm taking Spencer to the airport."

"Afterwards then." He flicked his tongue over her earlobe. "It'll be worth your time."

She shivered and tilted her head, giving him better access. "I don't think a date is the right way to handle this situation."

Keeping his mouth on her, he ran his hands up her sides. "What would be?"

She thunked her head back against the wall. "A bucket of cold water over my head."

He grinned and lifted his head. "You need a bucket of cold water around me?"

"With ice." Seeming to gather her thoughts, she straightened and shook her head. "I think it's best to forget it. I'm leaving, and whatever we'd do will just make it that much harder to go." She jabbed him lightly in the chest. "Don't follow me."

He took her finger from his ribcage and entwined his fingers with hers. "Does that work for you in your ER, that point and demand thing?"

"Yes, actually. In my world, I'm quite intimidating. It's how I get what I want."

With a smile, he shook his head. "It's okay, Emma. You don't have to throw your weight around with me. You keep thinking. I'm sure the longer you think about loosening up and relaxing and connecting, the easier it'll get. Maybe by the time you get back to New York, you'll have it down."

She just stared at him. "Maybe you could just write down the instructions."

"Come out with me tonight and I'll make you a list."

She walked to her father's truck, then turned back. "A list?"

"Sure."

"On how to be more easygoing and relaxed? On how to fit in? How to connect?"

He was quite certain that she had no idea how vulnerable she looked, and how utterly irresistible. "Yes, I will. Think of it as an Olympic event. I'll be your coach."

"A training session then."

"If that makes you feel better."

She stared at him, then let out a breath. "I'm insane. Hell, you're insane. But yes."

When Emma got back to the Urgent Care, Missy Thorton was there waiting for her, claiming to need her dish. The older woman sat in the kitchen while Emma transferred the Thai food to another container and washed out the casserole dish.

"I didn't really come back for the dish."

Emma looked up. "No?"

"No. Well, yes. But mostly, I wanted to tell you something before you leave."

"Okay."

"Your momma came back here once. Did you know that?"

Emma looked up from the sink. "What?"

"About ten years ago now. The rumors were she came back to reunite with your daddy, but that's not what she wanted. She wanted one hundred thousand dollars. It wiped him out, but he took out a second mortgage on this place and gave it to her."

Emma set the bowl down and stared at her.

Missy nodded and her blue hair bounced. "It's why he doesn't have any large retirement funds. He never built them back up. We all figured your mom wanted a trip around the world or something like that, but she had a fancy husband to pay for such a thing, so that didn't make sense."

Ten years ago, Emma had been turned down for financial aid for medical school because her stepfather had been making a fortune. But he hadn't offered to help her. Emma had looked into student loans. Four years of pre-med at twenty-five grand each would have put her at her BS degree with a hundred grand in debt and four more years of medical school still to get through.

At the time, Emma had panicked. She'd thought maybe she should do something other than become a doctor. Taco Bell was always hiring, and she did love their food. Or Target. She could get good clothing discounts, plus she looked good in red and khaki.

Her mother hadn't been amused. She'd bossed, yelled, cajoled, and demanded Emma not give up, so Emma had tried for grants, but she'd been denied.

Then her mother had shown up with a check, written from

Sandy's own personal account. She said it was a gift, one Emma wasn't to question or ponder or give another thought to.

Emma had never been so grateful or felt more love in her life.

Her mother had never brought it up again, though Emma had. Plenty of times, including the day she'd gotten her first job in the ER, when she'd begun paying her mother back from each paycheck.

Her mother had always taken the checks with a sweet, grateful smile, and never once, not one single time in all these past ten years, had Sandy let on that the money hadn't been hers to begin with.

Sick, Emma turned her back on Missy and closed her eyes. *Her father had paid for her education.*

"Dr. Sinclair? You okay?"

Emma drew a deep breath. He'd never once asked for a thank you, or thrown it in her face, or even so much as mentioned it.

In return, what had she done?

She'd griped about being here, thrown it in *his* face at every turn, and had mentioned, oh a million or so times, how much she wanted to get back to her own life.

She'd thought Serena was the bitch. Ha! Serena had nothing on her.

"Dr. Sinclair?"

Emma closed her eyes. *Dr. Sinclair.* All those weeks she'd been wanting a sign of respect, some sort of verification that the people in Wishful knew how important she was, and she'd just gotten it.

Yet it was *she* who owed the respect. "I'm okay, yes."

"I debated about telling you the truth."

"Why did you?"

"For him. So that before you leave you know what kind of a man he is."

"You know I'm leaving?"

"When will you learn? I know everything."

Emma could do nothing but laugh. After she gave Missy the dish, they walked out to the reception area together, where Missy pulled out her checkbook and asked for a pen. "For my last two visits. I know how you like your money."

Emma gently pushed the woman's checkbook away and offered a smile she hadn't known she had. "I'd rather have another Thai dish if you don't mind."

Later Emma walked upstairs, took a good long look at her mom's picture on the mantel and sighed. "You should have told me."

What does it matter where the money came from?

"It matters to me." She knew it mattered to her father as well—oh not that he'd given the money to her, but that she'd followed in his footsteps. That she'd become a doctor like him. "You should have told me," she said again to Sandy's face, and then lifted her gaze to the mirror and looked at her own reflection. She had one foot out the door now, the freedom in sight.

For the first time, she hesitated. She'd come for her father. This is what she'd been telling herself for two and a half months now. She was in Wishful for him.

Except she'd just realized that it wasn't one hundred percent true.

She'd also come here for herself. For her lonely restlessness. For the part of her that said she was missing something. Someone.

She thought maybe she'd found it, found him.

Chapter 23

Emma and her dad met at the clinic that afternoon. They went over the offers on the place, and picked the one they planned on accepting. It'd been made by a South Shore investor who owned fifteen other properties in the area. He was well-known and respected, the numbers were fantastic, and it was an easy decision to sign on the dotted line.

Relatively speaking.

Spence was giving her father a check up before Spence left for the airport so that Emma would feel better about following in a few days.

Or as okay as she could manage.

In the meantime, she was updating the records while keeping one eye on the examination door, and thinking of a certain expedition guide with a certain amazing mouth and who knew how to use it—a guy who was taking her out tonight.

On a training session to relax.

The front door opened and the cowbells jangled together. They no longer drove her crazy, Emma realized as Serena walked in with a black and white bag. "My specialty good-bye chocolates. For the doctor."

"Wow, thanks." Emma reached for them, but Serena held the bag up with a laugh that brought Emma back to first grade so fast her head spun.

"The *other* doctor," Serena said with a sweet smile. "The one I want to have sex with. Not that you're not sexy. If I swung that way, I'd totally do you."

"Um, thanks. I think. Spencer's busy right now."

"No problem, I'll just wait." Serena looked uncharacteristically unsure of herself. "So . . ."

"Is everything okay?"

"Yeah. No." Serena leaned in. "Spencer wouldn't sleep with me this afternoon. I mean we were having a great time. We went out to lunch and talked and laughed for hours. We played with the kittens, which certainly closed the deal for him, but then he took me home."

"Sounds like a nice day."

"Okay, you're not listening. He didn't sleep with me. Is there something wrong with him?"

"Of course not. He's leaving is all. He was being a gentleman."

"Him leaving is what makes it perfect. No ties."

Emma had no business judging anyone, especially when at the moment, Serena's philosophy seemed appealing. Casual sex; no pain or messy emotions . . . seemed better than her way.

"I'm going to try one more time," Serena said, sounding determined as she applied some lip gloss while looking at herself in her own cell phone's camera lens.

"Now?"

"No, tomorrow when he's gone. Yes, now."

"He's with my dad."

"I can wait." She crossed her legs, and picked up a magazine.

Emma tried go to back to the books but her mind wandered

to Stone. And tonight. And whether they'd be having casual sex.

God, she hoped so. "Serena?"

"Yeah?"

"What do people in Wishful do on dates?" Not that it was a date, because it wasn't.

"As everywhere else, City Girl. Whatever you want. With Stone?"

"Yes."

"Well, lucky you. He's a hot one."

Yeah. Yeah, he was. She opened her mouth to say something, she had no idea what, but the examination door opened. Spencer came out, his nose in her father's chart.

Emma moved around the front desk and into the hallway, pulling him with her. "Well?"

"His latest EKG is good. We need to run labs to check liver function and cholesterol levels, but you already know that. He's taking his beta blockers, Plavix and Niacin, and following your strict dietary restrictions. He's also exercising. He reports no chest pain." He smiled. "I see no signs of post infarction syndrome indicating either recurrent MI or heart failure. He's good."

"You see him going back to work?"

"He certainly wants to. He told me he's planning on working here as much as he can."

Relief had her leaning back against the wall. "Okay, then."

"Which means you could fly home with me if you want."

"No." She needed a few more days to help her father close up.

No, that wasn't true.

She needed her night with Stone. "I'll wait until Friday."

He smiled. "Used to be you couldn't wait to get out of here."

"Yeah." She sighed. Now she suddenly wasn't in a hurry. It

didn't take a genius to know why. It did take a genius to understand it. "Are you ready to head out in a few?"

"One thing left to do." He waggled a brow suggestively. His favorite cue for "let's have sex".

"I thought we'd discussed that."

He laughed. "I didn't mean you, Em. We dumped each other, remember? I wanted to say good-bye to Serena is all."

"Well then you're in luck," Serena purred, and with eyes only for Spencer, came close. "How about I drive you to the airport? It'll give us extra good-bye time."

"I don't want you to go to any trouble."

"It isn't." She turned to Emma. "Okay with you?"

"Sure. Thank you."

Like a cat in cream, Serena smiled. "Oh, you are most welcome."

Spencer gave Emma a kiss and a long, hard hug "Friday, babe."

"Friday." She went into the examination room to see her father.

Spencer watched her go, then turned to Serena. "I appreciate this. She had enough on her plate."

"Don't thank me yet."

He laughed. "Should I be scared?"

"If you like." She had a pretty black and white bag from her shop in one hand, and with her other, linked her fingers in his as she led him outside.

Spencer was very aware that she was watching him closely. "Something wrong?"

"Are you going to miss her?"

"I'll see her soon enough. Is that really your question?"

"No. But I'll get to it when I'm ready."

"All right then. So what were you at the clinic for?"

She lifted the black and white bag. "Bringing you a good-bye present."

"I hope it's chocolate."

"Oh, it's better. It's *my* chocolate."

He dug into the bag as they got into her car, then moaned heartily at the fantastic fudge melting on his tongue. "My God." He looked at her in a new light. A fellow foodie . . . "People should bow down to you in the streets."

"Yes, they should." She wore a skirt, longer than the other night, and pencil thin. Her top was white and fitted. She looked professional and untouchable.

And hot. So damn hot. It'd been almost impossible to resist her earlier, especially when she'd made it clear that she wanted to sleep with him, but for some reason he couldn't have explained to save his life, he didn't want to be just another guy she'd had.

"So you like chocolate."

"I like good food."

She was smiling at him, and he could have added that he especially liked her red lips, and was locked on those when she said unexpectedly, "I'm ready to ask you my question now."

"Go for it."

"Are you in love with Emma?"

She waited while he adjusted to the abrupt subject change, her gaze filled with a brutal, open honesty. "That's a pretty personal question," he finally said.

"I know. But it's something I'd like to know before I take you home and pour chocolate all over your body, and then lick it off."

He went from zero to sixty in less than two seconds. "I have a flight."

"Yeah." She looked out the windshield at the stark, blue, cloudless sky. "Not good flying weather. A storm's moving in."

He blinked, but the sky was still cloudless. He looked back

into her steady, heated eyes and felt his blood stir. He didn't
know a man could resist this. Her. "So . . ."

"I'm thinking a delay would be a smart move."

"Are you."

"Actually, it depends on the answer to my question. Because I screwed up love once. I don't do that anymore."

Yeah, she had claws, sharp ones, but she also had heart. And
big eyes. Eyes that weren't nearly as tough as she pretended
to be. "I love Emma," he said quietly. "But I'm not in love
with Emma. Does that count?"

She stared at him, then smiled slowly, warmly, and he stared
at her in return, a little blown away by how just that one smile—
her first real one he'd bet—affected him.

"It counts," she whispered.

He looked at her. She was beautiful, she took his breath
away. He ate another piece of fudge, chewing slowly because
it was so mind-boggling good he couldn't believe it, and because he wasn't sure what was happening. He usually went for
the good girls, the ones who followed the rules and were nice
to others and who didn't challenge him.

Serena was none of that.

He liked it. He liked her, a whole hell of a lot.

"Decision time," she murmured. "Left to the airport, or right."

To her place.

He was a careful man. Methodical and just a bit nerdy. He
knew this. He accepted this. But right now, he had a chance to
be more with a woman who saw something in him that made
him feel like Superman. "Right."

She smiled and pulled up to her shop. They walked into
her bakery, which had a mouthwatering scent and a décor to
match. It was done up like an old-time French café; wrought
iron tables and chairs, pale pink and white stripes on the walls,
which were covered with charming pictures of the French
countryside. It was warm and cozy and elegant.

"I have an apartment in the back," she said. "It's small. My own port in the storm."

"We could go out for dinner, or a movie."

She looked surprised. "You're not interested in the whole licking the chocolate off our bodies thing?"

"A dinner offer isn't a rejection. It's like the opposite of a rejection. You know that, right? It's my way of offering you respect and companionship."

She just looked at him. "You're unusual. You look like a hot guy, but on the inside you're sort of . . ."

"A nerd."

"Yes."

"True. But trust me. Nerds? They always get their way and win the girl in the end."

"You're going to win the girl, Spencer."

"Good." He took her hand. "So how about I cook dinner?"

"You cook?"

"Oh, sweetheart." He grinned. "Listen, we started with your most excellent dessert, but let's finish with my main course."

"And you don't mean sex?"

"First things first."

She stared at him for the longest moment. "I can't figure you out."

"Being figured out never works out for me."

She stared at him some more, then smiled. "Well, then. To a night of surprises. For both of us."

Emma and her father looked at each other over his chart. He was still sitting on the examination table, looking deceptively healthy. His hair was crazy wild but he had a nice tan and an easy smile. Spence says you're doing good," she said.

"I told you."

"I wanted to be sure."

"That's the doctor in you." He patted her knee. "I love that you're a doctor. I'm so proud of you, Emma. Have I ever told you that?"

The words slid down like warm milk and honey. "No."

"I am. Very proud, and very happy that we ended up doing the same thing with our lives."

If he'd said that even a month ago, she'd have denied that they were doing the same thing with their lives. After all, she'd been in an ER saving multiple lives every single day, and he'd been here in a small town of several thousand, treating rashes and sprained ankles.

She'd have been wrong.

So wrong.

What her father did was just as important as what she did. More so. Because in New York, she was a dime a dozen. If she couldn't show up for work, there was an entire staff to pick from of others exactly like her.

Just that easily, she'd be replaced.

But here in Wishful, her father was the only one. Irreplaceable.

"You feel good about the sale?" he said.

"It's not about me."

"I'm asking what you think."

He'd never asked her what she thought before she'd come here to Wishful, but he was asking now.

As she knew all too well, now was all that mattered. "I think it's a good offer," she said carefully. "And the easiest route to take."

He took a deep breath and nodded. "Easier because you won't feel responsible for me or this place, if something else happens?"

He meant if he had another heart attack. The thought made her gut clench and put a lump in her throat. That they'd had a tough time in the past finding a relationship didn't matter. Not when he was all she had left. "It's not about that. It's not about me at all. It's about you and your health and being happy."

"I've always been happy here, always."

The lump in her throat expanded. He'd paid for her college. He'd tried to see her. Wanted her. She couldn't keep quiet. "Dad." She shook her head. "You paid for my college education. You gave up your savings, your retirement fund. You were there for me, and I never knew it. I feel so selfish, so regretful that I—" To her surprise and horror, her voice cracked. "That we—"

"Hey. Hey . . ." Reaching out, he put his hand over hers. "Listen to me. A dad visits his kid. A dad gives his kid a leg up when they want to go to college. Both of those things were my job, and it's the least of what I should have done. In any case, it's all in the past."

"Yes, but Mom—"

"Did the best she could."

She stared at him, grateful beyond words that he wasn't asking her to make a choice between him and her mom's memory. More than that, he didn't want her to. She'd grossly underestimated him, and that was her own shame, but like him, she wouldn't look back.

But she could fix the now.

And the future. "I'm actually going to miss this place."

He looked up, startled. Hopeful. "You are?"

"Dad," she started regretfully, and he squeezed her hand.

"It's okay, Emma. It's all going to be okay."

But it wasn't. She was leaving, and she didn't know what that would mean for them. Would they go back to being polite strangers?

Would he really be okay without his clinic?

Suddenly she didn't think so, and she started to say something but he rose to his feet, a little slow to straighten. He creaked and groaned, then shot her another little smile. "Getting old isn't what it's cracked up to be. I don't recommend it."

He was giving her a moment, letting her skip over the big elephant in the room. But if she'd learned one thing from being here, from Stone actually, it was that sweeping emotions under the carpet never worked. We both know I wasn't exactly in my element here, that I never planned to stay."

"Yes." A wry smile twisted his lips. "You've mentioned a time or two."

"Or a thousand." She sighed at herself. "I planned to hate every single day and be resentful while I was at it."

"Which seemed to work for you for a while."

She had to smile. "I know. I really did pull that off for a good long time, didn't I?"

He cocked his head. "Is that a past tense I hear?"

She paused. "I don't know," she admitted. "I don't fit . . ."

"You look like you fit to me." He looked her over. "You're not nearly as pale as when you first got here, which means you're not all work and no play anymore. You sure as hell aren't as edgy and in such a hurry as you were, which means you've learned to let your hair down." He smiled. "I'd say you fit in just fine."

"Let's just say that this place and I have come to an agreement. Of sorts."

"Which is?"

"I stopped taking myself so seriously, and it stopped mocking me. People don't care where I got my degree, or that I run an ER, or even what my specialty is. They care that I open the Urgent Care at eight sharp, that I'm flexible when it comes to payment . . ." She shot him a long look that had him choking out a laugh and scratching his head with a wry/guilty expression. "But mostly, they care about you, Dad. And they care about each other." She shook her head. "It's truly the oddest place I've ever been, and honestly?"

He grinned. "You will. You'll miss it."

"Yeah. And you. I'll miss you."

"Same goes, Emma. Same goes." He cleared his rough throat. "I have something for you." He pulled a small gift bag from a pocket of his jacket.

"What's that for?"

"A good-bye present."

Her gaze flew to his. "I don't need a going away present."

"It's not a going-away present. It's a *good-bye* present. There's a difference."

There sure as hell was. "I'm not pulling a mom here, Dad. I'll come back. I already figured out the weekends over the next six months where I could grab three days in a row. There's at least one every other month."

"Look at you, with all your careful plans." He smiled. "I've made my own careful plans."

"You don't know the meaning of the word," she teased joking around the ball of emotion in her throat.

"I didn't, no. But you're not the only one who could block out dates." He reached into a different pocket and pulled out a small calendar, flipping through it, revealing several highlighted weeks. "I'm going to try to work two to three days a week. Here's the weekends I can get to you. We won't be strangers again. Now open the bag."

He'd sent gifts over the years. Sometimes a medical book, sometimes a piece of jewelry. She'd liked everything while secretly wishing for his presence instead. She opened the gift bag and pulled out a T-shirt, which read: I SURVIVED THE SIERRAS.

She stared at it for a moment, and then looked at him. There was a sparkle in his eyes as his mouth slowly curved, and she laughed.

Laughed with her father.

And in that moment, she felt a new inner peace. She could leave, it was going to be okay. He was going to be okay.

The question was, was she?

That night, Stone knocked on Emma's door, feeling both anticipatory and a little off his game knowing this was, in all likelihood, their last night.

She opened the door looking a little unsettled herself.

"Hey," he said.

"Hey. I didn't know what to wear for our . . . training session."

Ah, yes. Not a date. A *training session*. Interesting that she felt the need to play word games with herself to keep from jumping in with both feet.

As for the attire, she'd settled on a simple white t-shirt, denim shorts and sandals. She looked good enough to eat, and his evening, spent on paperwork, was most definitely beginning to look up. "You're a sight for sore eyes, Emma."

"I didn't know I'd feel this way, but right back at ya."

Doc had stopped off to see Stone earlier, so he knew father and daughter had spent some time together. There'd only been one thing Doc hadn't wanted to do—sell—and yet in spite of doing it anyway, he'd seemed in relatively good spirits, which meant the visit had gone well.

It meant something else, too, something he'd already figured out—that though Emma was adept at hiding her soft side, it was there.

Too bad they didn't have more time to explore it, and not for the first time he wished he'd found a way to help Doc convince Emma not to sell. "Were you busy today?"

"A case of chicken pox and a well-baby check," she said. "Oh, and Missy Thorton letting me know that my dad paid for my entire education. Yeah, that's all."

He lifted a brow. "I take it that was news to you."

"Uh, yeah. Big news." She blew out a breath. "Listen, I really need to get out of here for a while."

"I have just the thing. I asked you once before and you said hell no, but let me ask again." He held out his hand. "Trust me?"

Chapter 24

Did she trust him? Emma stared up at Stone.

Hell, no, came her mom's voice. *Don't trust any man that good looking with those wicked badboy eyes and the smile that promised all sorts of naughtiness. Say no and get the hell out of Dodge, darling.*

Emma had always listened to her mom, always.

But she'd also always followed her gut, and her gut happened to have the louder voice. It was saying that her mom had always acted out of love but that she hadn't always been right. It was saying that Emma had to decide for herself what was right.

But mostly, it was saying you aren't done with this man.

"Emma?"

"Yes. I don't trust me, but oddly enough, I trust you."

With a smile, he took her hand and pulled her outside. "You should know, I'm grumpy," she said.

"Shock," he said.

"And irritated."

"More shock."

That tugged a laugh out of her. "And I don't think anything

about us being alone together is a good idea, much less being naked."

He slid her a speculative look. "No one said anything about being naked except you. And you keep saying it." He flashed one of his slow, killer smiles. "You're going to miss me."

"You think so?"

"Oh, yeah."

Oh yeah was right. She was going to miss him. So damn much it hurt to think about, so she'd managed not to think at all for the most part. "Did you bring me the instructions you promised?"

"Worked all afternoon on it," he said, and gestured for her to get into the Jeep.

"Isn't this TJ's vehicle?"

"Yep. He has my truck." The top was off, but the evening was warm enough. She got in and let the light wind roll over her as he took off. "Where's my instructions on relaxing?"

"Coming."

But he just kept driving.

Just outside of town, on the narrow two-lane highway cutting up through two majestic mountain peaks, he finally handed her a folded up piece of paper.

She unfolded it. He'd written only one line:

Close your eyes.

"Sort of self explanatory," he said when she just stared at him.

Fine. She closed her eyes.

"How do you feel?" he asked.

"Silly."

"That's because you don't like to follow directions, you like to make them."

True enough.

"What else do you feel?"

"Dizzy. The road is curvy."

"You can get car sick if you need to, it's TJ's Jeep."

She laughed, and heard the smile in his voice when he said, "What else, Emma?"

"Well . . ." Sometimes after a day off from her ER, she'd come back and stand in the middle of the place and close her eyes, just breathing it all in. The rush of rubber soled shoes, the sounds of the equipment beeping, the scent of antiseptic and rubbing alcohol . . . It'd always been nirvana to her.

It couldn't be more different here. She could feel the warmth from the remnants of the setting sun on her face. She could hear the whistle of the wind, the screech of a bird, the hum of the Jeep's engine. She could smell the fresh dirt, the pine trees. "The air up here always makes me think of Christmas."

"Yeah, that's the thing I miss the most when I leave here, and the first thing I notice when I come back," he said, and turned down a dirt road, shifting into four-wheel drive, taking her up a trail she wasn't sure she'd even be able to hike.

She opened her eyes again. The Jeep rocked from side to side, and on the next turn, she'd have sworn two of the wheels left the ground. It wasn't what she'd expected, the whole four-wheeling thing, but in truth, she'd never been, never even thought about it, had only seen pictures in a magazine, or the occasional story on TV, but the reality was . . .

Bigger.

The Jeep was versatile and tough, taking the roads with ease. Or maybe that was Stone himself. He handled the wheel as if he'd been born with it. She watched his big hands, one on the wheel, one on the stick shift, not white knuckled like she was, but handling the job while remaining cool, calm and collected.

In easy control, as she would be in the ER.

Yet unlike how she'd be at work, he was also relaxed. Laid-back.

All the things she wanted to learn to be. "What's next?"

He handed her another little piece of paper, which she un-folded.

Be patient.

Ha. "If I knew how to be patient," she said, "we wouldn't be doing this."

"Wouldn't we?"

She met his gaze, his clear and green, and so direct it was hard to take. He allowed her to see his affection, his need for her, the heat, and she found herself swallowing hard. "I meant, I wouldn't be here in Wishful. I'd have hired someone for my dad instead of coming to help him out."

"Would you have? Really?"

She blew out a breath. "No."

He smiled and reached for her hand. "Hi."

"Hi?"

"Hi to the *real* Emma. Now stop thinking so hard and look around."

She didn't want to, because she instinctively knew that she was vulnerable to him, but she did as he asked and looked around. They were surrounded by woods, deep, dense, over-grown woods, and she could see nothing but pine and Man-zanita bush and—

And suddenly, with one last turn, it all fell away and they were on the edge of a cliff.

Looking down. And down. And down . . .

It was staggering. Heart-stopping. She'd never in her life seen anything like it.

"The Tahoe Rim Trail," he said quietly, turning off the engine so that the air was filled with nothing but a bird's cry, the hum of unseen insects, the light brush of a breeze.

He hopped out of the Jeep and she followed him, walking to the edge of the drop-off, where hundreds of feet below, she could see the huge expanse of Lake Tahoe, spread out like some magnificent feast for her eyes.

"This way." He led her along a very narrow trail that had her huffing and puffing in two minutes flat while his breathing remained perfectly steady.

"I could have relaxed easier at a spa," she said, huffing like a freight train.

"Consider this the Wilder spa, and you've booked the Stone Special."

She gasped for breath for another few hundred feet. "I think I'm dying."

"It's the altitude." He opened his backpack and pulled out a water.

"You came prepared."

"Don't look surprised. It's my job."

It was, she realized, not just to have a good time, but to be ready for anything. Like her job, his required him to have whatever they'd need. She might have just gotten in the Jeep without thinking much about their plans, but he'd put thought into it, as he did into every trip he made because it was up to him to be in charge.

It was odd to think of his work that way, to compare it to hers, even in broad scope. But it reminded her that when she'd first come here, she'd seen him as a mountain bum. How perceptions change. She couldn't help but wonder, had his perception of her changed too?

He pulled a third piece of paper from his pack and handed it to her:

Stop over-thinking.

"You think you know me pretty well, don't you?"
Smiling, he handed her another.

Go with your gut instincts.

He'd kept walking while she read that last one. She eyed him just ahead of her, moving along with an easy confidence that was so sexy he made her mouth dry. His shirt was stretching the limits at the shoulders, playing over the muscles of his back, half tucked into his Levi's, which were all in themselves a gift to her eyes. The jeans were loose and low on his hips, nicely taut across his extremely fit butt, and emphasized his long, powerful legs. "Go with my gut instincts on what?"

He kept walking.

With a huff, she shoved the notes in her pocket, downed some water, and followed. "Are there people up here?"

"Not on this trail, it's hard to find."

"I think TJ could probably find it."

Stone flashed her a grin over his shoulder. "He's in Desolation Wilderness on a group trek."

"Ah. A great date trail, then."

"You're the first woman I've brought up here."

She stared at his back in surprise, and then tripped over her own feet.

"Careful. I have an in with the doctor, but she wields needles and knows how to use them." When he stopped, she nearly plowed into the back of him. He shifted to the side and she saw that they were in a sort of rock alcove, once again looking down at the Tahoe Rim Trail but from a far more private, secluded spot.

"My God," she whispered, feeling like they were on top of the world. "It's the most beautiful thing I've ever seen."

"Agreed," he said quietly at her side, but when she turned to him, he was looking right at her.

"Stop." She ran a hand over her hair. "I'm dusty and hot and icky."

He smiled and grabbed her hand. "You can be the boss of your world all you want, Dr. Emma, but even you can't tell me how to think."

"I'm merely questioning your eyesight."

"Twenty-twenty."

"Ah." She sipped some water. "Then you're warming me up, thinking you're going to get lucky up here in the middle of nowhere. Luckier than the last time you had me in the wilderness."

He looked at her and slowly arched a brow. "You have it all figured out then?"

"Yeah. But let me assure you it's not happening. My mind would be on all the bugs, and where they could crawl into, and you wouldn't get very far with me."

"Trust me, your mind wouldn't be on the bugs."

While her knees wobbled over the inevitable truth of that statement, he slid an arm around her. "I realize you like to be in charge, Emma. Always in control. But you're supposed to be working on that. That's what we're doing here. Relaxing. Letting go."

Right. Per the written instructions, she closed her eyes and actually *heard* him smile.

"You reaching for some patience?" he murmured.

"I am. And it would help if you could possibly shut it while I do so."

She heard his low laugh, then felt him step into her. "Bossy," he whispered. "Pissy, stubborn as hell, and . . ."

"And what? Annoying?"

"Well . . ."

"Always right?"

"I wouldn't go that far."

She snorted out an unexpected laugh and opened her eyes, catching a new light as it came into his, more than simple affection, more than casual fun. "Stone."

"You're beautiful, Emma." He slid a hand around the back of her neck, stroking her jaw with his thumb. "Made all the more so because you don't even know it."

Things were happening inside her—besides just the physical response of his touch. She was softening, unveiling the real Emma, without her protective walls. It brought an edge to her arousal, and an odd sort of panic. "I don't need pretty words."

"No? Maybe I do." A callused fingertip ran over her cheek, skimmed her ear.

She shivered. Pretty words, amazing touch . . . she was a goner. "Seriously, Stone."

He was looking at her as if she was so important. And also as if he was amused. "I'm afraid of needles, Emma, which is ridiculous enough, but look at you. You're afraid of niceness."

"Am not."

He let her have the lie, moving onto a devastatingly tender, gentle sexiness she had no defense against. "You have the most amazing eyes," he whispered.

Oh, God.

"Yeah, and a smile that always puts one on my mouth as well, and a way of looking at me that weeds through all the bullshit and sees the real me. You make me laugh, you make me think. You turn me on, Emma, in every way." As proven when he settled his hands on her hips and pulled her into him so that she could feel him, fully aroused. "You are truly the most beautiful woman I've ever had the pleasure of kissing." He kissed her then, and God his mouth. He made a sound deep in his throat and turned deeper into the kiss.

He had a way of making her feel like there was nothing but

her, but them, and by the time he pulled back slightly, she wasn't worried about bugs, but how fast she could get her clothes off.

Which was bad. Very, very bad. Her knees were liquid, her body revved for action.

"Your eyes are closed, what's next?" he asked.

"Be patient."

"And . . ."

"Don't over-think it. Go with your instincts," she repeated obediently. "But my instincts . . ."

"What are they telling you?"

To strip naked. "Nothing."

"Liar," he chided gently, looking at her from sexy, heavy-lidded eyes, his mouth still wet from hers, his hands—

God, his hands.

They were spread wide on her ribs, his fingertips almost brushing the undersides of her breasts.

"I blame the kissing," she decided, her voice a little shaky.

"For . . . ?"

"For me losing my head. Look, you need to back way up."

He merely smiled and pulled her closer in, and somehow her brain got mixed signals from her body and went with the flow, which wasn't good. Not good at all. She was going to miss him, miss him so damn much, and that thought wasn't comforting. She'd miss his humor, his voice, how he made her laugh, the way he looked at her, everything. "Stone."

"Emma," he said sweetly.

As if he was sweet! "Okay." She fisted her hands in his hair. "You know what? Fine. Have it your way. I'm going with my instincts."

"I like the sound of that. What are they saying?"

"They're saying we should have sex right here, right now." She smacked a hand to his chest when his eyes flashed with triumph. "But you should know, we are not cuddling after-wards. Not this time. Not—" She'd been about to say ever, because she was leaving, and cuddling with him messed with her head big time, but he smiled soberly, whispered, "Shh," and kissed her again.

Chapter 25

Ah, yeah, Stone thought. This. This is what he'd wanted, Emma melting in his arms, her tongue down his throat. Leaning back against the rock, he pulled her with him.

"You should know," she murmured against his mouth, hands still fisted in his hair, wrapped around him like a pretzel. "This is just instincts talking. Not my heart."

"Okay," he said, hoping like hell that was just her trying to convince herself.

Behind them, the thick growth of pines protected them from the breeze. In front was nothing but a staggering view of Lake Tahoe and a three hundred and sixty degree view of majestic, rugged, isolated peaks.

A fact that Stone was most grateful for, especially the isolated part. He nudged Emma down onto their rock alcove, stroked a strand of hair from her face, tucking it behind her ear and pulled her neatly tucked in shirt from her pants.

"Really?" She blinked up at him, clearly surprised. "So you believe me? That this is just sex?"

"Hell, no." He shook his head with a low laugh. "It's not even close. But I didn't want to argue with you until I got you naked again."

She choked out a laugh. "Stone."

"Now see, I know that tone. It says that if I let you finish that sentence, we're not going to get naked." He gently kissed one corner of her mouth as he unbuttoned her top, then the other corner as he slid it off her shoulder.

She cupped his face between her hands until he looked into her eyes. "You know that I'm as good as gone. Tell me you know that."

"Today?"

"No."

"Then shh."

In response, she nipped his lower lip with her teeth, and when he hissed out a pained breath, she soothed the ache by sucking it into her mouth, running her hot tongue over it as she shoved up his shirt.

He was goners. He slid his hands down the back of her pants, loving how she felt in his hands, loving how when he slid his fingers even lower, he found her hot and wet, for him. "Just sex, my ass," he murmured in her ear.

"Speak for yourself," she panted, tugging his shirt over his head.

Then she stopped his heart when she spread her legs a little to give him more access.

"It has to be just sex, because . . ." She stopped to moan as he stroked his thumb over her. "Because I'm leaving in two days. That's all we have."

With a sigh, he pulled his hands free of her and met her gaze, somehow managing to speak evenly. "So you're not even so much as looking back?"

It was a tricky question, one that could have stopped the proceedings cold, but it didn't. At least not *her* proceedings. She pressed her mouth to a pec and just breathed him in for a moment. "I'll look back plenty." She ran her hand up his abs.

"You should know, I'm planning on taking something with me. A piece of you."

"What?"

"Yeah." She ran her mouth over his chest, a soft, light, erotic caress. "Your spirit. Your sense of adventure. Your loyalty."

Unbearably touched, he slid his hands into her hair and lifted her face to his. "Emma."

"You give yourself, Stone, to everyone you meet. Hell, you'd give a perfect stranger the shirt off your back. I've seen you do it."

"You give yourself, too."

"No. No, I don't. My time, yeah, but that's my job. Outside the hospital . . ." Her mouth glided over one of his nipples, and he quivered. "Outside the hospital," she whispered against his flesh. "I'm closed off. I don't give myself to my stepfather, never have. I don't give myself to Spencer, much as I say I do. I don't give myself to my friends. And I didn't give myself to you." She lifted her head. "Until it was almost too late."

He could scarcely breathe. "What changed?"

"You. You offering your heart and soul to everything you do. It changed me. You changed me."

He stared at her, heart pounding as he realized the truth in that. He'd given her his heart. His soul. He opened his mouth to tell her that, but she kissed him, long and deep and warm, and he lost himself in her. Still goners, he let her unzip his jeans while his hands slid up her belly to her breasts, which knocked a gasp out of her, and a groan from him.

She was warm and full and perfect.

Beneath his palms, her nipples were already hard, and he rasped his thumbs over them, feeling them pucker even more. Not enough. He flicked open her bra and tugged the straps down her arms, sucking in a breath at the sight of her. Lowering his head, splaying his hands on her bare back to pull her even closer, and opened his mouth on her.

"If I get bit by a mosquito," she gasped, "I'm coming after you."

"Come after me."

She huffed out a laugh as she tugged open his pants. Making herself at home inside of them, she wrapped her fingers around him, stroking . . . squealing—which was very ego-boosting, until he realized the squeal was for the bee that buzzed by them.

"*Did you bring bug spray?*"

"You'll be okay," he promised.

"How do you know?"

He rasped his thumbs over her bared nipples. "I'll keep you covered."

"I'm pretty uncovered, Stone."

He spread out his shirt on the rock behind him, lay her on it, and then towered over her, his gaze sweeping down the length of her gorgeous body as he pulled a condom from his pocket.

"Always prepared," she murmured. "Like a Boy Scout."

"Not quite." He slid down her body, spreading open-mouthed kisses as he went, loving the taste of her, the scent of her, the way she arched and writhed beneath his touch. He could feel her heart pounding in excitement, in arousal and need, and his own matched it, beating in tune to hers.

Just sex? Hell, no.

But he could admit he understood why she wanted to believe it. That she was leaving certainly played into it some, though actually that worked in her favor.

It gave her permission to try to keep her heart out of this.

Good luck, he thought, because his heart hadn't had any such luck at all. He knew it. He accepted it.

Just as he accepted that this scared the living shit right out of her. This connection, this bond.

She didn't do connections or bonds, at least not effectively.

It wasn't all her fault. She hadn't had the best of luck keeping people in her life. They didn't tend to stick.

But he did. He was good at it, too. Good at a couple of things, he thought, kissing her belly, her ribs as she inhaled sharply, going tense beneath him, quivering with anticipation. Beneath his mouth, her skin was heating up, flushing with arousal. His fingers wrapped around her ankle, bending her knee, placing her foot on the rock so that she was open for him.

Oh, yeah. She wanted him. He let his thumb glide over her creamy heat and she shivered.

"Such a bad idea," she murmured, even as she rocked up to meet his touch.

"Bad is relative."

"Yes, but I'm here to learn to be laid-back and chill." She came up on her elbow and jabbed a pointy finger toward him. "All you ever do is rev me up."

"Sometimes, you have to rev up first."

"You just made that up."

"Nope."

"Seriously, you just pulled that right out of your ass."

He laughed and shook his head. "Pay attention. The instructions. You have to repeat them to make them stick. Do you remember them?"

"I'm not an idiot."

"Then close your eyes."

She was looking up at him with a mix of heat and irritation and affection. She hadn't looked away, not once, and that was so damn attractive. She was a woman who wasn't coy, a woman who might take a hell of a long time—weeks, thank you very much—to decide to give him a shot, but once she made up her mind, she was on board. Need and yearning and lust swirled in his gut at that, and then she smiled at him and stopped his heart.

Stopped it on a dime. "Emma."

She sighed, rolled her eyes, and then obediently closed them, her face still tilted up to his in a trusting manner that reminded him that this was about far more than hormones and lust. "You are so damn beautiful," he murmured, taking in her creamy skin, her mouth, including that full bottom lip he wanted to nibble on for his next meal. "What comes next?"

"Be patient."

"Yeah." Leaning in, he kissed her temple, her jaw. Brushing the tip of his nose along her cheek, he kissed the sweet spot beneath her ear, and absorbing her shiver, gently sank his teeth into her earlobe.

She drew in a quick breath, and shivered again as her fingers closed around his biceps. "Stone . . ."

Cupping her face, he kissed her. Kissed her until he couldn't have come up with his own name if his life depended on it.

She opened her sleep, sexy eyes. "Go with my instincts," she whispered.

It took him a moment to realize she was quoting the third rule. "Yeah." His voice was husky and a little thick. He didn't know exactly what her instincts would be, but he sincerely hoped it didn't include pulling her clothes back on.

She surprised and shocked him by pulling him down on top of her, rolling so that he was lying flat on his back on the rock and she was straddling him. Wrapping her fingers around him she lifted her hips. Then, slowly—so slowly she almost killed him—she sank over the top of him, threatening to blow his mind *and* his wad as he entered her, and he gripped her hips in desperation when she rocked against him. "Wait," he gasped. *God.* "Don't move." He was a fraction of a second from coming. "Christ, Em, don't move or I'll—"

The woman never listened. She moved. She rocked her hips again just as she sucked his lower lip into her mouth, and that was it for him. He thrust up into her, and then again, until with a panting cry, she came, and he was right there with her.

The next morning, Spencer stepped into Wishful Delights from Serena's living quarters.

Serena was behind the counter, her back to him, stirring something in a large bowl, and his mouth watered.

For the woman, not the chocolate, though he happened to know that she made the most amazing chocolate, as he'd spent some time last night licking it off her body. As he'd already known, she was truly the hottest, sexiest woman he'd ever met. What he hadn't expected . . . she was also the sweetest, warmest woman he'd ever met. "Hey."

"Hey yourself." She looked at him, and the duffle bag hanging off his shoulder. "I was thinking the weather was going to be really bad again today."

"I have to get back, Serena."

She nodded. "Well, I guess all fun has to come to an end some time, right?"

"Yeah." He set the bag down and moved toward her. "I was hoping you could take a little break before I go."

"I could, but you should know, I only take breaks for orgasms."

He laughed, then pulled her out from behind the counter and flipped the OPEN sign to CLOSED.

She laughed. "Aw, now you're just teasing me—"

He put his hands on her face and kissed her. Kissed her until he didn't know his own damn name, until she was clinging to him, panting for breath, until it took everything he had to pull free and reach into his pocket for the envelope he'd put there.

"What's this?" she whispered, still breathing heavy.

"I called a cab."

Her eyes flew up to his. "So that was a good-bye kiss?"

"I hope not." He kissed her again, softer this time. "More than anything I can think of, I'd like this not to be a good-bye. Come see me in New York, Serena. We'll go to amazing restaurants and moan over food together."

"Come to New York?" She sputtered over that for a moment. "Are you crazy?"

"Uh huh. And you are too. You're bored here. Take a vacation, come visit me."

She looked at him as if trying to find the catch. "And then what?"

"And then I'll come visit you. We'll take turns."

"That sounds so . . . civilized."

"It won't be, trust me."

She didn't laugh. She stood there, stunned. "It was just one night."

"Yes. One really great night."

She softened. "Yeah."

"We could have a lot more."

She just looked at him, beautiful and gorgeous.

"Tell you what." He leaned in for another kiss. His last, he promised himself. "When you're ready, you open this." He pressed the envelope in her hands and took one last long look at her. "Good-bye, Serena."

She lifted her face from the envelope she held between tight fingers. "This isn't a Dear John letter?"

"Of course not."

"Good. Because *I* do the dumping."

He smiled, his heart panging at the look of bewilderment on her face. "Would you like to dump me before I go? Would that make you feel better?"

Her eyes got suspiciously bright at that. "Shut up, Spence."

He gently tugged on a strand of her hair, and smiled. Though it was the hardest thing he'd ever done, he turned around and walked away.

Emma woke up entangled in Stone's warm, strong arms. Not a bad way to wake up. They'd gotten back to her place late last night and had somehow ended up in her shower.

Together.

And then in her bed.

Also together.

He was still out cold, sleeping deeply, and she leaned in, pressing her nose to his throat, inhaling deeply before pulling back to stare at his face. He had the longest lashes she'd ever seen on a man, thick and inky black. His jaw was rough with a few days growth of stubble. She remembered wondering how it would feel on her skin, and now she knew.

Amazing.

She'd always tended to sleep alone, and she honestly couldn't remember the last time she'd woken up with a man. She'd been missing out because there was definitely something about waking up like this, so close she could feel the slow and steady beat of his heart against hers. If she'd been the canoodling kind, she might have been tempted to snuggle in even deeper.

Even as she thought it, his arms tightened on her. In his sleep, he let out a shuddery sigh, burying his face in her hair as he relaxed.

She was leaving. He'd come visit her. She knew this. But she also knew he'd hate it in her world. She had no idea where that thought came from but suddenly it was front and center.

Her world.

She hadn't thought about it in awhile . . . yet she was going back to it, tomorrow.

A knock came from the front door. With a last look at the gorgeous man in her bed, she slipped free, threw on sweats and made her way to the door. Serena stood on the top step in her black and white, sunglasses on, nose in the air as usual. "Serena." Emma ran a hand over what was undoubtedly a very bad hair day. "You get Spencer off?"

Serena blinked, for a minute looking . . . guilty. "What?"

"You get him to the airport okay?"

"Oh! Right . . ." She flashed a smile. "Yes. He . . . appreciated the ride."

"Good." She looked and sounded like the same old Serena; gorgeous and sharp, but something was off. Emma pulled the sunglasses off Serena and looked into her eyes, and then nearly staggered a step backwards at the emotion blaring there. "What's wrong?"

Serena shook her head and turned away.

"If this isn't a business call, I'm going back to bed."

"Okay, fine, if you're going to browbeat me about it." Serena turned back to Emma, who raised a brow. "He asked me to New York, and of course he's crazy, but I just wanted you to know I'm . . . thinking about it."

"Spence?"

"No, the postman. Yes, Spence! Keep up. Jesus."

"Spence asked you to New York."

"Yeah." Serena thrust a bag into Emma's hands. "The best croissants on this side of the Divide."

"Is this a bribe of some kind?"

"Yes. Yes, it is."

"If I said I was fine with you and Spence, that I've always been fine with you and Spence, can I still keep the croissants?"

Serena's face filled with relief. "So we're good? I can still be my mean old self, and you'll still be your stick-up-your-ass self? We'll co-exist?"

Emma took a bite of a croissant rather than dwell on the

stick-up-her-ass comment, and nearly died and went to heaven. "We're good, Serena. For better or worse."

As Serena drove off, a set of arms surrounded Emma from behind, pulling her back against a hard, warm chest.

She turned in the circle of Stone's arms and faced him.

"I'm glad," he murmured, his voice morning gruff and bringing tingles to her erotic zones, of which she had far more than she remembered.

"About?"

"That you're okay with her and Spencer knocking boots."

She just soaked up his warmth and breathed him in. How terrifying was it that she could do this every morning and not get tired of it?

"Our last day," he whispered, his hands all over her. "Right?"

"Yes." She was leaving tomorrow, come hell or high water. She waited, expecting him to say something or maybe to try to talk her out of going. Instead, he pulled her back inside, kicked the door closed and pressed her back against it, holding her hands in his, pulling them high above her head as he kissed her blind. God, his mouth. And those hot, demanding kisses—

"Love it when you hum like that," he murmured, his lips against hers. "I came when you made that sound last night, did you know that?"

She smiled and rocked against his most impressive morning erection. "Should we go back to bed?"

"Not going to make it that far."

"No?"

"No."

"Here then?" she asked breathlessly.

"Yeah. Oh, yeah." He let out a rough sound of pleasure when she rocked again. Gripping her hips, he swiveled his head around to eye the small desk where she'd been tossing her purse and keys whenever she walked in. Twisting them both around, he set her on top of it and slipped his hands up her top to cup her braless breasts.

"Stone." Her need level ramped up a notch. "I don't think it'll hold."

"It'll hold." With another rough sound, he easily and efficiently stripped her out of the sweats she'd so hurriedly slipped into.

She was amused at his hurry, and turned-on beyond belief. He produced a condom, and in the next minute, his sweats were down, her legs wrapped around his waist, and all her amusement fled, replaced by a desperate hunger. He slipped his fingers between her thighs and let out a heartfelt groan that she was already wet for him "Hold onto me. Yeah, like that—"

He switched his fingers for something better, bigger, harder, and when he pushed into her, he groaned, dropping his forehead to hers. "Oh, God, yeah. That's just what I needed. You."

She swallowed hard against the ball of emotion suddenly in her throat, because wasn't that the truth. All her anxiety, her rush, her need to be so driven, it all came down to what she needed, and she knew what that was now.

This.

Him.

Chapter 26

Emma spent the morning sitting at the bank with her father. They were officially in escrow, and because the buyer had requested an expedited seven day escrow, the Urgent Care was going to be closed for the week so that some work could be done on the place to the new owners' specs.

Emma would have loved to see what that work would entail, but she was going home.

Home.

It'd been all she wanted for the past few months, yet suddenly the word had taken on a new location.

The building she'd just sold. She looked at her father as they walked out of the bank together. He took one glance at her face and reached over and patted her hand.

Reassuring her.

Her heart tightened.

"Here," her father said, and steered her into Wishful Delights. "We need a sugar fix," he announced to Serena. "Cookies, cakes, pies . . . whatever you've got."

Serena brought out a tray of to-die-for brownies and slapped it on the counter. "Have at it."

Emma frowned at the pastry chef. "Something wrong?"

"I'm overworked, under-appreciated, and I need a damn vacation."

"I'm sorry if you're overworked," Doc said very gently. "But if it helps, these are the best brownies I've ever had."

"Thanks." Serena leaned against the counter, propping up her head with a fist. "I hear you sold. Think your investors would be interested in this building too?"

"You selling?" Emma asked in surprise.

"Thinking of it."

It was so unlike her that Emma reached out to put her fingers on Serena's wrist to check her pulse.

"Stop it. I'm not sick, just tired."

"Maybe you should take a vacation off the mountain. Get your mojo back. I hear Mexico is good this time of year."

"Yeah, you're right on getting out of here. But I was thinking New York."

Emma blinked, then set down her brownie. "New York. As in my New York?"

"As in Spencer's." Serena paused, looking first at Doc, then Emma. "He left me this." She pulled an envelope out of her pocket with the words written DO NOT OPEN UNTIL READY on the front.

Spencer's writing.

"On the day I didn't take him to the airport," Serena finished.

"Okay, what?"

"Yeah. I kept him overnight and had my merry way with him until yesterday. Sorry, Doc," she said to her father.

He shook his head. "No apology necessary."

Serena watched as Emma opened the envelope and peeked inside. "A ticket to New York. Wow. He must really like you."

"It's a one-way," her father noted, looking over her shoulder. "Must have been a nice night."

Serena smiled dreamily. "It was."

Emma eyed Serena in an entirely new light. "You're thinking of doing it, you're thinking of going."

"Would that be so odd? Me in New York, crushing the competition with my off-the-charts desserts?"

"No." Actually, Emma could see it quite clearly, and it worked. Just as Serena and Spencer would work. As her father had earlier when she'd needed it, Emma reached out and squeezed Serena's hand. "I'm happy for him."

Serena looked down at her hand in hers. "And me? Are you happy for me, too?"

Emma smiled and went with her trademark honesty. It was all she had at the moment. "No. You, I'm jealous of."

"Because I'm going after what I want, which is Spencer, and you don't have the guts to go after Stone?"

"Actually," Emma said dryly. "I meant because Stone isn't likely to follow me across the country."

"You could follow him," her father said.

"And stay here," Serena finished for him, nodding.

"My life is in New York."

"Yeah." Serena took back her envelope. "Well, if Stone hands you an envelope that says DON'T OPEN UNTIL YOU'RE READY, don't open it, cuz you're not ready." Without giving Emma a chance to respond to that, she turned to Doc. "So it's a done deal?"

He took another brownie. "Done deal."

"Too bad Stone couldn't talk her out of it, huh?"

Emma looked at her dad in disbelief. "What?"

Serena winced in Doc's direction. "Sorry. That slipped out. I shouldn't have said anything."

Her father stuffed a brownie in his mouth.

Emma didn't blink. "You wanted Stone to talk me out of selling?" she pressed.

Her father grimaced. "Not exactly."

Oh, boy. She set down her second brownie, her heart kicking hard. "Then what exactly?"

With a sigh, he set down his brownie and faced her. "It's not a big deal. I just thought maybe, if things worked out between the two of you, that you'd want to stick around."

"So you wouldn't have to sell."

"So I wouldn't have to sell."

Oh, God. "Dad, I asked you a hundred times if you really wanted this. A *thousand.* I asked and asked, and you never—"

"I wanted you to *want* to stay. To want to not sell. To want to run the clinic." His smile was solemn and heartbreaking. "I wasn't going to ever ask it of you."

Oh, no. He didn't get to pull the martyr card. "You weren't going to ask it of me directly, you mean. Instead, you were going to have Stone talk me out of it, a nonmember of the family, a virtual stranger—"

"Is he?" her father interrupted softly. "A stranger?"

He hadn't trusted her enough to tell her the truth. "I can't believe this. You sold your own business, and you didn't want to. Do you have any idea how . . . *frustrating* this is?"

"Really? You want to know frustrating?" Her father stood up. "Frustrating is your livelihood being taken away from you by the turning of time and bad genes. Or watching your child choose a world that is slowly sucking the life and joy and heart and soul right out of her, three thousand miles away so that you can't help. *That's* frustrating."

She shook her head, devastated for him, wracked with guilt. "I've got to go."

"Emma, wait."

She turned back, unable to keep the tears out of her voice. "I'm sorry, Dad. So damned sorry you sold when you didn't want to. I'm sorry you felt you could tell Stone the truth when you couldn't tell me."

"Don't leave, Emma. Not like this."

"That's my point. I always was going to leave, always. I thought you knew that."

"Yeah. I knew it." He sighed. "I just didn't want to."

Stone and TJ took a group up Rockbound Summit. When they got back, dirty and exhausted, Stone headed straight to his cabin, planning to shower, then head straight to Emma and get her naked.

And somehow make her want to stay.

Instead, he stopped short on the trail in front of his cabin, surprised to find her on his porch, waiting for him. His entire body reacted at the sight of her, even his knees went weak. A dead giveaway, in his book, about how he truly felt about her. "Emma." He moved in to touch her but she stood up and held him off with a hand.

Okaaaay. "Something wrong?"

"My dad didn't want to sell and you knew it. In fact, he asked you to talk me out of selling the clinic."

He blinked at the last thing he expected to hear come out of her mouth. "What?"

"You heard me. So when did he ask you? Before or after we'd slept together?"

Okay, this wasn't going to go well, he could tell, and he stepped toward her. "Emma—"

"Don't." She pointed at him, her own voice a little shaky. "Don't 'Emma' me in that soft, sexy voice of yours, the one that can talk me into or out of anything."

"Out of?"

"You know damn well you've talked me out of my clothes on several occasions now. When, Stone. When did he ask you?"

He looked into her eyes and found not temper, but hurt. And it killed him. "In the very beginning, but it's not like you think—"

She made a soft sound that might as well have been a knife to his gut. "In the very beginning," he repeated, "he told me he wasn't going to tell you about the severity of his heart attack because he didn't want to guilt you into coming. I told him that was a bad plan, that no matter what he should be honest with you."

"Which he wasn't. And neither were you."

"I told you, it wasn't my story to tell. When it became clear he wasn't going to bounce right back, and when you were still so unhappy here, he knew you weren't going to stay."

She stared up at him, so many things in her eyes it hurt to look at her.

Or maybe that was his own hurt.

"He couldn't ask you to stay," he said quietly. "Whatever you think you know about this, I'd never ask that of you. Never. I know what your life in New York means to you. The sale of his place just came . . . quick. Quicker than he thought it would."

She stared at him, and then deflated, sank back to the porch bench. "Dammit." She covered her face. "Dammit."

With a sigh, Stone sat next to her. "This isn't your fault, Emma. You know that. Just as you know that if you want something, you have to go out and get it. If things haven't worked out the way you hoped, then change them. You of all people know you can do or get anything you damn well want if you want it bad enough."

She lifted her face and studied his. "Except that I don't know what I want," she whispered.

"Well, then, that's a problem."

"Do you know what you want?"

"Yes. I want to keep running Wilder, leading treks, volunteering with Search and Rescue, hanging out with my brothers, and until very recently, that list also included whatever sweet smiling woman came my way. Until a not-so-sweet smiling woman came my way, one who threw everything in my life upside down, proving that life isn't easy at all, and shouldn't necessarily be."

She sighed. "Oh, Stone."

He smiled solemnly. "Is this good-bye, Emma?"

She paused, not taking her eyes off him. "I once told you that we'd be a mistake."

His heart took a good hard knock. "Yes."

She surprised him by cupping his face and kissing him, a warm, heart-wrenching kiss, because he knew what it meant.

It *was* good-bye.

"I was wrong," she whispered against his lips, holding still for a heartbeat, breathing him in.

Destroying him.

"Being with you was the best thing that's ever happened to me," she murmured, and with one last touch of her lips to his, walked away.

He watched her go, rubbing his aching chest, knowing she was the best thing that had ever happened to him as well, given that he was head over heels crazy in love with her.

It took her a lot longer to pack up than it had to unpack, Emma thought putting her clothes into her bags. First, she had to keep stopping to blow her nose because her eyes kept watering.

Damn allergies.

Except she didn't have allergies. What she had was a broken heart. A fact she had to hide every time the stupid cowbells jangled, which they did often. Not by patients needing treatment, but by the people stopping by to say good-bye. Missy came by with handmade tea bags.

"For stress," she'd said genuinely.

Yes, that would come in handy. Tucker came by with a small, perfectly constructed wooden box. "For some of your doctor stuff, Dr. Sinclair. I made it in wood shop."

It was so beautiful, and just looking at it made her ache. "Thank you," she whispered.

"You hate it."

"No, I love it." She hugged him hard. "Thank you."

He awkwardly patted her back. "Dr. Sinclair?"

"Yes?"

"If you love it, why are you crying?"

She let out a watery laugh. "Because I'm female. Thank you for the box, Tucker. I'll treasure it."

He nodded and escaped, and she sank to the stairs. When she'd first got here, she'd resented being called Dr. Sinclair in that formal, almost awed tone, but it wasn't irreverent anymore. They meant it.

It was then, when she was all packed to go, that she realized. She wasn't just Doc's daughter.

Or that woman that Stone was seeing.

Or that fancy city woman with all the airs.

She was Emma Sinclair, and she fit in.

Hell of a time to realize it.

Chapter 27

New York, two weeks later

Emma jumped right back into work and everything was just fine.

Except it wasn't.

She picked up extra shifts at the hospital so she didn't have to go home and be alone. She ran herself ragged so that she didn't have to think outside of medicine.

Yet every single moment of every single day for fourteen days she felt alone. The city was noisy, crowded. Everyone was in a hurry.

And it didn't smell like Christmas trees.

She'd told Stone that nothing was ever easy and that everything came at a price. She hadn't been kidding.

As unbelievable as it seemed, she missed Wishful and its slow pace. She missed the people, even Missy Thorton and her shockingly delicious homemade Thai food. She missed her father. Hell, she even missed Serena.

But most of all, she missed Stone, a man who'd shown her the fine art of smelling the roses, of being happy in the moment, a man who kissed like heaven and looked at her like she was his world.

After her shift, she went to Spencer's, hoping a home-cooked meal would take her mind off Wishful. It certainly smelled delicious when she walked into his place. How he found the time or the energy to cook after a long day at the hospital, she never understood, but she was grateful.

But this scent was different, not a main course, but a baking scent.

Chocolate.

Her mouth watered. "I'll take two of whatever that is," she said, entering his kitchen, where her smile gave way to shock when she found Serena stirring something on the stove.

"Hey," Serena said. "Just in time." She lifted a wooden spoon dripping in chocolate. "Taste this. Too sugary?"

"Can chocolate ever be too sugary?"

"Hell, yes. If you go right into a diabetic coma, I took it too far." She waited while Emma took a taste. "Good?"

"Amazing. What the hell are you doing here?"

"She opened the envelope." Spencer joined them, clearly fresh from a shower. He looked happy and relaxed.

Very relaxed.

She took a closer look at Serena. Yep, they both have afterglow all over their faces. "So you used the one way ticket," Emma said to Serena.

"Yep, I took the plunge." Serena pulled out a fresh spoon from a drawer and resumed stirring. "I'm selling my place. Going big city." She beamed at Spencer. "Opening a pastry shop not too far from the hospital. You can come on your breaks and I'll take care of your sugar rush for you, any time."

Spencer pulled Serena in close and Serena closed her eyes and hugged him tight.

The two of them seemed so happy it almost hurt to look at them. "You're selling your place," Emma said. "Uprooting your entire life. For a *guy*."

"Hey," Spence said, insulted.

"A guy you hardly know," Emma went on.

Serena ran her fingers through Spence's hair, her eyes on his as she smiled. "I'm not uprooting anything. I wanted a change. New York is it. Spence is just the bonus."

He smiled at her. "Admit it, I'm a fairly big bonus."

"The biggest, baby."

Gobsmacked, Emma sank to a chair. "You're selling your business."

"Well that's just good sense. It won't run without me. Your father did the same thing. No one could run that place like him. Well, you could have, but it wasn't your thing. Sometimes it's just time to move on."

"Yes, but he's still going to work there."

Serena shot her a funny look. "No, he's not. You guys sold."

"To a group of doctors."

"Yes, who are turning the clinic into a hoity-toity vacation B&B for other doctors."

"No. My dad's going to work there. He—" She broke off as Serena slowly shook her head.

"Sorry," she said. "But it's a done deal. They were demoing when I left yesterday."

Emma whipped toward Spencer, who gave her a sympathetic look. "I'm sorry, babe. I didn't know. But it's what he wanted, so—"

"No." She shook her head, grabbed her purse, and headed toward the door. "It's not. It's not what he wanted at all. It's what he thinks I wanted. And I was wrong."

"So let me get this straight," TJ said, standing in the middle of an empty Wishful Delights. "We live in the boondocks, and yet Serena sold this place off in one day, and now the new owner has already hired you, sight unseen. You're okay with that?"

"The building predates the 1907 fire," Stone said. "It's one

of the oldest historical sites in town. The buyer wants to restore it to its former glory, which is right up my alley. Plus, I
was prepaid in cash. So yeah, I'm okay with that. I'm meeting
the owner here in half an hour." He looked down at his clipboard and the notes he'd taken. "Besides, it's keeping me
from losing it."

"Used to be that mountain biking would have done that."

Stone lifted a shoulder. "Things change."

TJ looked at him for a long moment, his eyes unusually
solemn. "Are you going to be okay?"

"I'm not sick."

"You're in love. Same difference."

"I thought you didn't believe in love."

"Just because I don't believe in it for myself doesn't mean
that I don't believe in it. Cam found it. You found it."

"And lost it."

"So I'll repeat. You going to be okay?"

Stone tossed aside the clipboard. "Aren't I always?"

"Yeah, which is what worries me. You're the glue that keeps
us all together."

"I'm fine. I'm the easygoing, laid-back one, remember? Nothing gets me."

TJ eyed him for a long moment. "That's actually technically not true. This got you. She got you. But true to form, you
let it bead off your back. Instead of—"

"Instead of what, pouting for a year like Cam did? Instead
of shutting out all emotions like you did after—"

"This is about you," TJ interjected. "All I'm saying is stop
trying to be okay for us. Stop being everything for everyone
else and Jesus, go get what it is you want. For once, get something for yourself."

"Like?"

"Like whatever it is *you* want."

What he wanted was three thousand miles away.

"The question is," TJ said quietly. "What do you want?"

A car pulled up out front, saving Stone from having to answer.

TJ cocked his head. "What time did you say your meeting was?"

"Half an hour. The owner's bringing the final plans for us to go over."

Just as he said so, the door opened. TJ had asked what Stone wanted, and what he wanted walked in. His heartbreak in her trademark elegant trousers and fitted button-down, looking like a million bucks.

In the stunned silence, TJ turned to Stone with a raised brow like *what the hell*, then smiled at Emma. "Hey, Doc."

"Hey right back at you." She had eyes only for Stone. "I see you've both taken a good look at my new place."

"Your place?" Stone managed.

"Yes." She cleared her throat, looking unaccustomedly nervous as she set down a set of plans. "Since Serena decided to keep Spence, and go be a fancy NY pastry chef while she was at it, I figured this building was perfect."

"For what?" TJ asked.

Stone knew. "For a new Urgent Care," he said softly, watching her face.

"Yeah." Looking relieved that he got it, she smiled. "Since I so badly screwed up the other one, I figured I'd give it another whirl. And actually, this building is better suited. It's right smack in the middle of town, it's bigger, and we can update to the latest and greatest in technology while we're at it."

Stone couldn't take his eyes off her, questions bouncing in his head. Was she staying, was she going, and even more pressing, could he drag her into the back and rip off their clothes and bury himself deep within her, because that had been when he'd last been happy, buried deep inside her.

She was staring at him, too, with a bunch of stuff swirling in her gaze. He didn't know what any of it meant, and he needed to know. "TJ?"

TJ divided a look between Stone and Emma. "Let me guess. Get the fuck out?"

"No," Emma said politely. "Of course not."

"Yes," Stone said, not politely. "Get the fuck out."

TJ nodded and turned to Emma. "I can't tell you how good it is to see you."

"Same goes." They hugged, and over her head TJ pointed at her. "Don't let her get away again."

In answer, Stone pointed to the door, and TJ went through it, leaving a very heavily weighted silence.

"So . . ." Emma smiled awkwardly and lifted a shoulder. "What's up?"

Stone just stared at her. He hadn't slept, hadn't eaten, hadn't been able to do anything since she walked out of his life, and she wanted to know what was up? "You bought this place."

"Yeah."

"You're here to renovate it."

"Yeah."

Neither of which had a single thing to do with him, and yet . . . and yet *she'd* contacted *him*. She'd made sure he'd be here. "You hired me."

"Yeah." She flashed another nervous smile. "I have a problem. I thought I could just put a Band-Aid over it and be done, but as it turns out, a Band-Aid isn't going to cover it."

He blinked. "Was that in English?"

She let out a breath. "You don't get it. I was trying to be poetic, mirroring our first Meet Cute."

He just stared at her, and she laughed a little and shook her head. "It's the way all the screwball romantic comedies start— the contrived encounter of the two leads, like when you first came to the Urgent Care, bleeding and hurting, and all you wanted was a damn Band-Aid."

"I don't remember that being cute."

"No." She spread out her arms. "And I'm not bleeding, not on the outside anyway, but I'm hurting like hell, and I thought a Band-Aid would do it. I thought going back to New York would be that Band-Aid, but I was wrong."

For the first time in weeks, the fist around Stone's heart loosened slightly. "Okay," he said very calmly, when he wanted to snatch her in his arms and never let her go. "Okay, I think maybe we're getting closer to speaking the same language. Keep going."

"I first came here to save my father. That's what I told myself, that it was for him. It took me a very long time to realize that I'd come for me. To ease the loneliness, the fear of truly being alone, and my seeming inability to have a long-term relationship with anyone other than my doctor's license. But I did figure it out, Stone."

"But you left."

"I did." She nodded in agreement of that. "And that was my mistake. When I found out the clinic had been closed, that my father wouldn't have a place to go back to work when he wanted, I put a set of plans in motion and told myself that was for him, too." She shook her head now. "Another mistake. Because this time I knew I wasn't coming back to save him. I was coming back to save me."

He couldn't take his eyes off her, and even though she was only a foot away, it was too far. He put his hands on her hips and pulled her in so that they were toe to toe. "Tell me what you needed saving from."

"My own stupidity," she whispered, and finally, God, finally, touched him, reaching up to cup his face. "I thought I had it all figured out when I was here before. It was temporary, everything was temporary. But then my father turned out to be . . . well, wonderful. And the people here in Wishful let me become one of them. And I made friends. Annie, TJ, Harley . . . you."

Friends. That's not all he wanted.

She ran her thumbs along his jaw. "Only you . . . you turned to be much more. More than the ski bum I mistook you for, and much more than just a friend. Somehow . . ." She went up on tiptoe to look him in the eye. You looked right through me when no one else could." She let out a small smile that wormed directly into his thudding heart. "With you, I found myself. *You're* the one I was waiting for, when I didn't even realize I was waiting. I fell in love with you, Stone. You completely snagged my heart when I wasn't looking, and now I'm wondering . . ."

Anything, he thought, barely breathing. *Anything you want.*

"If I could possibly have snagged yours as well." She offered a self-conscious smile.

He pulled her in hard, burying his face in the crook of her neck, just breathing her in, relief nearly buckling his knees. "Are you kidding?" He pulled back to meet her gaze. "Emma, you've had my heart in the palm of your hand since day one."

"I have?"

He set his forehead to hers. "Jesus, Emma, I'm so in love with you I can't even see straight. If you hadn't come back, I was coming after you."

"To New York?"

"Yes. To New York. To wherever you wanted to be."

"But . . . you would have had to start all over there."

"That would have been fine. It could have been Mongolia for all I care. Together, Emma, you and me. That's all I care about."

"I want to be together." She smiled, her eyes shiny. "Here, with everyone at our side."

"I can't think of anything better." Unable to hold back, he picked her up and headed toward the back room.

She laughed breathlessly at his purposeful stride and the look in his eyes. "Here, Stone? Now?"

"Here. Now. And forever."

She curled into him. "And forever . . ."

Read on for an excerpt from the first book
in Jill Shalvis's Wilder series,
INSTANT ATTRACTION,
Now on sale!

Chapter 1

"Live life balls out," Katie Kramer told herself every night, and even though she didn't own a pair, she hoped the mantra would keep the nightmares away.

It didn't.

Death and destruction and horror still dogged her dreams. Until tonight, that is. Tonight she'd miraculously been nightmare free. So when she opened her eyes sometime just before one, she felt . . . confused. She wasn't screaming about the bridge collapsing, about being trapped in her car, hanging upside down by her seatbelt fifty feet over the side of a cliff with flames licking at her. . . .

Which meant something else had woken her. And whatever it was, she wanted to kill it for interrupting the first solid sleep she'd had in four months.

There was a fatal flaw with this logic, of course. Because most likely it hadn't been an *it*, but a someone.

She wasn't alone.

Not prone to hysterics or drama, she shook her head in the dark. She'd locked the cabin door. She was safe. Plus, she wasn't in Los Angeles anymore. After the accident, she'd gotten into her brand-new used car and left town to fulfill her "balls out" motto. She didn't know what adventures were ahead of her exactly, but the not knowing was part of the plan. She'd gone north because Highway 5 had been the only freeway moving faster than fifteen miles per hour and she'd needed to move fast, needed to get as far from her old, staid, boring, careful life as a tank of gas could get her.

Eight hours later, she'd found herself in the Sierras, where it was *real* winter. None of LA's lightweight weather where flip-flops were risky for a few weeks in January, but the real deal complete with snow piled high in berms on either side of the roads and frost on her windows.

When she stopped for dinner in a tiny old west town named Wishful, she'd nearly froze her fingers and toes right off. And yet, after all her nightmares of heat and flames, she loved it. Loved the huge wide-open sky, loved the way her breath crystallized in front of her face, loved the way the trees smelled like Christmas.

Then she'd seen the want ad.

> LOCAL OUTDOOR ADVENTURE AND
> EXPEDITION COMPANY SEEKING TEM-
> PORARY OFFICE MANAGER, ADVENTUR-
> OUS SPIRIT REQUIRED. CALL WILDER
> ADVENTURES FOR MORE INFO.

That had been it for her; she was sold. She'd been working for Wilder Adventures for a week now, the best week in recent memory. Up until right this second when a shadowy outline of a man appeared in her room. Like the newly brave woman she was, she threw the covers over her head and hoped he hadn't seen her.

"Hey," he said, blowing that hope all to hell.

His voice was low and husky, sounding just as surprised as

she. With a deep breath, she lurched upright to a seated position on the bed and reached out for her handy-dandy baseball bat before remembering she hadn't brought it with her. Instead, her hands connected with her glasses and they went flying.

Which might just have been a blessing in disguise, because now she wouldn't be able to witness her own death.

But then the tall shadow bent and scooped up her glasses and . . .

Handed them to her.

A considerate bad guy?

She jammed the frames on her face and focused in the dim light coming from the living-room lamp. He stood at the foot of the bed frowning right back at her, hands on his hips.

Huh.

He didn't look like an ax murderer, which was good, very good, but at over six feet of impressive, rangy, solid-looking muscle, he didn't exactly look like a harmless tooth fairy either.

"Why are you in my bed?" he asked warily, as if maybe he'd put her there but couldn't quite remember.

He had a black duffel bag slung over a shoulder. Light brown hair stuck out from the edges of his knit ski cap to curl around his neck. Sharp green eyes were leveled on hers, steady and calm but irritated as he opened his denim jacket.

If he was an ax murderer, he was quite possibly the most attractive one she'd ever seen, which didn't do a thing for her frustration level. She'd been finally sleeping.

Sleeping!

He could have no idea what a welcome miracle that had been, dammit.

"Earth to Goldilocks." He waved a gloved hand until she dragged her gaze back up to his face. "Yeah, hi. My bed. Want to tell me why you're in it?"

"I've been sleeping here for a week." Granted, she'd had a hard time of it lately, but she definitely would have noticed *him* in bed with her.

"Who told you to sleep here?"

"My boss, Stone Wilder. Well, technically, Annie the chef, but—" She broke off when he reached toward her, clutching the comforter to her chin as if the down feathers could protect her, really wishing for that handy-dandy bat.

But instead of killing her, he hit the switch to the lamp on the nightstand and more fully illuminated the room as he dropped his duffel bag.

While Katie tried to slow her heart rate, he pulled off his jacket and gloves, and tossed them territorially to the chest at the foot of the bed.

His clothes seemed normal enough. Beneath the jacket he wore a fleece-lined sweatshirt opened over a long-sleeved brown Henley, half untucked over faded Levi's. The jeans were loose and low on his hips, baggy over unlaced Sorels, the entire ensemble revealing that he was in prime condition.

"My name is Katie Kramer," she told him, hoping he'd return the favor. "Wilder Adventures's new office temp." She paused, but he didn't even attempt to fill the awkward silence. "So that leaves you . . ."

"What happened to Riley?"

"Who?"

"The current office manager."

"I think she's on maternity leave."

"That must be news to his wife."

She met his cool gaze. "Okay, obviously I'm new. I don't know all the details since I've only been here a week."

"Here, being my cabin, of course."

"Stone told me that the person who used to live here had left."

"Ah." His eyes were the deepest, most solid green she'd

ever seen as they regarded her. "I did leave. I also just came back."

She winced, clutching the covers a little tighter to her chest. "So this cabin . . . Does it belong to an ax murderer?"

That tugged a rusty-sounding laugh from him. "Haven't sunk that low. Yet." Pulling off his cap, he shoved his fingers through his hair. With those sleepy-lidded eyes, disheveled hair, and at least two days' growth on his jaw, he looked big and bad and edgy—and quite disturbingly sexy with it. "I need sleep." He dropped his long, tough self to the chair by the bed, as if so weary he could no longer stand. He set first one and then the other booted foot on the mattress, grimacing as if he were hurting, though she didn't see any reason for that on his body as he settled back, lightly linking his hands together low on his flat abs. Then he let out a long, shuddering sigh.

She stared at more than six feet of raw power and testosterone in disbelief. "You still haven't said who you are."

"Too Exhausted To Go Away."

She did some more staring at him, but he didn't appear to care. "Hello?" she said after a full moment of stunned silence. "You can't just—"

"Can. And am." And with that, he closed his eyes. "Night, Goldilocks."

Cameron Wilder tried to go to sleep, but his knee was killing him, and his bed buddy was sputtering, working her way up to a conversation he didn't want to have.

"You can't just . . . I mean, surely you don't mean to . . ."

With a deep breath, he opened his eyes and took in the woman sitting on his bed. She wasn't a hardship to look at, even though he'd much rather be alone. She had light brown hair, which was currently in bed-head mode, flying in crazy waves around her jaw and shoulders. Her creamy skin was pale, with twin spots of color high on each cheek signifying either arousal or distress, of which he'd bet on the latter since he hadn't exactly been Prince Charming.

And then there were those slay-me eyes, magnified behind her glasses. They were the color of her hair, and also the exact color of the whiskey he wished he had straight up right now.

Clearly, she needed him to reassure her, but he didn't have any reassurance in him. She'd asked who he was, and the fact remained—he had no fucking clue anymore. None. He'd spent some time trying to figure it out, in Europe, South America, Africa . . . but there were no answers to be found. He hadn't felt anything in months, and yet there she sat staring at him, wanting, *needing* him to feel something.

They were both shit out of luck.

"I can't stay in the same cabin with someone who . . ." She waved a hand at him, at a loss for words.

He had the feeling that didn't happen to her very often. "Could be an ax murderer?" he offered helpfully.

"Exactly."

"I told you I wasn't."

"But you didn't tell me who you *are*. Whoever that turns out to be, you should know, I'm a black belt in karate. I can kung fu your ass."

Uh-huh. And if that were true, then he really *was* an ax murderer. He didn't challenge her, though. He couldn't summon the energy, not for a fight. Which was a sad commentary on his life all in itself. Not that he started fights as a rule, but he'd sure as hell never walked away from one.

She pushed up her glasses and stared at him with cautious curiosity. And he couldn't help but wonder if she liked her sex cautious too. He liked his—when he could get it—a little hot and sweaty, and a lot shameless. And definitely, decidedly, *not* cautious. "You can relax. I'm a Wilder. Cameron Wilder."

She said nothing, his favorite thing ever, so he leaned back and closed his eyes again, so damn exhausted he could sleep for a week.

And then, finally, the reaction. "Cameron *Wilder?*"

Yeah, there it was. Once upon a time, at the height of his career, he'd been a fairly common household name. He'd made a lot of people excited. Mostly women. They'd gotten excited and wanted an autograph, a picture, even just to look at him, anything. Any piece of him that they could get.

But those days were long gone. He was damaged goods. Now, apparently, he was reduced to scaring the hell out of women instead of turning them on, and if he hadn't been so tired, he might have laughed at the irony.

"You're related to Stone."

It was a sad day in hell when his brother was better known than he, but he should be used to the bitter taste of humble pie by now. "I'm his brother."

"And you . . . you live here? In this cabin?"

"Used to anyway."

"So you're the boss as well."

He hated the idea of being in charge of someone else, had always hated it. Hell, he could hardly be in charge of himself. But fact was fact. At the moment, he was nothing more than part owner of Wilder Adventures. A regular Joe Blow. "For better or worse, I suppose."

"I threatened to kung fu you. Oh my God."

"Don't worry. I didn't believe you."

"And I'm still in your bed! *Crap.*" This was accompanied by a flurry of movement. "Maybe we can just forget about all this and start over."

He'd have said he was too tired to care what the hell she was doing, but curiosity got the better of him and he cracked open an eye.

She was hopping out of his bed, small but curvy in a pair of plaid boxers and a dark blue tank top—no bra, which he noticed because one, hello, he was male, and two, he'd gone one full year without sex.

"So can we?"

He blinked and brought his bleary vision back up to her face, which was fixed in an expression that clearly said they were going to be talking for quite a while. Oh, yay. "Can we what?"

"Forget about the kung-fu thing? And the bed thing?"

"Absolutely, if we can also stop talking." Leaning back again, he snuggled into the chair, enjoying the blissful silence—until she cleared her throat politely.

He ignored her.

"Excuse me. Mr. Wilder?"

Jesus. Mr. Wilder? That had been his father. Not him. Never him. He didn't need to throw his weight and authority around, demanding respect but getting none. "Look, Goldilocks—"

"Katie."

"Fine. Katie. You should know that I don't care if *you're* an ax murderer. I need sleep. Kill me while I'm at it if you must, but do it quietly."

"So you're just going to sleep right there? Really?"

"Yeah. And I'll give you a raise to be quiet, very, very quiet."

"You don't even know what your brother is paying me."

No, he didn't. He didn't because he hadn't talked to his brother. "I'll double whatever it is."

"Well, that's just crazy. It's only a temporary position, a month, until your regular office manager comes back, and—"

"I'll *triple* it," he vowed rashly. "Just please, *please* stop talking."

She fell into what he hoped was a lasting silence, and he let out a sigh.

"You're too big to sleep in that chair," she murmured.

"Are you offering to share my bed?"

"No!"

Yeah, he didn't think so. "Hence the chair."

"I'm sorry, but you really need to leave now."

"Or you'll what, kung fu me?"

"You said we could forget that," she said with disappointed censure.

Wow, that was new, disappointing someone. "If you stopped talking. Which you didn't."

Indignant was a good look on her. Her eyes were flashing, arms all akimbo. And he was really enjoying that tank top, especially since she'd gotten a bit chilly in the past few minutes.

"I can't sleep in your bed while you're right there staring at me."

Yeah, pissy too, and actually sort of hot with it.

"I'm sorry about the mix-up," she said stiffly. "But—"

"You. You're the mix-up. You're in my cabin."

"Fine. I'll just go to another cabin."

"Perfect." He stayed where he was, happy to have her do just that and leave him alone with his own misery. Oh, he'd accepted his new limitations . . . well, almost. But the not knowing what to do with himself, *that* got to him.

Move on.

If he had a penny for every time some well-meaning asshole had told him that, he'd buy each and every one of them a fucking clue. He wanted what he'd lost, and short of that, he planned to continue to wallow in peace.

But she didn't leave. He knew this because he could feel her whiskey eyes boring holes in his face. "What now, Goldilocks?"

"It's dark out there." She was peering out the window into the admittedly dark, cold night. The sharp wind whistled through the trees and rattled the glass. "It's so secluded." She turned to him. "A gentleman would offer to walk me."

He didn't know how to break it to her, but he was no gentleman.

"Cameron?"

"Shh, he's sleeping."

She let out a sound that defined annoyance. "You are the singularly most unhelpful man I've ever met."

Yeah, He already knew that.

She was shifting around again and bumped into his legs. "Please move so I can get by."

He didn't. Interesting that he usually shied away from touch—with the exception of sex, that is—and yet he remained utterly still now, absorbing the fact that her legs were knocking into his.

The sensation was shockingly pleasant.

Unlike her talking. That was distinctly not pleasant. He wanted silence. Needed silence. Needed that more than his next breath.

"Excuse me."

Without opening his eyes, he dropped his legs down so she could pass him, then settled in again, his hands linked low on his belly, head back, eyes still closed.

The front door opened, then shut.

Ah, yeah. Perfect. Finally alone, where he could contemplate how he'd tell his brothers and Annie that he was back—

"Dammit."

He shook his head and opened his eyes. Yep, there she was, still with him, leaning against the door, chewing on a thumbnail, her hair wild around her face, her eyes filled with misgivings, her body—

Well, wasn't that a shame. She'd dressed.

She'd put on white jeans and a pink soft fuzzy sweater that zipped from chin to waist, with two tassels hanging down stopping just short of her breasts, pointing to them as if in emphasis of how long it'd been since he'd last seen a woman's breasts.

"It's really dark out there."

"Yes," he agreed, looking to where the stars littered the

black velvet sky like a sea of diamonds. There was no sky on earth like a Sierra night sky. He waited to be moved by it, as a sort of test, a gauge of his emotional depth. He waited for the mystic wonder to hit him like it used to.

Waited.

And waited . . .

Nothing. Not even a twinge. "Which means it's also too dark for any ax murderers to find you," he pointed out.

"That may be, but there's something else out there, something that always lurks in the bushes and makes this sort of rustling noise. It's done it all week."

He met her gaze. Those pale, clear depths could really haunt him, could make him yearn. Except he no longer did things like get haunted or yearn. "Nothing's stalking you. Unless . . ."

"Unless what?"

"Well, there's been some sightings of Big Foot over the years."

She looked horrified but spoke bravely, "There's no such thing."

"Tell that to the people who reported seeing him. Or to the bushes next time they . . . rustle?"

She nodded in confirmation. "There must be an explanation."

"Sure there is. It's Old Pete. He runs the gas station in town. He grew up on a commune and hasn't shaved since the seventies."

Her gaze narrowed. "Is this amusing to you?" Her hands went to her hips. "Making fun of my fears?"

What was amusing was his own reaction to baiting her. Why it was so much fun, he had no idea, but he was enjoying the spark in her eyes, the attitude all over her, and for some stupid reason, loved her crazy bed-head hair. "I'm sorry."

"You are not."

Okay, he wasn't. "Look, I'm tired. It's like three in the morning. I'm feeling punchy."

"It's one. One in the morning."

"Well, it feels like three. I've been up for thirty-six hours straight and I'm dead on my feet."

"Does that mean you're not moving?"

"Not a single inch." He closed his eyes again.

"Maybe Annie—"

"Go for it. But fair warning, she's cranky when she doesn't get her sleep."

A sound of frustration left her, but Cam was already drifting off, dreaming about his knee *not* aching, dreaming what Annie would be cooking for breakfast in the morning up in the main lodge, dreaming about his feisty Goldilocks sleeping in his bed and whether he could coax her to share the bed tomorrow night . . .

Huh.

Seemed as if maybe he was feeling plenty of things, after all.

And keep an eye out for the third book
in the Wilder series,
INSTANT TEMPTATION,
available in October 2018

Prologue

If you asked TJ Wilder to choose between a warm autumn night in the Sierras or a warm woman, he knew that most people would put money on him taking the woman.

And while that might have been true in his wild, unchecked youth, tonight they'd have been wrong.

Not that he didn't love women. He did. Short or tall. Willowy or curvy. Sweet or hot-as-hell sexy—actually, make that *especially* hot-as-hell sexy. Over the years he'd loved plenty.

Yet he loved the Sierras, too. While it was true that the tall, rugged, remote mountain peaks could be deadly dangerous to both life and limb, the mountains couldn't break a man's soul.

At least not without permission.

TJ no longer let anything break him. He didn't let anything break him or get to him, period. He was cool, calm, and prepared, always. Cam and Stone had long ago accepted, that as the oldest brother, TJ just knew things, like which direction to go on the mountain whether on skis or a bike, or in the helicopter. He knew which of their outdoor expedition clients would be a pain in the ass, and he could sense trouble a mile away.

Usually.

But, as he walked through Moody's Bar And Grill after a quick dinner with Cam and Stone, feeling full and surprisingly content for the moment, something plowed into his chest with the force of a cyclone.

Not something. Someone.

Harley Stephens—the one source of trouble he'd never managed to avoid.

Absorbing the impact, he prevented them both from tumbling to the floor, and as his brain registered how warm and soft she felt in his arms, she lifted her face, the scent of her filling his head. That's when something else hit him, too, the same inexplicable sense that he always got with her, the déjà vu feeling that he'd been there before. Not there in the doorway of Moody's with the fiery Indian summer sun setting behind her and the sound of the dinner crowd behind him, loud and rowdy . . . but there, as in having her practically wrapped around him.

Which made about as much sense as the head-buzzing physical reaction he got from the feel of her against him.

Wishful was a small mountain town. TJ knew every person in it fairly well, and Harley was no exception. He knew her layered blond hair, silky and straight and not quite touching her shoulders, even as a strand of it caught on the stubble of his jaw. He knew her face, always soft and pretty, though tonight it held more than a hint of fatigue and anxiety as well.

And just like that the sexual punch faded, replaced by concern. "Harley? You okay?"

Twisting free, she turned from him so quickly he was barely able to catch her hand. "Hey. *Hey*," he murmured when she fought him pulling her back into him. His hands were on her arms as he bent to look into her face, which did him little good. Her eyes were covered by reflective sunglasses.

He pulled them off, exposing her warm chocolate eyes, but whatever expression he'd caught a quick flash of was gone, carefully and purposely gone.

"Did I hurt you?" she asked, staring at his throat, always so tough on the outside, yet so soft on the inside.

"No, I'm fine. You?"

She wasn't. He could feel the tension of her body against his, in the quick quiver of her limbs, though that might just have been the same unwelcome erotic awareness he'd felt.

Still felt.

With Harley, he'd *always* felt it, though he'd gotten good at ignoring it since they subscribed to two very different philosophies in life. His being to live as uncomplicated as possible, including romantic entanglements. Hers being the opposite. She was complicated as hell, and she played for keeps.

"I'm fine, too," she murmured, flexing her shoulders beneath his hands. "Really."

He wasn't surprised at her statement. She was proud and she didn't need anyone. Just ask her. But he took a second, longer look at her, saw the exhaustion in the paleness of her skin, and the worry in the tight lines of her mouth. God, he loved her mouth. She wore gloss on a pair of lips that had given him more than a few dirty fantasies over the years. Then there was the milk chocolate depth of her gaze, which could warm anyone else's soul but sliced right through his. She wore faded, snug Levi's low on her hips and a pretty stretchy knit top that hugged the curves she was so often forced to hide beneath her mechanic overalls when she was working. "Harley, what's wrong?"

"Nothing."

A bullshit answer and they both knew it. Once upon a time, they'd been close enough that he could have called her on it. She was still close with his brothers, but TJ had never been able to put his finger on exactly when things had changed between them.

"Sorry about the collision," she said.

Wow. Four whole words, willingly given. "No problem. Watch out." He pulled her back up against him to let a customer move through the door, and for the second time in as many minutes he felt an undeniable . . . zing. And for the *first* time, he saw the mirror of it in Harley's gaze before she could mask it.

For a deliciously long beat she stayed plastered up against him, and he began to think she was enjoying the connection, but proving the ridiculousness of that, she snatched her glasses from him and turned to walk away.

"You telling me you didn't feel that?" he asked her back, having no idea why he pushed, or why he cared. Since when did he push for anything, especially something as nameless and intangible as what he might want from Harley Stephens?

"Feel what?"

"The thing that happens when we get too close."

She froze, then slowly turned to face him. "It's Indian summer, TJ. We're all a little overheated. It's natural."

"Is that right?"

"Yes." She broke eye contact, her gaze skittering away. "It's Wishful, you know. High altitude. And it's hot, it's really, *really* hot. It's normal to feel so . . ."

"Hot?"

She bit her lower lip. "Yes."

"So is that what happens when we get too close then, Harley? You get really, *really* hot?"

Her eyes jerked to his, clearly realizing she'd just given away far more than she'd meant to. "What are you even doing here anyway?" she asked. "You're usually in Alaska, or Wyoming, or anywhere other than here."

True. He took all the long treks for Wilder Adventures, which usually had him gone for weeks, even months at a time. He liked it that way. Always had. "I'm in between trips. So do you get really, *really* hot with Nolan, too?"

Nolan being Nolan Lightner, the owner of the car and truck garage where Harley wrenched part-time. And Wishful, being Mayberry-With-Attitude, loved its gossip mill, which meant that everyone knew she'd gone out with Nolan twice.

Not that TJ was counting.

"Yes," she said firmly even as a blush bloomed on her cheeks. "Nolan and I get . . . hot." She crossed her arms, as always, ready and willing to do battle when backed against a wall. "Is that what you wanted to hear?"

Hell, no. But TJ watched her fidget, and suddenly he felt a whole hell of a lot better.

Because she was lying.

"In fact, if you must know . . ." She stabbed a finger into his pec for emphasis, "there are so many sparks between me and Nolan that our clothes catch fire every time we're near each other."

He registered the abrupt change in the pitch of her voice and her overly defensive stance and grinned. Yeah, he was feeling *much* better, and leaned in close enough to whisper in her ear. "Liar."

A low growl of temper escaped her and once again she pushed clear of him, heading toward the pickup counter, bad attitude spilling from her with every swing of her sweet hips and sweeter ass.

Feeling a mixture of amusement, at himself, at her, he let her go.

Stone came up behind him. "You're supposed to ask them out, not scare them off."

TJ turned to his brother, standing tall and lean and tanned from long days on the mountain, his stark green eyes flat-out grinning, looking like what TJ knew was his own mirror image. "You think I scared her?"

"No, I think you do something else to her entirely." Stone shook his head. "Though I have no idea what she sees in you, man. You're ugly as sin."

Ignoring that, TJ twisted to look at Harley again.

"You going to run off on yet another long trip to get away from her again?" Stone asked. "'Cause that's only a temporary fix and we all know it."

"Stone?"

"Yeah?"

"Shut up."

Stone clapped a hand to TJ's shoulder and didn't shut up. "Face it, man. You're as drawn to that woman as you're drawn to the mountains. One guess as to which is more lethal."

Connect with Us

Visit us online at
KensingtonBooks.com
to read more from your favorite authors, see books
by series, view reading group guides, and more.